KISSED BY THE DARK

Ollie Wit #3

DONNA AUGUSTINE

I'd never been this happy, truly *happy, the kind of happy that seeps into all the nooks and crannies and fills the gaps in your soul, soothes away the pain, and stitches together the wounds. Before now—before him—I'd been merely surviving. Not that surviving was a bad thing. It was what you did. It was what most people did. It was the everyday struggle you saw everywhere, as people clawed their way through the day and then the next, all in the hopes of finding a better alternative. Like so many others, I wasn't sure that alternative existed. Well, it did, and I had found it.*

This was living. This was effortless joy. I woke up breathing in sunshine and went to bed sleeping on the clouds.

It was the best feeling I'd ever had. While it lasted...

Ollie

Chapter One

PERFECT WASN'T PART OF MY WORLD. HAD NEVER BEEN. I'd never aimed for perfect because it had always seemed so out of reach. I'd always strived for what others would consider ho-hum, like waking up without a monster staring down at me and things not blowing up.

But somehow I had ended up here, with something that felt suspiciously like perfect. I had the greatest man interested in me. The crawlers, the monsters that had haunted me, were keeping their distance. I even had friends who didn't think I was a freak. Like I said, I had something near perfection. That was how I knew disaster was looming right around the corner.

Instead of relaxing and enjoying this newfound happiness, I was in a panic most of the time. I didn't know what to do with this life. Disaster? Oh, yeah, had that one in the bag. No problems. I could do disaster every day of the week and throw in a couple of cartwheels for fun as I navigated the nightmare. Nightmares were my wheelhouse. I knew what to do with them. Survive. The same way I'd been surviving my whole life.

I didn't know how to handle *this* life. I had no experience at happy. No training. What was one supposed to do when everything was going right? Smile and forget that monsters existed? Pretend that life wasn't fragile and people died every second of every day? Especially when it didn't make any sense and I barely knew how I got to this place?

No. That wasn't me. I didn't put my head in the sand. I stared straight ahead, even if it made me squint and my eyes water. But I was staring at nothing. I didn't know what was going to hit. Even as I sat in the booth in the Underground, surveying the crowd, I couldn't find the trouble on the horizon. I'd made enemies, too. I'd killed some vampires and rained on some witches, but that seemed to be blowing over. I couldn't see what was coming for me, and something must be, because it always did.

This perfect shit had me looking over my shoulder, trying to figure out what I was missing. I was so on edge, waiting for a disaster I knew had to be looming, that I would've sworn I felt the breeze on my ankles as my feet dangled over the abyss.

Maybe I needed to keep things in perspective? It had only been a week of perfect. And things hadn't been *that* perfect, right?

A not-so-gentle kick nailed my shin under the booth's table. I glanced up to see everyone's coffee and juice jiggling around in their glasses, and three sets of dirty looks aimed my way. I didn't know who to curse at. It could've been anyone. I did the only acceptable action. I gave Flip, Butch, and Leon all nasty stares before I asked, "Who kicked me?"

"I did," Butch said, the sun streaming through the window behind him making his red hair glow. "You were doing it again."

I clamped a hand to my knee under the table. You know what happened to people who were on edge, besides the nice breeze from the abyss? They became twitchers. My foot had been tapping as if I were playing the drums for a rock band on speed.

"We're going to tie weights to your legs soon," Leon said, before he shot a look toward Butch, as if making mental plans with him. Those two had known each other so long that it seemed talking was sometimes optional. Leon's gaze turned back to me, as if he'd forgotten something. "And don't punch me in the face for that," he added quickly, referring to my inadvertent violence toward an unsuspecting witch not long ago.

Good reminder of another reason things were too perfect. I had a mark on my hand from being shadow kissed by a crawler. That was what they'd called it, but in reality, it had been much more bite than kiss. And not one of those *ooh, make it hurt so good* bites. That little bastard had dug in. Who knew what it had done to me.

Things seemed calm, but they also seemed calm right before a tornado dropped a house on you, too. I'd grown up on *The Wizard of Oz*. I knew how quickly things could go downhill. If my apartment hadn't blown up, I'd be watching that DVD right now. That Dorothy chick knew some stuff about surviving.

I got another nudge, this time from Flip, my favorite half-fairy, half-leprechaun. "You've got to stop. You're killing us." She was the only mutt of her kind in existence. Leprechauns didn't breed well and fairies didn't intermingle, but apparently both breeds got drunk on occasion.

I put my hand back on my knee so I couldn't tap without realizing. I'd only moved it to take a sip of coffee and decided I didn't really need any more caffeine anyway. "Just so you know, I didn't mean to punch Dana." It had crossed my mind, as she was one of the witches who'd relished in aggravating me, but I never would've done it on purpose. Well, maybe I would've, but I hadn't meant to at that moment.

"Oh, then I'm sure it didn't hurt much." Leon rolled his eyes and the three of them laughed, as if the only problem they had was their food shaking and watching me punch people by accident.

"Don't you guys feel it at all?"

Butch shook his head. "I don't know what you're worried about. Everything's good." Flip and Leon nodded before the subject moved on to some other frivolous topic I tuned out of.

This wasn't a time to make jokes. It was time to build bunkers and stockpile supplies. Why was I twitching alone? We should've all been rattling the table. It didn't matter if we didn't know what was coming. It was. Things were way too peaceful.

I looked out into the field of other diners, in all their different shapes and sizes, all eating their breakfast too. Witches cackled a few tables over about something that wasn't funny. Their jokes never were. I'd overheard enough of them to be able to judge. Wolves were sniffing bacon and getting fat instead of honing their hunting skills. Vampires—yes, vampires at breakfast, because the Underground had some weird windows that blocked the harmful rays—admiring the other diners' jugulars. I couldn't see the dwarves, but I had to assume that they were doing whatever it was they did too.

When the heads swiveled toward the door, I didn't have to look to know Kane had just entered the room. No one else here got that much attention. If there were ever a group that fit the word jaded, this was them. Although they thought they were much cooler than they were. But even this group gave Kane his due. As soon as he set foot in the place he became the new center of gravity, everything orbiting around him, including myself. I tried to fight it, but you can't fight gravity.

I turned and watched Kane stride across the room, his dark hair gleaming, his eyes intent, looking like a king among men. I'd seen him walk through a group of vampires the same way. Into a den of leprechauns without being fazed. Even the crawlers paid him deference and backed out of the room when he entered. Maybe the monsters keeping tabs on him and backing away should've warned me off. Maybe, but it didn't.

I couldn't help myself. When he stopped halfway up the stairs and looked in my direction, his eyes nearly yanked my heart from my chest. He tilted his head in the direction of his office. I gave him a subtle nod that I'd be right over, not that there was a doubt, at least in my mind. My body moved toward him of its own volition, and I worried that I'd follow this man right into hell.

I made my way through the crowd and toward his office, all eyes now focused on me. There was a big difference in the appraisals, and I wasn't delusional about it. When they'd watched him, it was sort of like *wow, wish I could be that badass when I grow up.* As they watched me, it was more along the lines of *she might be bad news. Better not get anywhere near her before shit blows up.* I tried to comfort myself with the fact that we were both considered bad, but his was just a touch more flattering.

I shut the door to the office and left all the stares behind me. Kane was leaning on the front of his desk, shirt sleeves rolled up and the button at his neck undone. I strolled toward the couch, trying to quash my need to touch him. I was waylaid by a hand on my wrist that tugged me back toward him until I was standing between his legs.

I didn't mind. I liked being there, even as I'd made every excuse I could to avoid going beyond some heavy petting. Kane wasn't a stupid man. He'd probably caught on after my third night of excuses. Probably after my second. Maybe even the first. I wasn't very good at them.

It wasn't like I was a virgin. I'd had more than one night of using a warm body to try and chase away the nightmares. But he wasn't a random man used for a purpose.

He wasn't like the others. Being near Kane was like being in an inferno, burning warmth surrounding you, and when he wasn't there, everything felt cold and lifeless. And when that fire died, it would leave you dead in the ashes. That scared me worse than a horde of crawlers.

He was giving me space, or as much space as I wanted. He didn't press, beyond a little pushing here and there, like what he was doing right now. His hand was on my ass, hoisting me against him, making it very clear that one of us was definitely ready.

My head dropped back as I moaned, and he shifted slightly, his lips falling to the open neckline of my blouse. One hand came around and dragged the shirt loose from my waist, and then cupped my breast as his lips and then teeth nipped and slightly tugged. Nothing had ever felt like when he touched me.

His leg glided in between my thighs, and I found myself so close to orgasm that I didn't know if I was going to rub myself against him or run from the room to hide how quickly he could arouse me. I pressed against him, breathing in the scent of sandalwood and man. It had been an easy choice.

A loud cracking noise sounded behind me, and I jerked around to see that the large window overlooking the Underground had shattered.

Shit. That was the second window this week. We might as well hang a tie on the doorknob.

I turned around and I dropped my forehead to his shoulder, closing my eyes. Screaming, "Oh God, yes," for the whole place to hear would have been subtler that the shards of glass now littering the lower floor.

I felt his hand rub the length of my back, the mood switching over to something more lukewarm and comforting than hot.

"You'll get a handle on it."

I lifted my head in his direction and then narrowed my eyes.

"Trust me. I've been around a while and have seen some things."

I dropped my head into the nook of his neck, because if I didn't stop staring, I might break another window. "Maybe we shouldn't mess around in here, though, until I get this control you think is coming."

Before he could agree or not, someone knocked on the door.

I could feel the grumble in his body before he snapped, "What?"

"The leprechauns are here," Jerry said from the other side of the door. "Wanted to give you some warning, you know, since the window and all."

Jerry tended to be stuck on door duty more often than not. I had a feeling the beach boy lookalike pulled the short straw a lot because he couldn't keep his other stick in his pants when needed.

Kane trailed a hand down my spine as he yelled back, "Put them in the room off the hallway. I'll be there in a few minutes."

I held back a sigh. I'd really needed some more time with him. He was the only person who seemed to calm the nerves, but I wouldn't make him stay. I was still shocked he wanted me in the first place. I wasn't going to run him off by getting clingy and neurotic. He straightened, and I moved back a few steps, letting him go do his thing.

"I've got to go handle this, and then I've got to run out and smooth the vampire feathers. I'll be back by eleven. You better be lying in my bed or I'll hunt you down and drag you there." He looked like he was about to leave, but he stopped, cupping my cheek, his eyes softer than I'd thought possible. "What is it? Are you still nervous?"

I shrugged. "I'm fine. Go take care of business."

He stepped closer. "Ollie, it'll be okay. Whatever comes, I'll take care of it. I promise you."

I nodded, smiling for him. Wanting to believe him.

But I just couldn't.

Something was coming. I felt it like you could feel a storm brewing in the air before the first drop of rain fell.

Chapter Two

A HAND RAN UP AND DOWN MY LIMBS, WHILE AN ARM circled my shoulders as someone kept speaking insistently.

"Ollie? Come on now, open your eyes for me."

I recognized the voice pulling me back to reality. From where, though?

"Come on, Ollie, wake up. It's Kane."

Kane? Shock brought my eyes open faster than smelling salts. Why was that arrogant asshole from last night holding me? After his thugs had dragged me to that strange place, I'd told him I'd think about his offer. I hadn't agreed to anything.

I struggled in his arms, fighting back the dizziness. "What the hell are you doing?"

His face was much softer than the last time I'd seen him, but that didn't stop me from pulling out of his arms. I rolled myself onto the cement and got to my knees. He'd let me go, and I thought it had more to do with confusion than willingness. Why he'd think I'd want to stay in his arms was beyond me. It would be like leaving my arm in a lion's mouth to use as a chew toy.

"Where am I? What did you do to me?" I got to my feet, my hands stinging from the cement and my head feeling as if it were bobbing on my shoulders.

He stood with me, leaving a buffer of space but taking a step every time I did, as if prepared to grab me at any second. "Ollie, you've been missing for a week." He spoke softly, as if I were daft.

I bounced off the side of one of the buildings that formed the alley we were in and then settled against it. "Missing from where? Did you have your goons follow me again?" Wasn't it bad enough they'd already kidnapped me once? Had they attacked me again? They'd probably been sitting across the street staring at my building, or something equally creepy. I couldn't believe I'd even thought of taking him up on his deal.

His whole body tensed, like a flash-freeze sort of deal. It was a slight overreaction on being called out on his bullshit. Maybe nobody ever did that to him, though? Handsome bastard was probably used to getting away with all sorts of stuff. Well, not with me. I didn't care. It was bad enough he'd sent them out to stalk me and kidnap me once. This was too much.

His eyes narrowed. "Ollie, how many times have we met?" he asked slowly, as if I were a spooked horse.

What was up with this guy? He knew very well how many times we'd met. Now he wanted to play mind games or something? "You were there. You tell me."

"I was there," he said, more to himself than me, as if I'd just given him some vital information. "So you remember meeting me once?"

"Of course. I'm not daft. I told you I'd think about the offer. If you people try and stalk me again, or *grab* me, I'm not doing it. I don't care what you do."

I could see the thoughts flying around in his head. It was strange how different he was acting compared to last night, as if *I'd* lost my mind. He was the one acting unbalanced.

He shook his head, looked upward, and said, "Fuck." It wasn't long before his attention landed on me again. "You're injured. You need to see a doctor."

"No, I—"

"Before you argue, look at yourself." He took a step forward and looked over the length of me.

I looked down too. How didn't you after someone said something like that? My jeans, a pair I didn't remember owning, hung in shreds below my knees. My hands and arms looked like I'd crawled my way out of a forest, and the fresh scabs made me think there'd been some barbed wire, too. I didn't know what my face looked like, but my head was pounding and I didn't think I would've been on my feet this long if it weren't for the brick at my back.

"I can't let you stumble away like this."

In other words, *I'd like you to come with me, nicely, but you'll be coming with me one way or another.* I looked about the place for my purse as he watched on. Then I felt my pockets. I didn't even have a phone to call for help, not that I'd be able make the phone call if he didn't want me to.

He was right, though. He hadn't tried to force me to stay when I'd wanted to leave. And the doctor suggestion wasn't so off the mark either. I didn't know what had happened, but I was a mess.

I nodded. "Okay. Maybe that's not a horrible idea." I looked up and down the empty road. "Where are we?"

"A block from… We're a block from my building." He held out a hand.

I took it, knowing I was going to need a little help. A couple of wobbly steps later and his arm was around my waist. I wasn't stupid enough to argue that one either.

Then the strangest thing occurred to me. "Why is it so warm?" It had been thirty degrees last night. Today I didn't even need a jacket.

"Because it's almost summer."

Summer?

A WOMAN IN A WHITE COAT, who *looked* like a doctor, was listening to my heart. She had all the bells and whistles you'd expect of a doctor, and seemed to know what she was doing. She wasn't what had made me suspicious.

I wouldn't have doubted her credentials for a minute if I'd been at a doctor's office. But I wasn't at an office. I was sitting on the couch in somebody's apartment above that weird Underground place.

Kane was standing across the room with the Thug Brothers, the ones who'd kidnapped me. Although I doubted the big redhead and his even larger blond buddy were actually connected by blood. More likely their only connection was their life of crime and past of abducting unsuspecting women, like myself.

A small woman, with frizzy yellow hair, and a very odd way of moving, as if gravity didn't affect her the same way as the rest of us, was with them. They all whispered to each other as they took turns glancing my way.

Kane was watching the doctor run her fingers over my scalp as the big blond guy called Leon turned to Butch, the redhead, and said, "She's been gone a week. Who knows what happened? The timing looks bad. *Really* fucking bad."

Butch's eyes swung to mine as he elbowed Leon in the ribs. Kane's attention also turned to them. I couldn't hear what he said, but Leon dropped his gaze.

I'd been gone a *week*, according to them, and I couldn't remember anything that had happened in months. My last memory was walking through slush as I left here the first night I'd met Kane. And then poof, I'd shown up a block from here. I'd been mugged or something. Maybe my mugger had dumped me there? How else would it have happened?

The doctor finally stood and began packing her things into a leather bag. Kane walked over to get the verdict. He said the least, but he was definitely the one in charge. I would've known it even if I hadn't remembered that.

The doctor spoke without any prompting. "She's got a pretty bad bump on her head that looks to be fairly fresh. Other than that, and a lot of cuts and bruises, she looks fine."

The small blonde was edging closer to Kane and the doctor, listening in on the verdict. I glanced over as Leon was shaking his head at Butch.

"There's no way she didn't have something to do with it," Leon said.

All heads swiveled toward him.

"Leon," Kane barked from across the room.

Leon immediately nodded and mumbled, "Sorry." He put up his hands and glanced at me, not meeting my eyes.

"Had something to do with what?" I asked Kane, seeing how he had the ability to put a gag order on everyone else.

Kane turned his attention to me. "Nothing." He turned back to the doctor before I could ask another question. "She's not fine if she can't remember anything."

The doctor looked at me and then turned to him. "Her memory loss is probably the result of whatever caused her injuries. Nothing can be done about that but time and patience."

Kane turned toward the little blonde.

I didn't hear him say anything, but she nodded, and I had a feeling he'd just ordered her to keep an eye on me. Kane nodded to the doctor and walked her out.

One of the few things I did remember from that first night was that the monsters, or crawlers, as they were called, didn't like Kane.

As soon as he left the room, I waited for them to come hover, but they didn't. I could see them in the far-off corners of the large room, but they stayed away. Why were the monsters, the ones that seemed to become more invasive every day, all keeping their distance and giving me space?

I only had a moment to think it over before Kane came back and they disappeared altogether. They didn't like him at all. That was clear, but why? I'd never seen anything like it in my life. What was the deal with him?

Kane stopped in between me and the others, as if he couldn't decide what to do. I got the feeling this wasn't something that happened to him a lot. The three other people in the room, staring at him, seemed to feel the same way.

I was waiting too, but mostly for everyone to stop noticing me so I could sneak out. I'd had about enough of this circus.

Leon nudged Butch after a minute and then nodded toward Kane. Butch gave him a shrug but then stepped forward.

"It'll wear off," Butch said as he stopped beside Kane.

"What if it's a spell or something?" the little blonde asked. "Then it might not."

"Flip, it's not a spell," Butch said. "We checked. That concoction would've turned black. It didn't."

Flip glanced at my arm. I looked at it too now. The big redhead had splashed some sort of funny-smelling liquid on me earlier then acted like he'd spilled it on me by accident. Should I be relieved my arm didn't turn black and fall off?

My exit was becoming long overdue. The more I sat there, the crazier these people made me feel. I hadn't started off in a good place to begin with, considering that I was being stalked by shadow monsters.

I looked about the place, locating exits. It was a nice setup, high-end without being flashy about it. The place screamed comfort and quality, not *look at what I have*. I didn't care what the place said, though. All I wanted was out.

I didn't have a set of keys to my apartment, but that didn't matter. I'd get my superintendent to let me in. He was a bit on the slimy side but was always ready to help me. One of the few perks that came along with the looks he gave me that made me want to strip out of my skin.

Now the big question was, did I tell these people I wanted to leave or just stand and be assertive about it? Kane and the pixie-looking girl were back across the room talking to the Thug Brothers. Maybe they wouldn't even notice me leaving?

I stood, ever so slowly, and not just because my head felt like a TV that still used an antenna with bad reception. Slow movements might not attract the crazies.

Kane's head snapped toward me as soon as my butt left the seat.

"What are you doing?"

I knew instantly this wasn't going to work out how I wanted, but I would persist anyway. "I appreciate all the help, but I've got work tomorrow, so I should really get going." I was fairly certain I'd been fired from my cashier job. I'd gone on a bit of an impromptu sabbatical. I hadn't shown up since my world had imploded along with the explosion that killed my family.

Leon groaned loud enough that I could hear him across the room. I couldn't imagine why my having to work would illicit that kind of response.

Kane, the dark-haired devil himself, walked back over to me.

I took a few steps away. He instantly faltered, and I heard a soft sigh come from Flip, as if I'd just made a grave faux pas. A few seconds of silence fell, as if he were trying to determine the right step forward. Indecision didn't seem like something he was used to.

Finally, he seemed to resign himself, standing a good

five feet away from me. "You haven't been a cashier for months, and you *are* home."

What? No, this wasn't all me being crazy. This was them. They were trying to trick me. My life hadn't changed that much, that quickly.

I nodded, more in placation than belief. "Like I said, I appreciate your help, but I really need to be going. This is *not* my home." Or I'd started off with the idea of placation.

"Ollie, what is the last month you can remember?"

I paused. I wanted to say January, but I knew that couldn't be right. It was more than Kane having said it was almost summer. I'd felt the heat of the day myself.

I sucked in my bottom lip, wondering if I should lie, and say May or June. But I remembered nothing and knew my answer wouldn't hold up.

"January." As soon as I said it, I saw the Thug Brothers give each other a look that didn't appear to be flattering in nature.

"It's the beginning of June." Kane reached into the pocket of his pants and drew out a phone. He held it out to me.

I took it. His phone wasn't locked and the date read June second. Maybe you could set the date of a phone to months ahead, but you couldn't fast-forward the seasons. It had been too warm outside. I looked at my clothing. Even if I'd lost my jacket, I wouldn't have been wearing a t-shirt.

Maybe there had been a warm spell? You never knew. It could happen. I opened his browser as he watched, not trying to stop me, and typed "Google." I clicked the news tab and hit the first story that popped up, not bothering to look at the title. I didn't care what it was about. I only wanted the date.

JUNE 2ND.

I WOBBLED ON MY FEET.

"Stay here and relax. You can worry about running out of here after you can stand again." The dark devil was supporting me by my elbows and helping me back down onto the couch.

I glanced in the direction of the door. Considering that my legs had wobbled as if my bones had dissolved, it was a safe bet to say I wasn't going anywhere at the moment.

"I can't stay long. I really need to get home."

Kane's expression was blank, as if he were purposefully hiding whatever he was thinking. I turned to the others, looking for a possible ally or at least a clue. All eyes were fixed on me like I was a car crash on the highway they'd slowed down to see.

"I need the room," Kane said.

The place cleared as if the car that crashed was about to explode. Kane had moved a few feet back, as if allowing me space that he didn't really want to give. He took a walk to the other side of the room, where he stood looking away from me, arms crossed.

If I'd had leg bones right then, I might've had a chance to run. Except that the onlookers were probably waiting outside the door.

"Fuck," Kane said, under his breath but loud enough I

could hear him anyway. He turned, seeming to have made some decision.

When he walked back, resolve was on his face, and remorse, as if he'd helped cause this crash somehow. He walked closer but stopped four feet shy of the couch I was sitting on.

"A lot has happened since January. There are things you can't afford to forget, not for a week or a day or however long this lasts."

"Like what?" He didn't have the look of a man about to tell me I'd won the lottery and forgotten.

"The creatures you see, they're called crawlers. You're a Shadow Walker; you can walk in the Shadowlands and get spells—"

"I remember that part." It was only last night—or felt that way.

"You also have a trove of spells stored in your mind from when a crawler bit you. That's called being shadow-kissed. It hasn't happened in a long time, so we don't know the full ramifications."

He shifted to the other arm of the sofa, settling in, as if this was going to take a while.

Once he continued, the details kept coming. And coming.

He told me how I collected spells in the Shadowlands and the leprechauns had kidnapped me. I'd teamed up with a werewolf but gotten stuck in the Shadowlands. I'd lived with a crawler masquerading as a man called Asher, but then killed this same creature I'd tried to protect. And that hadn't been my first kill, either. I'd stabbed a vampire in the middle of a mall.

It was the murdering parts that put me into overload.

"Please, stop." I held up a hand. I didn't want to hear any more. I couldn't. It was too much. How could this all be true? I'd cared for a monster enough to try and shield it, and then I'd killed him after he kidnapped me. Was this some sort of strange game? Maybe this man had drugged me and hit me over the head? These couldn't all be accurate. Could they?

I got to my feet, adrenaline feeding strength back into my legs, even as my head felt like it was spinning so fast it was about to break the light barrier. Kane rose as well.

And then the couch I'd been sitting on snapped in half behind me with a loud cracking noise. I jumped away from it, inadvertently moving closer to Kane. Then I jumped the other way.

"How did you do that?" I demanded, pointing at the broken furniture, while making sure to keep a buffer between us. It was telling enough that the crawlers hid from him. If he could break things with his mind, who knew what else he was capable of?

He stared at the couch, a frown marring his brow, as if maybe he regretted he'd broken it now.

He ran a hand through his hair. "I didn't do that. You did."

I wrapped my arms around myself, unsure whether to believe what he'd just said. Had I done that? What kind of monster had I become?

"The bedroom is over there." He pointed to a room off to the side. "No one will bother you. Maybe you should rest for a little while and we'll see how you feel after." He was looking at the door as if he were the one who needed a moment.

He was standing in between me and the exit to leave,

so I did as he said and made my way to the bedroom.

I would've gone and sat in the bathroom to be alone for a second.

"Ollie."

I turned, my hand on the doorknob, so close to being alone.

He hesitated a moment before speaking, as if uncomfortable with the words he was about to utter. "I don't know what happened, but I'm going to fix this. I'm sorry I didn't listen to you."

"Sorry you didn't listen?" What was he talking about?

"You thought something bad was going to happen. I thought I could handle whatever it was. I should've been more careful."

It was a bucket of cold water on already chilled skin. "I warned you?"

He nodded.

I didn't know what to say, so I said nothing. I turned and shut the door. I couldn't handle one more piece of information.

Chapter Three

I DIDN'T KNOW HOW I'D MANAGED TO SLEEP ALL THE WAY to the next morning, but I had. As soon as my head hit the pillow, I'd been out. Before my eyes opened all the way, I tried to remember the gap of time that was missing, only to find it still gone. I don't know why I'd thought maybe it would magically come back after I slept, but that wasn't the case.

As I sat up in bed and waited for the barrage of crawlers, I realized they were still keeping their distance. Other than them, it seemed as if I were alone.

I let my gaze roam the bedroom, and a flash of color caught my attention. Yellow Post-its were stuck to the closet doors, telling me there were clothes within. I guessed it made sense, since Kane said I lived here. This place didn't look like mine. Maybe I had stayed here for a bit, but it was time for me to go back to my apartment now.

My head was still a little fuzzy when I stood, but it felt

as if a lot of the cobwebs had been wiped away by sleep. I desperately wanted a shower, but the idea of being naked and vulnerable overruled any desire to be clean. I'd have to settle for a quick wet towel in the bathroom as I got dressed, not wanting to tempt fate. A shower would wait until I was behind the row of deadbolts at my apartment.

I grabbed the first t-shirt and pair of jeans I found, which, luckily, were my size. Since I'd supposedly lived here, that at least made some sense.

I tore off the dirty shirt I'd slept in and gasped at the sight of my skin in the mirror. There were faded bruises all over me. I looked as if I might've jumped out of a car while it was speeding down the highway. Maybe that was where I got the bump on my head? Had I been trying to escape someone? But who, and were these people still after me? Or was I already back with them?

Only thing I knew for sure was that I had to get out of here right now before someone showed up and tried to stop me. If I could. Odds were, the exits were probably being watched. I'd find a way out. Even without a phone or a dollar to my name, I was getting out of here.

I heard footsteps approaching as soon I swung open the door that exited the apartment. My steps faltered for a second before I walked out confidently.

The redheaded half of the Thug Brothers was headed my way. "Ollie," he said, smile about as wide as it could stretch.

"Hi…" What was his name again?

His smiled drooped. "Butch."

"Butch." I nodded like I'd been on the verge of spewing forth his name. "Nice to see you. I'm in a bit of a rush right now, so I can't really chat." I smiled and headed toward the elevator, not caring if every little monster, or crawler, as Kane called them, climbed in with me. I'd bear it to get out of here quicker, as I prayed Butch would let me.

He followed me into the elevator. I guessed that was what happened when an atheist prayed. God and I had hit a real rough patch after my family had blown up, and he wasn't scoring any points today, either.

"Where you going? Do you have a ride?"

"I'm going home. I don't need a ride, but thanks anyway."

The elevator doors closed and not a single crawler got on. Well, that was weird. Why were they still keeping their distance? I thought back to all the stuff Kane said, but I didn't remember anything about keeping the crawlers from crowding me.

"Maybe I should drive you? It's no problem," Butch said.

My attention was jerked back to him. Was he really going to let me leave? If he was, turning down a ride might be idiotic, since I had no idea how to get home from here. I'd also have to walk the unknown distance. "Yeah, thanks."

The elevator opened to the hallway off what I remembered them calling the Underground, and I called the first level of hell. It looked like a cross between an old warehouse and a club. As we stepped forward, the music pounded, and half the people in there weren't eating. Most didn't have a normal look about them, either too pale or too hairy or just too—*something*. I decided maybe the second level of hell was more appropriate.

Instead of walking toward the exit, Butch paused.

"Why don't we get a bite to eat first? It'll only be a couple of minutes, and I'm prone to low blood sugar." His droopy smile had perked back up, as if willing me to agree.

My stomach was a knot and I only had eyes for the door. But if Butch was trying to keep me here, I couldn't take him one on one. There was another man standing by the door. I didn't think I could get past him, either. All that stuff about having spells and magic in my head was fine and dandy, but when I stared at the door and rattled my brain on how to get out of here, there was no magic jumping to my aid.

If I was stuck, it was better to pretend I was willing. If I got locked in a cell somewhere, I might never get out.

"Okay, just a quick bite." I tried for a wide smile, like the one he kept giving me.

"Two eggs over easy with a side of toast coming up." There, *that* smile.

"We eat breakfast together quite a bit?" He knew what I ate when I'd had trouble remembering his name. I was at a steep disadvantage in this place.

"More often than not," Butch said as we walked. "This is where we eat." He pointed proudly at one of the limited booths in the place.

I slid in, still working on my faux-smile. "Very nice."

He slid into the other side, no sign of the smile now. My faux-enthusiasm clearly reeked of cheap plastic, like a bad knockoff.

He leaned forward a bit, but without crowding me. "Ollie, I know this seems overwhelming right now, but I promise, you're safe with me. We were friends. We still are, even if you don't know it."

There was something about his soft, almond-shaped eyes that made me trust him, no logic involved. This was strictly my gut talking. He leaned back, not pushing for a response.

"Okay," I said, giving him one anyway. Maybe this wasn't going to end with me in a cell. Maybe this really would be a quick bite before a ride home.

"I'm going to call for breakfast. I'm guessing you won't remember this either, so don't get freaked out." He patted the air beside me.

Why would ordering breakfast freak me out?

"Gargoyle?" He was looking into the air as if he were speaking to someone.

A stone-looking creature popped in front of us, bright red hair appearing to be glued to a cement head, a hot-pink jumpsuit complementing three-inch-long pink nails.

"Ollie? You're back! Zee is going to be so happy to see you!"

I nodded. "That's great." I smiled again, hoping this one looked more genuine than the ones I'd given Butch. I tried to figure out what to say next, but was a stuttering mess.

Butch saved me by taking over and ordering us breakfast. The gargoyle winked at me with false eyelashes before she disappeared.

"Who's Zee?" I whispered, not sure if the gargoyle could still hear us.

"Zee was your girl. She's out on vacation until next week. She was freaking out so bad when you disappeared that Kane sent her away for mental duress. She was driving us all nuts."

The redheaded gargoyle popped back in, dropping off steaming-hot plates with a huge smile. "As soon as Zee is back on the grid, I'll let her know you're home."

"Thanks." I was all nods and fake smiles until she popped back out of existence. "Do all the gargoyles have this same sort of look to them?"

"What look would that be? The stone like skin, or the…" Butch quirked his mouth.

"The, you know." I nodded toward where she'd just been, waving my hand.

He let out a laugh, looking quite amused with himself as he cut into his sausage. "That look would be your fault."

My fork clattered to the plate. "My fault?"

"Yep," he said, making a small popping noise on the P.

After the slew of information I'd gotten from Kane last night, I decided I'd eat some more eggs instead of asking questions about the gargoyles.

I was a couple bites in when it occurred to me that Butch knew where my apartment was, as he'd visited me there. "How far are we from my place? I don't recognize the neighborhood."

He looked up, reminiscent of a deer in the headlights, before shrugging. "Not far." He seemed to dig into his sausage with gusto after that.

I pretended to eat some eggs. Butch seemed more intent on staring at his food than making small talk, so I surveyed the room of freaks around me. Some of whom seemed to be examining me right back. There was a group of women gathered a few tables over staring in my direction. They didn't look altogether unfriendly, but most definitely guarded.

"Butch, who's the group of women in the corner?"

He laughed, but it was of the nervous variety. "For someone who doesn't remember the witches, that question had an edge sharper than cut glass."

"You're saying I don't like them?"

"You've got some history with them." He held up a finger. "Although they did try to make peace with you." He stopped and looked over his shoulder. The women had all turned away, as if nervous of getting caught staring. "Did Kane mention them to you last night?"

"No."

He nodded, as if adding up some invisible tally.

"I was pretty tired last night." I waved a finger back toward the table of witches. "What did they do?"

His eyes went wide as he took in a big breath that turned into a loud sigh. "Well, there was the movie about your life's greatest failures and embarrassments. The clothes rotting away was a bit of a problem for a while. To give them their due, that was a bit—"

All the plates on the witches' table started rattling around until their coffees splashed upward like a geyser. The egg in front of one blonde exploded, catching her in the face, along with the other two women beside her.

"Oh fuck. Time to go." Butch shot out of the booth and grabbed my hand, dragging me with him toward the exit as the witches shrieked.

I didn't say one word. I didn't care if I'd exploded the witches' breakfast and that I had no idea how. Butch was bringing me exactly where I wanted to go. Out of this place.

We didn't stop until we were outside and he was walking toward the vintage Caddy I remembered.

"Are you driving me to my apartment now?" I asked when we were feet from the car.

His steps paused and he turned around. I immediately regretted speaking. I didn't want him to stop walking. I wanted him to get in the car and drive.

"Kane happen to mention anything about your place last night?"

"No. Why would he?"

The door clanged open behind me, and I turned to see Kane striding over. "Where are you going?"

Great. That one definitely didn't want me to leave. Why did I have to go and ask questions before we got out of here?

"She says she wants to go to her *apartment*," Butch said, and then cleared his throat as he tilted his head toward me.

"I'm going home." Which this place was not. This place was mayhem and crazy, shot up with some steroids and wrapped in a straitjacket. I was already plum full of crazy without them.

Butch's eyebrows rose as he whistled.

Kane walked the rest of the way over until he was right beside us. "I thought you were going to rest?"

I crossed my arms. "I did. Now it's time to leave." What was wrong with the two of them? I was getting the feeling that this wasn't about keeping me here, as much as keeping me away from my home.

Butch cleared his throat and took a couple of steps away, pretending he had something else to do.

Kane stood as still as the Rock of Gibraltar. "Ollie, it's not there anymore."

"What do you mean?" What rubbish was he speaking

now? I needed to get out of here before I was as crazy as they were.

"It's gone. A crawler destroyed it," he said softly, taking a half step toward me.

I took a half step back. I didn't believe him. He was crazy, and there was no way everything they said had actually happened.

"I'd like to go see for myself." I took another step away from him, ignoring the twitch in his jaw and the way he looked off to the side.

"I'll take her over there," Butch said from where he'd moved several feet away. "It might be easier."

Kane shook his head. "No. I'll do it."

"If someone insists on taking me, he can." I pointed to Butch. Him, I could handle. Kane was—too much. I didn't know how else to describe it. When he looked at me, it was like he was seeing something more than what I was. More than the person I was capable of being or had any desire to be. All I wanted was for them to leave me alone.

Kane froze, but it was still too much. I could feel the tension exuding from every tense muscle.

Butch stepped a bit closer to Kane and then turned to me. "Can you give us a minute?"

"Sure," I said, and made my way a little closer to the exit of the alley—just in case.

"I get it, but…" I couldn't hear the rest of what Butch said. I shifted, giving them my profile and angling my ear in their direction. I stared in amazement at the brick wall in front of me, as if it were the *Mona Lisa*. Still, I was only picking up on a word here and there. "She doesn't understand," and then "Overwhelmed."

Kane wasn't saying anything, and the tone Butch was using was a cross between cajoling and pleading.

I glanced over when Butch stopped speaking. Kane was emotionless and Butch looked like he'd just ran a marathon.

"Are we leaving soon?" I asked.

Butch shrugged the stiffest shoulders I'd ever seen.

Kane's jaw twitched. "I don't know how long this memory gap is going to last. While we're waiting, do not speak to the crawlers for any reason. It's very important."

He was being fairly reasonable, so I nodded. I had no desire to talk to them anyway. Truth was, I would've agreed to anything right then.

I nodded, waiting to see if there was anything else.

"That's all. If your memory doesn't come back soon, we'll worry about it then." He watched me in that way he did, the one that felt too knowing. I shifted back onto my heels, trying to hold my ground even as I wanted to run from him. His expression blanked and he looked over my shoulder again, at nothing.

For some reason, it reminded me of my family's funeral, all of those mourners standing around the caskets, not having the strength to look at all the people who had been so vibrantly alive a couple days prior.

He finally turned his attention to Butch.

Butch nodded and said, "We're good," even though Kane hadn't asked anything.

Kane turned on his heel and walked back inside.

I stared at the door for a minute, wrestling with this conflicting urge to follow him. Well, it had never been my style to be complacent. That's probably all it was.

"You okay?" Butch asked.

"Yeah, sure. Let's get going." I shook off the feeling the way a dog shook off the damp. I'd never wanted to get home so badly in my life.

Butch swallowed so loudly that I could hear him to my right. "Okay then, I guess we should get going."

Chapter Four

WE'D BARELY GOTTEN AWAY FROM THE BUILDING WHEN Butch started up his weird *did Kane mention this* questions again.

"Did...did Kane tell you anything about your past with him?"

Past? When someone had a "past" with someone else, it was usually one of two things, love or hate. Kane hadn't alluded to either. But last night, how many times had I gotten the feeling he wanted to touch me, even though he hadn't?

"No. Not at all." And I didn't want to hear about it, either. Not right now. Things were already too awkward, and all I wanted to do was get home to my apartment. How bad could it be? Odds were, it hadn't been an explosion so much as a fire. And it had been months. The place must've been repaired by now.

The car screeched as Butch hit the brakes and then swung the Caddy around in a U-turn.

"What are you doing? You know where I live, right?"

"Hang on a sec." He dug his phone out of his jacket and called someone. "You need to come take a ride," he said into the phone.

Butch fell silent. He let out one of those sighs, the aggravated kind. "Jerry can wait. You need to come. I'm around the corner. Hurry up."

He hit the end button and tucked his phone back into his pocket, plastering a smile on his face for me. This one was definitely *not* genuine.

"What are you doing?" I asked, not buying all the shining teeth.

"Leon likes to go for rides."

I didn't bother mentioning I'd heard enough of the phone call to know he definitely did not want to come on this ride.

"That's that blond guy, right?" Had to be the other half of the Thug Brothers. Why did he need backup? For a ride with me?

"Yes." He reached down and turned the volume on the radio up. It was death metal that increased my urge to whack my forehead on the dash, as if that were needed.

I was out of the crazy place. A few minutes more wouldn't kill me. And whatever had happened to my apartment probably wasn't that bad. I'd sleep with two-by-fours if needed.

Leon turned the corner and got in the back seat a couple of minutes later, yelling, "Turn that shit down," as he did.

Butch lowered the volume as Leon settled in.

"Why'd you need me to come?" Leon asked.

Butch didn't answer until after he'd hit the gas. He gave Leon his fake smile as he looked in the rearview mirror. "We're driving Ollie to her old apartment building while explaining to her what her relationship with Kane was."

"You fucker. You set me up." Leon leaned forward, looking out the window as if deciding whether to make a jump for it. "Why do we have to do this? Kane should be doing this."

"Well, we are." Butch hit the gas harder.

"Can you two stop bickering and tell me? Did I fuck him over, did he fuck me over, or did we just fuck? Which is it? Whichever way, it's not a big deal. Just spit it out." I didn't remember being such a liar, but I was doing a bang-up job of it now.

They bounced looks back and forth in the rearview mirror for a minute. When I heard Leon sigh and a genuine smile hit Butch's face, I knew who'd won.

Leon's back hit the seat with a whooshing sound against the ivory leather. "It was more of the 'fucking' variety, without the 'over.'"

So I'd been with him? How had I gone from hate at first sight to a relationship? He was handsome. Maybe I'd been filling my bed with a warm body? Not like I hadn't been guilty of that before. I half turned, leaning an arm on the back rest so I could get a better look at Leon. "So it was a one-night-stand-type deal?"

"I don't know the particulars, but it appeared to be a longer-type deal." Leon was looking out the window as he answered, as if he regretted not throwing himself from the car. You'd think it had been his sex life we were discussing.

I turned back around. "I find it very hard to believe I

would've gotten involved with him. He's…" My shoulders lifted as I tried to find the best words.

"He's what?" Butch asked.

"Arrogant and bossy, so…" I thought back to our first meeting. No. This didn't make any sense. "And he doesn't like me, either."

"I'm not saying it was love at first sight or anything," Leon said. "It took a while."

"*That* I believe."

I kept my eyes forward as I tried to imagine what it might've been like, but couldn't. They were making too much of whatever we'd been. Kane hadn't even mentioned it. It was probably a fling because we'd both been single.

I wonder what the sex had been like, though? Probably great. He was too hot for it to have been bad. Although maybe he was so hot that he didn't think he had to do any work, and lay there like a slab of meat? Still would've been good, considering what I would have had to work with.

BUTCH PULLED the Caddy over in front of a yellow curb and then threw it in park. I didn't bother to tell him to move it. It wasn't my ticket, and he could see the curb as well as I did.

I got out in front of the corner store where I'd get coffee in the mornings on my way to work, not caring if Butch and Leon followed me or not. I'd walked this path so many times that it was like breathing. I took off down the road, following my normal path.

And then I almost walked past my building. This was my street, that was my address, but that wasn't my building. I didn't know what building this was. The location was right, but it hadn't looked anything like that last time I'd been here. It had been brick. Had they stuccoed it after the fire?

I scanned several floors and searched for my window, knowing right where it should be. But it was gone. The window configuration was completely different. It wasn't a facelift. It was a brand-new building, and it wasn't even finished yet. When I glanced through the windows, it was just a shell. They'd been telling the truth. I didn't live here anymore. The last link to the only life I'd remembered was gone, and it shook me like nothing else had, not all the crazy stories or the bruises or couches breaking.

There was no me left. I didn't even know where the clothes on my back came from. It was as if my entire life had been completely erased in those months I'd forgotten.

"What happened? Couldn't they have fixed it?" I turned to Butch, one of the people who acted like they had all the answers.

Butch opened his mouth, then started chewing on his cheek as a couple of "ums" slipped out. He lifted a hand and ran it through his hair, stopping to scratch his scalp. "You really don't remember any of this? Not even a hazy sort of blur?"

"No." Did he think if I did I'd be standing here? Dumbfounded?

Butch looked behind him, where Leon was lagging a few feet away. Leon shook his head in an *I already took my turn* sort of way.

Butch scratched his head again and finally spat out,

"The explosion was *really* bad. It burned for a day. There was nothing left."

"How?" It shouldn't have mattered. It was gone, but I still wanted to know.

"You talked to a crawler. That's why Kane told you not to talk to them. They blow things up." He took a couple of steps and kicked a stone out of his way as I stared at the new building.

Was it true? Maybe the building had just burned down on its own. My whole life, no one believed me about the monsters, and now they were telling me they caused my building to burn down.

I was still staring as Butch made a loop around, stopping beside me. "You ready to go back yet?"

"Back where? That club?" Was that the only reason they'd brought me here? Get it over with, let me see I had nothing so I was easier to handle? Did he really think seeing this was going to make me want to skip back there?

He nodded. "Yep, that's the place."

I gaped at him, stunned, before I finally said, "No. Absolutely not."

Now he was the one with his mouth open, as he turned back to Leon.

"I don't know why you thought it would be that easy," Leon said, shaking his head.

Butch walked over to Leon. "Now what do we do?"

"I don't know. I've never dealt with something like this either."

I didn't wait to hear how they were going to fix me. I walked away, hoping I'd never see any of them again.

I kept walking for a while before the sad realization that I had no money and nowhere to go sank in. Then I walked back to my building, or where my building used to be, and sat on an empty stoop across the street. I leaned my shoulder and head against the concrete doorframe as construction workers walked in and out of the new building that had stolen my home.

Chapter Five

THE SUN HAD SET HOURS AGO, AND BUTCH AND LEON appeared to be gone. I wouldn't have been surprised if they were hiding around the corner, spying on me. I didn't care. As long as I didn't have to deal with them or see them.

The crawlers sitting across the block scattered, and I turned to see Kane a few steps away. I hadn't noticed him as I'd sat angled toward the building. Yep, the Thug Brothers must be lurking around here somewhere. I should've kept walking, but there was that damn problem of having nowhere to walk to. Probably wouldn't have mattered. They had two feet each to follow me with.

"You took a while," I said as I turned back to where my building used to be.

"Was hoping you'd figure it out on your own that you can't sit here all night."

He was acting more like he had that first night I'd met him, and it was something of a relief. Except when I turned toward him, I caught him in an unguarded moment.

He shuttered it quickly, but it was too late. It was that same look he'd had earlier, like he was in mourning or something. And all it did was make me want to run. That or scream, *I'm here. I don't know who you're looking for, but I'm here, me, Ollie. And if whoever I am isn't good enough, then stop looking at me.*

But I didn't say any of those things, because I didn't want to have that fight. I wanted to be alone, where people didn't look at me at all, and when I saw a stranger, they really were a stranger.

Maybe I really had been someone different during those months. A guy like him never would've been with a girl like me. It wasn't my looks, exactly. I knew guys liked the dark hair and grey eyes, and my body wasn't bad either. I was attractive enough to get interest, but I was also a mess, with crawlers stalking me. I'd gotten fired from my last job for being a no-show, and now I was homeless to boot, not to mention the psychiatrist on speed dial. Nothing about me was dating material.

I could see by the cut of the pants he was wearing and the quality of the fabric of his white shirt, the understated watch that I knew cost more than my apartment had, that he had it all. He'd get the pick of the litter when it came to women: looks, smarts, *and* mentally sound.

Didn't matter. He wasn't my type anyway. No man was. Not now. Maybe not ever. Having a husband and kids seemed a bit of a stretch when I was still afraid of the boogieman in the closet.

When I dared to look back at him, his expression was shuttered again. It was safe.

"Where are your buddies?"

He nodded toward the end of the street, and I leaned

forward to get a better view. The Thug Brothers weren't bothering to hide anymore, but standing a block or so away, sipping takeout coffee.

I leaned back, getting as comfortable as you could in a cement stoop. "You should've stayed away. I'm not going back there with you."

He walked the last few steps toward me. "Ollie, I know that this is rough on you, but we'll figure out what happened and it'll come back. But in the meantime—"

I shook my head. "You have no idea if it'll come back." I'd talked to my psychiatrist about amnesia once. It had been a random conversation born of desperation. I'd made a passing comment about some guy who had forgotten his entire adult life, and maybe it would be worth it for a clean slate. He'd told me that whether his memories came back was hit or miss, but it wasn't something he'd ever wish on someone. Thinking back now, maybe it hadn't been so random. And now I knew why he wouldn't wish it upon someone. I didn't get it then, but your memories *are* you. Losing them was like losing some of yourself.

"I know they will because I know..." He took a step away.

I know *you*. That was what he'd been about to say. It might've been true, but it made me want to run. My silence answered what I thought of that.

His stiffness said he was getting impatient. I just wasn't sure if he was getting impatient with me or who he thought I should be.

"Come on. You've been here too long. Let's head back."

I snapped my head in his direction. "Head back where?"

"To the Underground. The place you left earlier," he added, in case I'd forgotten the name. I hadn't.

"I told you in the meeting last…" Fuck. It hadn't been last night. I couldn't make slips like that unless I wanted to sound as unstable as I felt. "I told you that I wasn't staying there." I stood and took a couple of steps away from him. "I don't know what our relationship was, but I don't know you and I don't want to." I looked down the street. "Or them. I'm not staying there."

His jaw clenched, and there was nothing shuttered about his expression now. He shoved up his shirt sleeves and folded his arms. "Then where do you plan on going?" He cocked an eyebrow at me, and he might as well have added, *Go ahead, genius, you tell me.*

I narrowed my eyes and crossed my arms. "I don't need to inform you of that."

He walked toward me, narrowing the gap. "You mean you don't want to tell me what stoop you're sleeping on tonight?" Arrogance poured off him as thick as water over Niagara Falls. I could only imagine that standing in those cold waves was just as uncomfortable.

"I'm not going back to that place." I'd lost months of memories, and my home. The idea of being surrounded by crazy people, talking to me like they knew me all day, made me want to climb up to the roof of the new building and take a leap.

"Ollie—"

"Look, I know you're offering me a place to stay because I'm essentially homeless, but I can't go back there. I need some time—space." I needed a place where people I didn't know weren't looking at me expecting things.

He stood staring at me. Was he going to try and grab me and drag me back, or respect my wishes? I did remember him sending the Thug Brothers for me, but he had let me leave after the meeting. The longer we stood staring at each other, the more I wondered if he had no idea what he was going to do either.

He looked up and muttered something to the sky that sounded like "She's injured."

I nodded, even though I was pretty sure he wasn't actually talking to me.

I looked back over my shoulder at where my building used to be again. Why this too? I'd just lost my family, or it felt like I just had. Now I'd lost my memories. I was going to break. I could feel it. I gripped my arms with my hands so he couldn't see the tremble. I kept my gaze on the building until I could get the burning in my eyes to stop threatening tears.

I took a deep, unsettled breath and squared my shoulders, preparing to settle the issue with Kane and withstand the icy onslaught.

When I turned back to him, his expression was guarded, but I saw his eyes take in the way I was hugging my torso. I dropped my arms quickly, shifting my hand to my hips in a battle position.

But a battle wasn't what I got.

"I own some real estate around here and I've got a place a few blocks away."

My chin jerked up. "I'm not looking for a handout."

"I'm not giving you one. I'm offering you a compromise. You'll be alone there, but the place is secure. You can stay there until you clear your head and we figure out what happened."

More details from yesterday came flooding back, details Kane had given me. I'd been so obsessed with getting home that I'd pushed away the fact that, in the time I'd forgotten, I might've made some enemies. There was stubborn and then there was stupid. I definitely fell into the former occasionally, but I tried to avoid the latter.

I nodded, and then forced myself to say, "Thank you."

He nodded, looking as unhappy as I was. He took a few steps down the road while I tried to force my feet to move.

He stopped and turned back to me. "Are you coming?"

"Yes." I had to. I had nowhere else to go. I forced my legs into action, telling myself everything was going to work out as I did.

He waved off Butch and Leon when we got to the corner. Even though I saw them leave, I doubted they'd be far away.

He kept walking, and I followed without asking any questions. When he got in a black Mercedes, I got in the passenger seat without prompting, telling myself this was a lot better than a stoop.

And when we got out in front of a huge brownstone, I followed then, too.

"You own a unit here?" I finally asked. The only reason I spoke was I wanted to confirm no one else would be dropping by and looking for rent that I didn't have to pay.

"I own the building," he said as he opened the front door, waiting for me to walk in. "But I keep one of the units open. Sometimes I need a place to put people up away from the Underground."

Did he put women up here? Or criminals? There was yet another story that I wasn't ready to open the cover on, not when all I wanted was a bed, not a reason to leave.

We climbed to the second floor, where he opened a door and then handed me the key before he walked in.

The place had a high ceiling and classic dentil molding that contrasted with the clean lines of the furniture. I walked farther into the apartment, the kitchen opening up into a dining area and a living space beyond, a door to a bedroom on my left. Everything in the place had the look of quality, new but used, sparse and yet warm somehow. I chewed on my lower lip as I watched him walk into the place.

"Who owned the apartment I stayed in last night?" I asked, seeing a certain similarity between the styling of this place and that one.

"Mine."

He said I'd have the place to myself, though. Did it matter if it was his? No.

"I'll have someone run a few of your things over tonight to hold you over."

I nodded, not asking where my things were now. I already knew. That apartment I'd stayed at, the one that reminded me of this place. So I'd been staying with him. Maybe we'd clicked in bed, if nowhere else.

The windows that stretched nearly from floor to ceiling gave me the pretense of something else to stare at, even though I was glued to his every move, just as he was mine.

He leaned against the counter that divided the kitchen from the dining area, acting relaxed even as I could taste the tension flowing from him. Flowing from both of us. There was history here, just as Butch and Leon had said. I couldn't remember it, but I surely felt it.

I'd so hoped I'd wake up this morning and remember everything. I was still hoping that I'd go to sleep tonight and it would all flood back with the morning. But what if I woke and all the new sun did was bleach more of it away?

I was as lost as Alice in Wonderland.

"Here." He dug into his pocket and placed a phone on the counter beside him. "You need a phone."

"What kind is it?" I didn't care about the make, but I'd never seen one with that type of silver body before.

"Special line I have made. It's nearly indestructible. I programmed a few numbers into it."

I knew what numbers those would be. I nearly told him that it might've been simpler for me to stick my head out the window and shout if I needed. But I wasn't in the frame of mind for an argument. Let them play their games for now.

"I'll pay you back as soon as I get my banking in order." I knew that a couple hundred bucks, all that was probably in my bank account, would mean nothing to him. This wasn't about the money. This was about asserting my independence.

"There's no—"

"I'll pay you back." I didn't know how, exactly, but I would. My last memory was three hundred dollars and eighteen cents. I wondered how many pennies in interest I might've made?

He nodded, not looking as if he were in the mood for a fight either. "I'll bring— I'll have Butch bring you to the

Underground tomorrow so you can look through some of your things."

He'd been about to say he would, until he remembered how that had worked out last time. I almost felt bad until I saw the tension coming back in to his shoulders, as if he'd had enough of me pushing at him. He shouldn't have taken it so personally. We'd had a fling, and he'd surely gotten something out of it too. I wasn't pushing him away. I was pushing the whole crazy lot of them away.

"You should be okay here," he said, straightening.

I might've been safe enough, but I was definitely not okay, not tonight, anyway. I might've been acting like I was holding it together, but I was hanging by threads, my seams about to burst and show how flimsily I was put together. I'd see how the next sunrise went.

He moved toward the door, as if he were as ready to be alone as I was.

"Do you need anything else here?" He was almost through the door when he asked, obviously not expecting me to say yes.

"Yes."

He looked back toward me, and I thought I saw a glimmer of hope there, as if this were something personal. It was, but I didn't think he'd like it.

"When I told you that something bad was going to happen, why didn't you believe me?"

The glimmer disappeared and flattened. "It's not that I didn't believe you. I just thought I could handle whatever it was."

"But you couldn't." My voice sounded snappish, probably from being too tired and hungry. I didn't even know him. He'd probably been nothing more than a warm body on a few cold nights. I didn't have a right to be angry.

"I understand why you're angry." He gripped the door so tightly that his knuckles were pronounced, as if he were the one who was angry.

"I'm not angry." I wasn't. Was I?

"Goodnight." He left before I had the chance to ask anything else.

Chapter Six

A BEACH-BOY-LOOKING MAN OPENED THE DOOR TO THE Underground before I'd gotten within five feet. He'd probably known we were on our way because the Thug Brothers had reported in.

"Ollie! What's going on? Been waiting to see you all day."

"That's Jerry," Butch whispered from behind me.

"Hi, Jerry. I got hung up with some stuff." That "stuff" would be gathering up the will to come here.

"How's it going?"

"Pretty good." My voice sounded like you could buy me for five bucks in an alley, while his had the real label. As bad as I felt about it, there wasn't much to do but be a fake. I was surrounded by strangers who all knew me well enough to greet me with coffee in the morning, like Leon had today. He'd knocked on my door bright and early with a hot cup made just the way I liked it, with two sugars and skim milk.

I paused a second, fishing around in my head for small

talk, or even miniscule talk. Any kind of talk I could think of.

I was saved by a pouf of blond hair attached to a body. She wrapped an arm around mine and tugged me off. Flip, that was her name. She was there the day Kane had found me. But why she was towing me through the Underground was a bit less clear.

My face must've asked the question, because she started to explain. "Look, I know you don't know who I am. You don't have to. I don't care."

"Okay," I said, the way someone who wasn't quite sure it *was* okay would. But it did feel a lot better than having to pretend.

"We're friends." Her arm tightened around mine.

"Um…" Should I keep telling her it was okay, or did I say I needed some time? That might be awkward.

"We're friends, and you're going to have to deal with it because…" Her voice cracked as she kept walking forward, tugging me along. "You just have to, because not that many people like me." She pushed through the last words with a niggling wobble in her voice.

"Butch and Leon seem like they're your friends." I so wasn't up to propping someone else up today, while I was mentally hobbling along on crutches.

"They like each other better. Everyone likes everyone better than me."

The wobble was about to register on the Richter scale.

"Okay. We're friends. I might not remember you, but I'm getting good feelings. I must've liked you a whole lot." I was definitely overselling it.

"Good." She smiled at me, and I could feel the tension

in the arm looped around mine ease. And there might've
been a suspicious sniffle or two.

I pulled her arm closer, finding that not all of what I'd
said was a lie.

"Now that we've established that, we need to fix the
rest of the mess your memory is making," she said,
tugging me toward the bar that lined one side of the
Underground.

"That sounds like a really great plan, but I've got to go
speak to Kane right now." I tugged her back in the opposite direction, toward the stairs that led to Kane's office.

She patted my hand, nodding and walking with me.
"Good idea. You need to fix this. He's very upset."

"He is?" I'd gotten a couple of weird looks, but *very*?

"Yes. Very." Her voice dropped a few octaves on
the "very."

I smiled.

She cringed. "You're a really bad faker."

"Thanks." I stopped faking.

I marched my way up the stairs toward Kane's office.
This at least I remembered. I saw that Butch and Leon had
settled into their booth downstairs and were watching as I
knocked on the office door.

"Come in," Kane called from within.

There was a little shake in my hand as I reached for the
knob, but I shook it out. What the hell was wrong
with me?

He was seated behind his desk when I entered, calm
and collected.

The office looked a little different than it had last—
whenever it had been. There were still piles of paperwork
everywhere, but the windows that overlooked the main

floor seemed a bit shinier than I remembered. The wood framing had a fresh coat of paint, and it had a general remodeled feel, except nothing was really different.

I turned my attention to him. "Do you have a minute?"

He glanced over at the couch before pointing at the chair in front of his desk. "Have a seat."

I walked toward the chair but hesitated for a moment, glancing over at the couch, too. Why did I have this urge to go nap there? Did I used to do that? Was that why he'd looked at it?

I shut down that train of thought quickly, not knowing where it might drop me off. Just because I might've done something in the past didn't mean it had been a good idea. What if we'd had sex on the couch and that's why he was looking at it? I'd made a lot of bad choices in my life, and I didn't know if he'd been one of them yet.

I took the chair in front of his desk, and then shifted it so the couch was at my back, completely out of sight. I had more important things to worry about, one of them plaguing me since last night.

I sat stiff in the chair, afraid of getting too comfortable. "Do you have any idea why the monsters—crawlers—don't come close to me anymore?"

Kane kicked his feet up on the desk and relaxed back, one elbow resting on the arm of the chair, his shoulders looking too broad for my comfort. Why were the evil bastards always so good looking?

"Do you remember me telling you about Asher?"

How could I not? Of all the details he'd given me, that had been the worst. I was a murderer.

"That was the crawler who looked human that I

killed." I kept my aversion to the deed private. Might be better off to let Kane think I'd kill again—with ease.

"He did something to keep them at bay, but I don't know what." He stood, appearing as if he were going to come around the desk, but he didn't. He turned toward the window at the last moment and rested a shoulder on the wall beside it, leaving a large buffer between us. "How are you feeling?"

Do you remember anything? That was what he really wanted to ask.

No. I still don't remember you. I don't remember any of these people or this place. I wouldn't have even come here if I'd had somewhere else to go with my questions. I choked all of that down. "I'm good, thanks."

He looked out the window. Instead of seeing mourning, I thought I caught a glimpse of regret, like he was watching the sun set on a day he wished he could get back.

I heard a buzzing and saw his phone lying on the desk, facedown. He pushed off the wall and grabbed his phone but didn't answer it.

"I'll be back in a minute," he said, pocketing it.

"Sure." I pointed to his computer as he walked across the room. "Could I use your computer for a moment? I wanted to check some of my accounts."

"Go ahead," he said, like someone with nothing to hide.

He closed the door to his office on his way out, and I didn't waste a second sitting down in his abandoned chair. I kept an ear out for approaching footsteps but didn't hear any. Was he really going to leave me alone in his office?

I clicked on his shrunken windows, of which he had many. Real estate. And more real estate. Was it code for something else? I scanned the first few screens. If it was, it might be the most boring code ever. There were depreciation schedules and repair bills. Closing papers and title searches. If it was a code for something else, I'd never crack it. I'd fall asleep first.

I clicked into his file directory. He sorted them by date, and I scanned quickly to find, yes, more real estate. By the time the door swung open five minutes later, I hadn't had a chance to check my bank account, not that it mattered. I was fairly certain I was as poor as I had been back in January. I clicked shut every open file before he was two steps into the office.

"Done. Thanks."

"Did you get what you needed?" He took the chair in front of the desk that I'd vacated, leaned back, and kicked his heels up onto the surface. It was strange how I was the one sitting behind the desk but his spot had become the power seat.

"No. I forgot my password." Maybe it was the posture? I leaned back, like he was. The effect certainly wasn't immediate.

No. Not working. He was still hogging up all the energy in the room. I took the next step and kicked my feet up on his desk. It looked like it had been dropped out of a truck and rolled down a hill a few times, so I didn't think he'd particularly care about another set of soles on it.

Still wasn't working. Why was that? Was it me? If someone else walked in here, maybe I would seem to hold all the power.

Who the fuck was I kidding? No, I wouldn't.

He leaned his head back, watching me as he did. "Are you comfortable?"

"Eh." I shrugged. *Your position isn't so hot.*

"I'm glad you came in. We have some more matters to discuss."

Why had I come here? Did I really have to get the answer to why the crawlers were giving me space? I couldn't have left it alone and just been happy?

"You're not going to tell me I killed more people, are you?" Shit. I was supposed to pretend I didn't mind killing.

He paused for a second, and my heart began hammering at my chest like it wanted to build an addition. *Please, please tell me I didn't kill anyone else.*

He shook his head. "No, that wasn't it at all."

Weird way to phrase it, but I let it go. It was enough.

"I explained about being shadow kissed the night before. Have you thought about that at all?"

All night long. Somebody tells you a creature dumped a bucket load of spells in your head, how do you think of anything else? Well, that and being a murderer. "A little."

"You need to see what you can retrieve."

Not happening. The monsters were at bay. I had some peace from them for the first time in my life. "What if it shakes something loose and undoes whatever Asher did with the crawlers? All of that is linked somehow, right?" Before he could answer, I was already shaking my head. "I don't know if that's a good idea."

He nodded slowly, as if taking in my words and really digesting them. "I see your point with that—"

"Thank you," I said, cutting him off before the notorious "but" reared its head.

"What are you planning on doing about the magical outbursts?"

Both eyebrows shot up? "Outbursts?"

"Yes. Outbursts."

"It was one broken couch."

He tilted his head forward and stared.

Figured Butch had told him about a little spilt coffee and some egg crumbs. "That might not have been me."

His eyebrows rose as he continued to stare.

"You can stare at me all day long. I'm not retrieving anything. It's dangerous." I already had enough problems. Whatever was sleeping in my head could siesta until the day I died. I wasn't looking for trouble. I was running away from it.

"*That's* dangerous?"

"Yes." I stood, having no desire to have the upper hand in the room anymore. I wanted nothing to do with this room or this place. I knew I should've steered clear of him. What had I been thinking?

"Ignoring magic that might burst out of you every time you get emotional isn't?" He didn't rise, but his gaze followed me as I made my way around the desk, going the long way to avoid getting too close.

"I've got things to do. I can't discuss this right now."

"Yes, I can imagine your schedule is packed."

There he was, the man I'd met that first night, back again in roaring fashion. I didn't bother responding as I walked out of the office.

Chapter Seven

I HEARD THE NOISE AT THE FOOT OF MY BED AND TWO things hit me instantly. How was I *in* my bed when the last thing I remembered was walking down the street? And it was definitely my bed, or borrowed bed. I could smell the sachet of lavender I'd put under the pillow to help me sleep. But I hadn't gone to bed last night. I'd left the Underground on foot and couldn't remember a thing after that.

Second, someone was standing at the foot of my bed. Were they supposed to be here? Maybe I'd invited them back with me? I didn't know because I couldn't remember anything past walking down the street.

So now what? Did I feign sleep or fight?

I'd stashed a knife under my pillow, one I'd taken out of the utensil drawer and placed beside the lavender. It had looked like fairly good quality. It would probably butterfly a piece of chicken with ease, but I wasn't sure if it was up to carving a person, or vampire, or whatever else had come for me.

I jerked up in bed, fumbling for the knife. I spun around, about to dole out death, to find Kane standing in my room, not even alarmed enough to uncross his arms.

I dropped the arm holding the knife. "What are you doing here? Don't you know how to knock?"

"Where were you earlier tonight?" There was a razor-sharp edge to his voice and a hard look about his eyes.

I didn't think I was a killer, but I recognized it in him. He was what I was terrified of becoming.

I welled up all my panic and directed it into righteous indignation. I got to my feet, ready to go nose to nose with him, although failing by quite a few inches. Didn't let that stop me, though. "Seriously? You're going to barge in here while I'm sleeping and have the nerve to ask where I've been?"

He looked down his nose at me. "Yes."

Shit. I should've known that wouldn't work on him, even with the little I remembered. I took a step back, as if I were annoyed with him and not from my own nerves that were bubbling up.

"No answer? Let me guess, amnesia again?" Kane asked, as an even worse version of the man I'd first met reared his head.

Well, that pretty much ruled out telling him the truth, unless I wanted to risk finding out what kind of killer he was. Would he kill me quickly or drag it out? Yeah, no thanks.

"I was here." I forced my breathing to slow down, knowing he was watching every little move. I waited for him to call me a liar. Because I was. I didn't know where I'd been most of the night, but I didn't think it was here. I turned to the dresser and grabbed a pair of sweatpants I had in the drawers. Running down the street screaming might be more awkward in only a long t-shirt.

When I turned back, he quickly raised his gaze from my shirt.

I glanced down at myself. My nipples seemed to think there was a chill in the warm room. I crossed my arms over my chest.

He rested a shoulder against the wall, staring me down. "I thought you said last night that you didn't want to shake anything loose in your head by trying to use spells?"

What the hell had I done last night? "I don't."

"But you did a spell to evade Butch and Leon?"

"No, I didn't." That at least came out with conviction, or sounded like it.

"And yet you did." His eyes narrowed, calling me every bit the liar I feared he would. "Get your shit together. You're coming back with me."

His tone didn't sound like he was open to argument, and the set of his mouth compounded my assumption.

"Why?" I asked, arguing while I shoved the hair from my face, my eyes still struggling to focus in the dim moonlight. I couldn't go back there, especially not now. I didn't even know who I was anymore. "You said I could stay here until I got my head together."

Kane turned his head in the direction of the open bedroom door. "Butch?"

Was everyone here?

"Yeah?" Butch called back.

"Turn the TV on in there and put on a news channel." He took a couple of steps away from the door and then waved a hand toward it.

I didn't argue this time. He didn't tell Butch to turn on

a certain news channel, but any one of them. Which meant whatever happened, they were all covering it. *That* meant whatever had happened was really bad.

I glanced at the bedside table, where I would've put my phone when I went to sleep, but it wasn't there. Kane walked up behind me, and I moved to the living room without it.

Butch's massive head and shoulders were blocking the TV, but he stepped to the side as we came in. The terrified face of a reporter filled the screen. The mid-thirties blonde, with perfectly layered hair and flawless skin, looked about to crumble. Her lips trembled, and this did not look like it was going to be a pretty type of cry. I'd clung to the edge enough to know the look. This chick was about to crack.

A building on fire lit the backdrop. This wasn't a normal fire, either. I recognized it. I'd dug up the newsreel from the explosion that had killed my family and watched it at least fifty times since. It had never seemed quite real, and now I knew why. It was a fire started by a crawler. Once you really saw one, you couldn't miss the intensity that went with it, one that could only be created by a million gallons of jet fuel or a monster not of this world. It was a small apartment building in an area of town too far away from the airport for this to be jet fuel. That left only a crawler.

So, while I was having another memory gap, there'd been an explosion. That didn't necessarily mean I had anything to do with it.

But why did the reporter look like she was on the verge of hysteria? She wouldn't know it was a monster that caused the flames behind her.

"Carole Anne, when you got on scene, what was it that

you saw?"

"Uh," Carole said, nearly dropping her mic.

That was it. That was all she said. Most people could force out a single syllable steady enough, no matter how bad they were doing. The fact that I could hear the shaking in her "Uh," as bad as a four-year-old on their first two-wheeler, told me much more than I wanted to know. She'd seen it. She'd seen one of them, but I couldn't imagine how.

No one could see a crawler but Shadow Walkers, or that was what I'd been told. Shadow Walkers always had black hair and grey eyes, as if their DNA were somehow linked to that dark and shadowy world. That was what Kane had said that first night. This chick wasn't a bleached blonde. She was the real thing, with dark brown eyes, nowhere near a shade of grey.

But here she was, her spray tan not hiding the lack of blood flow to her face as she looked about to topple over.

After nothing came forth other than her initial "Uh," the anchor said, "Let's replay the video for our viewers who are just joining us."

The screen switched to an earlier scene.

Kane was standing by the bedroom door, Butch was by the windows, and I was standing dead center, none of us saying anything as we all watched.

The small building was in flames, bystanders watching as the prewar building lost its glory to a raging fire. A scream burst out of the crowd, different than the earlier ones. It wasn't someone in anguish, watching their life's belongings disappear. This was someone afraid they were about to lose their actual life. This was the visceral sound of terror.

Other screams quickly joined in, but you couldn't tell where they were coming from, as an already chaotic moment turned somehow worse. The camera that had been focused on the building swiftly shifted toward the crowds who were running away from where they'd been watching. They stampeded as if their lives depended on how quickly their feet moved. If what I thought was about to happen did, then their lives did depend on it.

"What is that?" a much calmer Carole asked, sounding like she was speaking to the cameraman.

"I don't know," he replied. The camera panned in the direction of a shadowy figure, backlit by the fire.

One of the largest crawlers I'd ever seen was suddenly on camera. How was this thing showing up on video? How was Carole seeing this? My entire life, no one had been able to see the creatures but me. I was traumatized for years by monsters no one acknowledged, told I had a psychiatric disorder. And now there one was, front and center for the world to see. I didn't know if I should call every doctor that had tried to put me on medication and stockpile happy pills or build a bunker, because surely this was the end of the world.

The creature turned and looked directly into the camera, as if knowing it was about to make its national debut, and opened its mouth. Flames shot out, burning several bystanders who hadn't been able to leap out of the way fast enough, and setting the nearby news van on fire.

The video ended and Carole appeared, a little more color lost from her face.

The anchorman spoke, having more confidence in Carole than I did. "Is there any word from the authorities? Do they believe this might be an alien?"

I watched Carole as she tried to form her words. It was going to be a while.

"So that's what those fuckers look like." Butch's voice was soft and somewhere in between shock and amazement. He glanced at me but turned back to the TV, as if he couldn't pry his eyes from the image. "No wonder you were such a mess when you first came to the Underground."

I knew the state I'd been in when I first met Butch. I was actually glad that I couldn't remember how that might've degraded.

Kane had moved from the bedroom door to a few feet away from me, arms folded, watching me now.

I didn't say anything as I sat there on the couch, letting the situation sink in. There was at least one crawler on the loose, and normal people could see it. I didn't know exactly how far down the scale that was, but it definitely registered as horrible.

Kane had told me that right before I'd lost my memory, I'd had a feeling that something bad was going to happen. I'd assumed my previous self had somehow known something was about to befall me. But seeing this, maybe it had been much larger than myself? This was a whole lot worse than losing part of my memory…unless the two were connected.

"Now we're going to switch over to Tom Anderson, who is at the other explosion site," the anchor said.

"Wait, this is the second explosion?" I asked.

Kane nodded, staring at me as if maybe I'd already known that for some reason.

The news was now playing a loop of another crawler

moving away from a roaring fire. This time it looked like a strip mall.

"Wow, that's another ugly fuck. Are they all that bad?" Butch asked.

"Yes, to varying degrees," I answered. Kane watched me, still saying nothing. "Any idea how this happened?" I asked, even as Kane was looking at me like I'd done it.

Worst part was, I might've done it. Still, asking some normal questions was the right move here.

"Somebody *helped* them out," Kane said.

No, asking questions definitely didn't throw him off the scent.

"Are there going to be more of those things?" Butch asked. I hadn't known Butch long, that I could recall, but he didn't seem the type to normally rattle.

"Hopefully not," Kane said, remaining calm even as Butch sounded like his shock and amazement was morphing into panic and revulsion.

"This is going to cause some problems," Kane said, sounding more put out by an inconvenience than worried that these creatures were loose. "You ready to leave now, or would you like to wait for a few more explosions?" he asked, his eyes hooded.

"Why do you think I'll be better off there?" Would I be safe there? Were these monsters going to come for me next? And if I was there, I'd have nothing but eyeballs on me while I was trying to figure out if I'd had some involvement.

"This isn't about it being better for you." He grabbed my wrist and then held it so my hand with the shadow-kissed mark was in between us. "See this? This means you are a liability to me. This is me doing you a favor."

He dropped my wrist, as if he didn't want to continue touching me.

"I can't imagine that I ever had anything to do with you." At that moment, I hated him. It wasn't rational. I knew how things looked, but I didn't care.

"Well, don't worry, because I'm not looking to revisit it."

Kane turned to Butch. "Talk to her." He then walked out, not bothering to say anything else to me.

"Talk to me about what?"

Butch sat beside me on the couch, and it didn't look like it was for my benefit. He looked like he needed to conserve his energy.

"What? I disappeared for a night and he loses his mind because of a coincidence?" Please let it be just that. I didn't want to find out I'd had something to do with this. The very idea I could have made me want to spill my own guts out on the ground.

Butch leaned forward, resting his forearms on his legs and sighing. "Ollie, you need to understand how bad this looks. The first sighting wasn't tonight. We got word of several crawlers being sighted the week you disappeared. Now you purposefully shake us off last night and another one shows?"

I narrowed my eyes. "What do you mean, I purposefully shook you off?"

"We were supposed to keep eyes on you because Kane was worried about your safety. You were walking down the street and you just disappeared, using magic of some sort."

They lost me on the street and their first thought was that I'd used magic? I was convicted before they'd even proven anything. "I can't use magic. I can't find any of it. You sure you didn't lose me in a crowd?"

He turned toward me, a frown on his brow. "Ollie, there was no crowd. We were the only ones on the street. You just up and disappeared. It's the truth that Kane's doing you a favor. People are starting to realize you aren't together anymore. If the other races think you've got something to do with letting the crawlers in, they might try and kill you. If you're back at the Underground, they'll know you're still under Kane's protection."

"Whether he wants to protect me or not." I bent forward, resting my forehead in my palm.

Butch's mouth ticked up in the corner as he gave a halfhearted shrug. "At least he's still willing to protect you while we work this out."

I closed my eyes. Don't ever, ever, think it can't get worse. Because it always can. How had I forgotten that lesson?

"Do you think I did it?" It was a bad question. I didn't know, and I was leaning toward guilty.

"No. I don't."

"Why not?" *Please say something that'll give me hope. Please, I need it badly right now.*

"I don't know why I believe you're innocent, but I do. The Ollie I know wouldn't do something like that."

I wrung my hands. "But I just disappeared."

"I didn't say I had a reason to believe you. It looks *really* bad." His eyes widened as he nodded.

Yeah, tell me about it. "But I was sleeping with him, and he thinks I did it."

Butch's face bunched up as if he had another unpleasant tidbit to tell.

"What now? Just tell me."

"Well, I figured you'd slept with him, and I actually used that in your defense. Turns out, you hadn't slept with him."

Why hadn't I slept with him? Had I been stringing him along? Had I turned into some sort of criminal mastermind that was trying to keep Kane close while I did horrible things? It surely looked that way. What was going on? What had I been up to?

I only had one option now. I stood. "I'll be right back."

"Where you going?"

"To pack." Before I headed to the bedroom, I looked back at Butch.

He turned toward me with a question on his face.

I pointed to the corner. "Can you see that?"

"That" was a particularly ugly crawler that loomed about five feet tall, complete with scales. Its lip pulled back, showing teeth as I stared at it.

"See what? The table?"

There was a small table in the corner beside the creature. "No. So, it's only some of them." I should've guessed that anyway, as I doubted Butch would've been so relaxed if it were visible.

"Is one of those ugly fucks over there?"

"Yep."

Butch shuddered a little and then stood and moved to the farthest point away from the corner. "Are they anywhere else?"

There was a small one right beside his feet. This was definitely one of those times that the truth probably wasn't for the best. "Nah, that's it."

Chapter Eight

KANE STOOD THERE, LOOKING EMOTIONLESS, WHEN BUTCH and I exited the building. Jerry and Leon acted as if the whole scene wasn't awkward.

It was. I felt like I was being escorted to jail without a trial, and it might've been better that way. I didn't know how I should plead.

Kane took my bag from Butch, who'd offered to carry it for me. Then the Thug Brothers and Beach Boy walked briskly to the Caddy, leaving me alone with their boss.

Kane walked over to the Mercedes I recognized from the other night and threw my bag in the trunk.

We drove in silence, mutually agreed upon without either of us having had said a word. As much as we were different, we were completely copacetic right now. Neither of us could stomach talking to the other.

He pulled into the lot and grabbed my bag out of the trunk before I'd gotten out of the car. There was nothing polite about it. He was holding my few belongings hostage. If I had the desire to speak to him, I would've told him he didn't need to bother. After I'd woken up after another blacked-out patch of history to find crawlers ravaging the city, I realized the Underground was my only choice. Butch laying out the finer details had only sealed the deal. I wasn't here just because he thought I should be. *I* thought I should be.

Another memory lapse and now another crawler out, this one blowing things up. Had it been me? The idea was revolting to my very core, but I'd been involved somehow. There couldn't be this many coincidences. That old saying about it quacking like a duck? Well, I was quacking my ass off and doing swan dives into the pond right now.

Too bad I had no one I could confide in. I certainly couldn't tell Kane. He looked like he was waiting for the smallest provocation to wring my neck.

There was no way I'd ever liked this man. I must've been on a drinking binge or something. Or drunk on lust. One of those would've made sense. I'd been so distraught about my family that I'd gone on a bender and grabbed the first hot piece of meat I saw. I'd never been prone to addiction before, but everyone had their buttons. Many sane people lost it for less than what I'd lived through. I must have finally cracked and been drinking nonstop, using his body for comfort. That might even explain the blackouts, or one of them. There were some big issues, though. Even alcoholics didn't black out for months, and according to Butch, I hadn't slept with Kane. Although there were a lot of things you could do that excluded intercourse.

The Underground door opening jarred me from my whimsical musings of being an addict.

Kane had my bag slung over his shoulder and carried it toward the door, without a glance at me. I told myself it wasn't rude when he walked without looking back to see if I was following. I was struggling with believing my own bullshit, though.

Kane walked through the Underground, the crowd all staring while pretending disinterest. I followed behind him as if I were some wayward orphan that had been brought home after escaping. The regular music was dulled as all the freaks in the room watched something bigger and badder than them on the TV, only taking a break to watch our spectacle.

Coming here was the best choice. I knew it even if I didn't feel it. If someone was using me, it would be a million times harder to get to me if I was here.

Kane walked into the elevator and the crawlers evacuated before I stepped in after him. Watching the crawlers steer clear of him made me wonder if I'd latched on to him because I'd found peace that way.

We stood a foot or two apart like we were strangers who'd never met. Had I been using him?

"The crawlers don't seem to like you." I left off "either," but I had to bite my tongue to do it. Yes, things looked bad, but you'd think I'd get the benefit of the doubt. The more I thought about it, the thicker his frost, the more I got heated. Who was he to condemn me?

He kept staring straight ahead as he flatly said, "Never noticed."

Sure. I got it. I was a liar, so why should he be honest? And I was supposed to spill my guts to him? When this was how he acted? For all I knew, he could be right. Maybe I was behind this. Maybe I'd finally snapped my cap. What if that Asher person had not only scared away the crawlers but jumbled my head? What if I had one of those split personality things? Hoped not, but you never knew.

The possibilities rolled around in my mind as the doors slid open. I pulled it together, or held it together with some duct tape, anyway.

I stepped out into the hallway and walked to my left, to the apartment I'd been brought to after he'd found me.

"No. Not there. That's my apartment." I turned toward Kane as he walked toward the door on the right. "This is your place."

So I'd definitely been shacked up with him and just officially been kicked out. He was keeping me close. But not too close. I hadn't wanted to stay in that apartment again, but being uninvited felt about as good as an eviction notice.

He opened the door, walked in, and tossed my bag on the couch.

He turned to leave, and I realized there was no one posted to keep me in.

"What? No guards at the door?" I'd intended to hide my sarcasm in a joke, but my words could've filled a thousand batteries.

"No." He turned and stood in the doorway. "I'm not wasting a guy on your door. This is it. I wouldn't disappear again, like you just did when Butch and Leon were watching you. If there's another explosion, you better have an alibi."

All the warm and fuzzy was sure making it hard to hold back my confidence, but I managed. "Sure. Message received."

His eyes dropped to the ground briefly as he stood still for a second, before turning and leaving.

I walked around the place, which looked like it had been redone fairly recently. In the normal world, redone meant things had been getting dated. Here, from what I'd already heard, it made me think of bloodshed.

There was a dining area and a small fridge but no real kitchen. A large sectional dominated the living room, and there was a door leading to a bedroom off to the side. It was similar to Kane's place, but a scaled-down version.

I sat on the couch and counted all my nos: no memory, no money, no cell phone.

My stomach growled, making me remember another no, as I wasn't sure if they had room service, and I wasn't going back downstairs. I'd rather my stomach howl like a wolf at the moon all night.

But as of tomorrow, I was going to get some answers, even if it meant talking to a crawler.

Chapter Nine

IT WAS NINE A.M. WHEN I MADE MY WAY DOWNSTAIRS, feeling like a zombie. Every time I'd started to drift off to sleep, I'd wake back up, afraid I'd find myself somewhere new with no memory of getting there. I felt like a bomb with a short fuse that was already lit, and if I didn't get some answers soon, something else was going to explode.

First place that I needed to go was the site of the explosions. There might not be any clues, but it was the only lead I had, unless I wanted to talk to a crawler. That had seemed like a good idea last night, but in the light of a new day, I acknowledged it was a last-resort kind of option, and I wouldn't do it here, among all these people. Either way, I needed to get out of here for a while, and I doubted it was going to go smoothly.

There might not have been a guard at my door, but Jerry was at the exit. His stance widened as he saw me. Then I saw the beginning of a cringe, like he was prepared for battle but hoping he wouldn't actually have to fight.

I stayed calm, in appearance, anyway. He was definitely going to try and stop me, but if I acted like it wasn't a big deal, maybe he'd do the same? After all, I'd agreed to come back here. I might've dragged my feet a little, but I'd done it because it had made sense. That didn't mean I'd agreed to house arrest.

Jerry shifted in front of the doorknob as I approached. He held up his hands when I was less than five feet away. "Before I say this, I want you to know something."

I crossed my arms, not wanting to hear it already. This was not going to go easily.

"You don't remember me, but you like me. You think I'm a decent guy." He put his hand to his chest, as if swearing.

"I'm sure I do, but I've got to go run some errands, so…" I smiled and waved a hand, hinting that he needed to get out of my way.

The cringe was back, and so bad I could see his upper teeth. "You can't."

"Because of him?" I asked, pointing to Kane's office, no longer feigning calmness. I should've known he was going to pull some upper-handed bull after last night.

Jerry jerked his head back unnaturally on his shoulders. "Please don't punch me."

"What are you talking about? I've never punched anyone." What kind of brute did he think I was? One thought I was blowing things up, another one thought I walked around punching people. And Jerry was twice my size.

There was a pause before he slowly nodded. "Okay. You don't."

He wasn't dropping the hands that were partially raised, as if I were about to attack him. Did Kane put him up to this? What kind of things was that man saying about me?

I turned on my heel and marched across the Underground, all eyes on me, but I didn't care.

I barged into Kane's office without knocking. Butch was by the Keurig machine. I gave him a brief nod and made my way to Kane's desk. Kane didn't say anything, but I had his full attention. He leaned back in his chair, acting relaxed as he tossed the papers in his hand on top of it. I would've bought the act, except his jaw wasn't tensing for nothing.

I put two hands flat on the desk. "I came here willingly and you're making me a prisoner? What happened to no guards?"

He rocked back in his chair. "Why is your phone going to voice mail?"

I swallowed so loudly that I thought Butch might hear me across the room. My phone had gone missing last night, along with my memory, and damn if he didn't know it.

But that might be useful right now. "I lost it. I was trying to go out and get a new one when your man stopped me."

"When did you lose it?" he snapped back quickly.

"Last night."

"You lost it while you were sitting in the condo all night?" he asked, eyebrows rising.

I was really beginning to hate when his eyebrows rose. "Before I got there."

He paused before he said, "Very convenient."

"Yes, my life has been so convenient."

He'd been trying to track me through my phone. Only

way he knew exactly when it had gone missing. He'd probably tried to pinpoint me after Butch had called in that they'd lost me.

Had I dropped it on purpose, just as I'd disappeared? What was going on? Maybe Kane was right—I was a monster. Maybe my personality had split and my other half was so atrocious that I couldn't bear to know her.

Kane stood, jarring me from horrible thoughts as he walked into a closet off his office. He came back out with a phone in his hand. He placed it on the desk in front of me. "I'll have it turned on shortly. Make sure it's charged and stays that way. As long as you have Butch or Leon with you, you're free to go wherever you want."

"So I need a babysitter?" How was I going to tell an escort that I wanted to dig around in the rubble of the explosions for incriminating evidence against myself? That if I found some, I might not be coming back, because everyone would rightfully want to kill me?

"Yes," he said, no hesitation. "You're mentally unhinged. You don't know where you were for months, and we have the small issue of buildings blowing up on the night you disappear again, *while* you're comfortably in bed."

He stood a foot away from me now, daring me to refute what he was saying. His words condemned me. I was glad this wasn't a court of law, because if I were the jury, I'd have declared me guilty too. It looked bad. I knew it, which was why I had to get the hell out of here and figure out what was happening before anyone else did.

But still, he was calling me crazy. Even if I was, I couldn't just accept that. "I'm not mentally unhinged."

He shrugged. "Not knowing what you did for months

certainly means something. If I were you, I'd check the mentally unhinged box. The other option doesn't have a good ending."

I leaned a hip against his desk, crossed my arms, and raised an eyebrow. "Being mentally unhinged would at least explain one thing that doesn't make sense." I kept my eyes locked on his. He was a smart man. He'd know I meant getting involved with him.

"If I didn't have an aversion to liars, I'd be tempted to prove a point."

For ice-cold eyes, he was throwing off a massive amount of heat. Or maybe that was me? It was a good thing I didn't like this man, or I might want him to prove all the points he needed.

Butch cleared his throat in that way made it sound like he was choking on unsaid words. "Still here."

I took a few steps away from Kane, grateful for the cold water that Butch had thrown on the moment. And where had that even come from? All our foreplay must've been really good, so good it was lingering in my lost memory.

Leon walked into the office, headed straight to the Keurig. He paused halfway there, took one look at Kane and I, then turned to Butch. "Ah shit. Is this a bad time?"

Butch rolled his eyes and nodded.

I gave them my back and turned to Kane.

"Fine. Give me one of the Thug Brothers." Then I'd lose him. I didn't care how long it took. I needed to get to the explosion site. And more, I needed out of this place and away from Kane for a while.

He walked back around his desk, reclined, and kicked his feet up. "I don't have anyone available."

"Really?" I hooked a thumb toward the Thug Brothers, who were both sipping coffee.

"Actually, we have pressing matters," Butch said. "I can't work without caffeine."

"Vanilla-flavored caffeine," Leon added.

"And don't punch us. It's not our fault," Butch said.

Why did everyone think I was going to punch them? I turned, wanting to get out of Kane's office more than I wanted to argue. "Find me when you have someone available."

Chapter Ten

I SPENT THE MORNING AND INTO THE AFTERNOON UP IN MY rooms, waiting for an escort. By three, I'd decided the wait had ended and no one was going to come. As I'd sat brewing for hours, it occurred to me that there might be another option to find out what happened. The witches. They'd replayed my memories once; they could do it again.

But I'd have to choose wisely. If they saw something incriminating, they'd probably run right to Kane with the information. And if whomever I picked saw me letting crawlers into the world, they'd be scared enough that it might be hard to keep them quiet. *I'd* be scared. Thinking about it, I wasn't sure I wanted to find out, but I had to. My life probably depended on me finding out what was happening before anyone else did. I needed one I could intimidate, someone smaller. I wasn't exactly a big girl at five feet four, so that might be tough. There were definitely some smaller witches, though.

It took about ten minutes to spot one in the Underground and then follow her into the hall. I had to wait until a vampire walked by. The blonde was about to get on the elevator when I grabbed her arm and dragged her toward the stairwell door.

"What are you doing?" She yanked on her arm but couldn't lose me. I was latched on to her tighter than a starving dog on T-bone steak.

I didn't answer until the door shut. "I need you to do me a favor." It wasn't exactly a favor, but presentation mattered.

She made a face, her skin crinkling so much that a pug would've been jealous.

"I'm trying to be civil about this." I let go of her arm. "See? Civil."

"You dragged me down the hallway." She rubbed the skin where I'd grabbed her, like it actually hurt.

"And I let you go."

She took a step back and glanced toward the stairs behind her, since I had the door blocked. I'd tackle her if she took one step.

"Look, I'm trying to do this peacefully. I'm sure you've heard what I can do, and grabbing your arm is the least of it." Or so I'd heard. Hopefully enough gossip had trickled down to the witches that she'd be wary.

"I don't care what—"

I threw my hand up over her mouth, muffling her yelling. She backed away from me. I followed her until her back hit the stair railing.

Hand firmly clamped below her owl eyes, I said, "Can you please keep your voice down? If you'd listen to me, you'd know this needs to stay between us."

The door creaked open behind me. Who was taking the stairs? I hadn't seen anyone come this way since I'd been here. I dropped my hand quickly. I didn't need any questions. I'd chase her down after they left.

"What are you doing?" Kane asked as he came and stood beside us.

Damn it. I should've known it was him when the little crawler on the landing above disappeared.

The little witch didn't waste a minute. "She's threatening me." Her eyelashes fluttered so fast that it looked like she was trying to take flight.

A fat tear ran down her cheek. Was that a spell, or had she trained herself to cry on command? It made me want to punch her in the nose to see what her real tears looked like. Except I didn't punch people, no matter what everyone else thought.

"I didn't threaten you. Theatrical much?" It was ridiculous. I hadn't been able to get the threat out yet.

She reached out and clung to Kane's arm, as if me merely speaking to her was harmful. If she fluttered those lashes one more time, I wouldn't punch her, but I might *accidentally* poke her in the eye. Then we'd see how pretty her tears were.

"Why were you threatening her?" Kane asked, as if there were no doubt I was the one at fault.

"I didn't threaten her." I might've been about to, but it was still insulting that I never got a trial.

Butterfly Lashes smirked, her body now positioned halfway behind Kane, as if she needed him to protect her. Actually, she might if she clung to him a little harder.

Kane turned toward Lashes. "What was the threat?"

"I don't know. She didn't get to it yet." She stared

straight at me as she poked her head clear of his arm. "But it was coming."

The entire encounter went from frustrating to so worth it when Kane shook his head. He let out a short sigh and took a step away from her, extricating himself from her clinging hands. "I'll handle Ollie. You should leave."

Butterfly's smile lit, and the lashes set to fluttering. Figured she'd misinterpret that as him taking her side, as opposed to him wanting to lose her. She walked out of stairwell, but not before she beamed a smile in my direction.

The door shut behind me, and I was fairly certain I wasn't getting out of the stairwell as easily as Lashes had.

He took a step toward me, tilting his head down. "What were you trying to get from her?"

"I heard I'd had problems with the witches. I was trying to clear the air."

His eyebrows rose, as if to say, *Bullshit.*

I shrugged. "You don't have to believe me."

He walked toward me, and as much as I told myself to hold my ground, my feet moved a few steps back until I got control of them.

He didn't stop until his shirt was grazing my long-sleeve t-shirt. "That's good, because I don't. You've had lots of problems with the witches, and you never cared if you cleared the air with them or not. Don't do something stupid."

The last thing I wanted to hear was how he knew what I did, or what I cared about, even if it might've been true.

"Stop expecting me to be her." Her. It was such an odd way to phrase it when "her" was me. But the things they told me about the person, the time I couldn't remember, it was as if they were telling me about a stranger. It galled me that everyone thought they knew *her* better than I did.

I put both hands on his chest and shoved, anger spilling out over the fact that I'd let him intimidate me into stepping away from him. How he believed the witch, even if she was actually right. Fury that he hadn't done something to stop this whole this situation before it blew up. I'd warned him something was coming, and he'd done nothing! Who was he to judge me at all?

I shoved again, anger boiling up in me. This time, instead of standing still in front of me, he put his hands under my arms and walked me back until I had the wall at my back and him at my front.

"I'm not your enemy."

"You're certainly not acting like my friend, either."

"Then talk to me."

And when he said it like that, so calmly and like he really cared, I almost told him that I'd lost another chunk of memory. How I was terrified of what I might've done and would maybe do again.

Then I thought about how he'd barged into the apartment as if I had blood on my hands. I might've been involved with him once, trusted him enough to reach out for help. Believed in him. But I wouldn't do that again. Look how that had turned out.

Fool me once...

I shoved at his shoulders, and whatever softness I'd thought I'd seen hardened. He stepped back a few inches, and I slid out from between him and the wall.

I opened the door, and right before I left, he said,

"Don't bother going after them again. The witches can't retrieve your memories. I've already tried."

Figured he would've already tried that.

Shit.

Chapter Eleven

THE SECOND I WALKED ONTO THE MAIN FLOOR THE NEXT morning, Butch and Leon waved me over to *the* booth. I didn't hesitate. I needed one of these guys to get out of the building. I made my way across the room, ignoring the people who watched me, as I slid into the booth.

"Still alive," Butch said, with a huge, hopeful smile on his face.

"Yeah?" I cleared my throat, wondering if he was going to say something more that would clarify it.

Leon coughed and looked the other way.

Butch leaned forward, his eyebrows both angling up. "Really? You forgot that too?" He sounded like I'd taken away a favorite toy.

I was tempted to lie, but I didn't know what to lie about. What was the importance of "still alive"?

Leon looked over at Butch and patted him on the shoulder. "You knew she wasn't going to remember."

Butch's gaze dropped and then shifted to the crowd. "I

know. I keep hoping something will click. I just don't know how to do this."

"It'll be okay. She'll remember us. Eventually."

"What if she doesn't?" Butch asked, turning to Leon. "She—"

"I gotta go. I forgot about something." There was no way I was going to be able to get them to take me out today and then purposefully lose them. I wasn't sure what my alter ego might be capable of, but I couldn't. Even the prospect of eating breakfast with them was too much at the moment. I had a bag of chips in my room. It would suffice.

Butch gave me a halfhearted wave, and Leon nodded, eyes down.

I made my way across the Underground and to the hall, where the elevators were. I'd meant to go to the elevators but found myself turning left instead, as if I were following a well-worn path.

I wasn't sure what the worst part of not remembering was. Having a list a mile long of things you didn't recall, having people know you who you'd just met, or feeling like there was an alien directing your actions. Sometimes it felt as if I were filled with urges that made no sense.

I made it to the first landing when a gargoyle popped in front of me. She had a side pony, perfect nails, a pink leather skirt with zipper up the side, and stilettos. "I hope you're ready to get back to work after disappearing on us all."

"Huh?" I jumped back. Here I went again. Someone who knew me, whom I didn't recognize. Although I had my suspicions this was Zee, the gargoyle I'd heard about.

Her side pony swung as she tilted her head this way and that. "I've been hearing all sorts of crazy talk." She looked as if she were about to go off on a tangent when she looked closer. "Are you kidding? It's true? I can understand you going daft, but you forgot me?"

I was too tired to deny something she already knew. "It's nothing personal. I've forgotten everyone."

"*Me*? Zee?" Her eyes narrowed and dust fell from her forehead. "Shit. This whole thing is stressing me out so bad I'm sweating."

She took a step away from me and appeared to be mumbling a pep talk to herself. She took a few steps to the right and then walked back again, occasionally glancing my way. I eyed up the door a half a flight down. Did I leave? She didn't appear to be done, but she wasn't speaking to me, either. Was this how that witch had felt? Nah, I wasn't *this* scary.

I edged a foot back, while watching to see if she noticed.

She spun back around. "How bad is it, exactly? Do you remember any of the stuff in your head, or is that all gone too?"

So, she knew I was shadow kissed. Everyone seemed to know about that, though. Didn't mean I'd been friends with her, did it?

"Nothing. I've heard that there's stuff in there, but I…" I waved a hand at my head and then shrugged. I inched back a little further. If this was what went down in the stairwells, I couldn't imagine why I'd wanted to come this way. Definitely taking the elevator from now on.

"Look, you might not remember, but we've got office space. We were about to be very profitable. You can't quit."

"I'm not quitting. I can't start. I don't know anything."

Then her words "very profitable" sank in. If I was guilty of what I feared, I was going to need money to disappear. A lot of it, and maybe quickly. I'd move to some island that was barely inhabited, so empty that the crawlers wouldn't have anything to blow up. "What exactly do you need me to do?"

Her eyes sparkled like newly buffed marble. "I'll bring some of the girls to our shop and you can experiment on them. Gargoyles are a hard bunch to kill. You can set us on fire, throw acid on us, it won't be a problem."

"What if I can't find anything in there?"

A noise near the first-floor door had us both waiting for someone to enter, but no one did. Still, Zee nudged me toward the next flight up. At least this time I wasn't the only one looking for secrecy.

"It's there. You're shadow kissed. That doesn't go away." She wrapped one very heavy arm around my shoulders as she kept me moving. Her arm jerked away suddenly, startling me.

"What's wrong?" I asked.

"Let me touch your head." She didn't wait for me to answer but backed me up against the wall as two massive hands with pink claws reached out.

Both palms landed on the top of my head, but instead of being crushing, they were quite gentle—and weirdly warm. Her eyes were closed. Since it wasn't hurting, easiest thing seemed to be to wait it out. And *never* take the stairs again.

Her hands dropped, and she'd lost the sheen to her marble.

"What is it?"

"We've got problems."

"What are you talking about? What problems?" Holy hell, did she see something in my head? Did she know what I'd done? Had I really helped those crawlers? I measured the distance between myself and the second-floor door, wondering if I was going to have to run for it now. Maybe I shouldn't run at all but let them kill me. If I'd had something to do with it, maybe I deserved death?

Zee didn't notice my panic as she eyed up the back of my head, then my back and my legs, examining every inch, it seemed. She backed up finally, and I waited for the verdict.

"This amnesia you have"—she kept shaking her head as she talked—"it's not normal."

Okay, verdict was still out on whether I was a criminal mastermind. That was good. The revelation that my amnesia wasn't "normal" didn't really rock my world.

"Is it ever?"

She tapped a shiny pink nail against her lower lip, making a clicking noise. "I'll get back to you."

Poof. Zee was gone.

Chapter Twelve

I WATCHED AS A BUXOM BLOND VAMPIRE STROLLED UP TO Jerry. It had happened several times tonight already. I knew because I'd been sitting and watching the door for hours. Butch and Leon had already eaten and left, and I still hadn't had the heart to trick one of them into escorting me. I was going to have to break out alone, and watching Jerry and this girl, I thought I'd found my way.

The female vampire would show Jerry something on her phone, grazing his arm with her cleavage as she did. *Accidentally*, of course. His eyes would go to the screen, but I didn't think whatever he saw was the real reason he was smiling like a kid on Christmas morning. She'd tilt her head this way and that, flipping her hair and swinging her hips just so. Her tongue would dart out, wetting her already glossy lips.

I'd seen this play out enough to know I needed to hustle into place, hoping she would follow the same pattern. I made my way around the room, glad everyone was watching the news and not me.

Boom, there went her big move. With a swish of the hips, she sashayed toward the alcove a few feet away. That was all I needed. He watched her every sway. Like a fish nibbling at the bait, she reeled him in until he disappeared into the alcove and I ducked out.

As soon as the door shut behind me, I jogged down and around the corner. The city had pretty much shut down, so grabbing an Uber wasn't going to be likely, especially here. Plus, there was something weird about this place. I didn't think it even showed up on a navigation system. It didn't matter. I'd jog the whole way to the closest explosion scene if I had to.

I'd only made it a block before a trio of young men, all with the color yellow displayed somewhere, approached me. I thought gang colors were blue or red, but I wouldn't put it past Kane to have his very own gang.

"Do you need help, miss?" one of the three called from across the street.

"I'm fine." This had to be a trap. Any second, they'd rush over here, grab me, and drag me into a dark alley. I'd be robbed and probably raped, too, unless whatever had broken Kane's couch decided to burst out of me and break some bones.

"You sure? Do you need a ride or something? You can take my car if you need." He dug in his pocket and pulled out a set of keys. He threw them across the street, and they skidded to a stop at my feet.

"That's my car," he said, pointing to a small blue Toyota, the only car on the street.

I stared at the keys like they were a snake at my feet. Then back to the guy who'd thrown them. Something didn't make sense here, or did it? "Why would you give me your car?" I asked, my voice raised enough that I could be clearly heard across the street.

"You're the boss's chick, right?"

I shrugged, not denying it. A ride would really come in handy. "I don't want your car, but I could use a ride." I picked up the keys and tossed them back at him. I hadn't driven in years, and I had no intention of banging up his car.

THE TIRES SCREECHED as the guys left me a block away from the location of the first explosion. I walked up the block to the building, which was now a charred shell in the center of a deserted block. I understood why everyone had moved out and in a hurry. It was hard to conjure up warm, cozy feelings of home sweet home when a monster had obliterated the building next door. I had a desire to run as well, but I couldn't afford to. There was nowhere safe for me to run. If these memory lapses had something to do with the explosions, I needed to know.

I ran my hand along the blackened building, not sure what I was looking for but hoping I'd find it anyway. There had to be something. I circled the perimeter and walked along until I was in the backyard. A swing set stood empty, only the breeze setting the empty seats to swaying. I knew there'd been deaths, but I'd tried to not listen to the head count. Now I couldn't help but wonder how many.

And why? What was the point of this?

The back entrance stood gaping open, the door scattered twenty feet away, as if it had been blown as easy as a playing card. The interior was even worse, like I'd stepped into the diseased belly of the beast. Everything was charred, the ground cracked and creaking under my feet as I walked upon the indistinguishable remnants of people's lives.

I'd knelt down, pushing a fallen piece of wood aside to see what lay beneath, when I saw a silhouette standing on the other side of the room. He was in front of one of the many blown-out windows, the moon at his back, casting his face and body in shadows. But even in the shadows, I recognized Kane. I froze, knowing how this could look, digging around in the ruins of the explosion after sneaking out of the Underground.

He wasn't moving. Did that mean he wasn't thinking the worst of me? Or was he not in the mood to murder tonight? Maybe he didn't like to exert that kind of energy until he'd had a good meal or something? I ignored him and continued to move around the room, refusing to act guilty.

"What are you looking for?" He took a couple of steps forward and leaned a shoulder against a metal support stud.

"I don't know. Clues? Considering I'm a Shadow Walker, I've got every right to check this place out myself." I kept picking around the debris, waiting for the shoe to drop. Any second he'd lay into me about how I'd snuck out and come here alone. Then I'd tell him he was arrogant and bossy, and voila, I'd end up homeless, in a cell, or dead. Couldn't quite put my finger on the ending yet.

"How did you know where I was?" I'd left the phone he'd given me in the apartment.

"I've got surveillance all around the building. You can't leave without me knowing." His voice was calm and he hadn't moved from his spot. "Are you almost done? I'll drive you back."

"Just a few more minutes." That was it? He was really going to let this drop? No harassment? No accusations? I kept my head down as I kicked debris this way and that with my foot, waiting. Surely he wouldn't make it that easy.

I swiped my shoe over another spot, not so much looking anymore, but buying time. The shock of how easy he was being was still probably plastered on my face, and I didn't want him to reconsider.

That was when a glimpse of shiny metal, one I recognized instantly, caught a ray of moonlight and gleamed. I stepped on it immediately, realizing how awkward my movement looked after the fact. I wasn't going to look at Kane and see if he noticed. I'd act normal and walk out as if I hadn't seen anything.

Except for one problem.

Kane walked over and stopped in front of me. "What's under your foot?"

His jaw was squared as he stared hard, waiting for an answer. He might've been willing to let my earlier duplicity go, but there was no way he'd let this go. It was as good as lifting my fingerprints from the bomb.

"Nothing." It was a waste to lie, but panic seized me. As soon as I moved, he'd see. And that look in his eyes—it wasn't mourning I saw this time, but betrayal.

"Move. Your. Foot."

"Kane…" I had nothing left to say. There was no defense. I'd been here. The phone put me here. I dropped my eyes, staring at my feet and his. I was a monster. There was no other explanation.

He didn't ask me to move again. His hands went to my waist, picked me up and then turned, so I was a couple of feet away.

He knelt down where I'd been standing, and, clearer now than it had been when I'd stepped on it, was my crushed phone. I took a couple more steps away from him, wondering if I should start running for my life.

He lifted the phone from the debris and stood back up, the phone, dented and a third of it missing, between us.

"Explain how this got here."

He wasn't screaming, or raging, but I wasn't delusional. I knew I might be a breath away from death. Right now, if I were him, I might have skipped the questions and gone right to the killing. People had died. Crawlers were loose in the city. I'd been here, and the picture was looking pretty grim.

"Talk," he said softly, but with straining patience.

I didn't know if he wanted me to give him an excuse or an admission. I had neither. All I had was a bone-aching sadness that I'd had some part in this.

"I don't remember anything from the other night, nothing after I left the Underground. I have no memory until you showed up." My voice cracked as I spoke.

"Are you saying you had another blackout and you're telling me now?" He leaned forward, his gaze intent.

I could hear the disbelief, but I didn't know if it was that he thought I remembered or that I hadn't told him.

Tears started to pour down my cheeks, and not from

fear. I didn't know what was happening anymore. Chunks of time disappeared. Crawlers were coming in, and I might be the reason why. People dead, and it might be my fault. Who was this person I was becoming?

"Don't fucking cry. Just tell me what you know."

"I am! I don't remember anything." I ran my sleeve across my face, trying to get the tears to stop, but they wouldn't. He made a growling sound, but that didn't stop the tears either. I couldn't get control of myself.

"You said you went to bed early. Those were your words. You lied. Now you say you can't remember?"

"How was I going to tell you? Look at you. You're ready to kill me." And that was the worst part of it all. I barely knew this man, but the way he was looking at me was tearing me apart. Why did I care if he thought I was a murderer and betrayer? We were nothing to each other. I'd made that clear. So why did his look of distrust eviscerate me, every—single—time?

He took a few steps away, giving me his back. With the destroyed phone in one hand, his free hand ran through his hair. With his back still to me, both his hands now at his sides, he said, "If it were only that fucking easy."

He was still, but I wasn't delusional. He looked about to explode.

"If you want to kill me then do it," I yelled at his still back. It was ludicrous to tempt him, but I couldn't stop this overwhelming feeling of betrayal that was rising up and choking me.

He said nothing, his back still to me. I turned, finding a half wall that was still intact and sitting on it, feeling a numbness settle over me even as the tears kept rolling down my face. I bent forward at the waist, burying my face in my filthy hands that had dug through debris as I tried to regain control of myself.

I didn't realize he'd come back toward me until I saw his shoes in front of me. I didn't move. Just sat there as broken looking as I felt.

"You tell no one about this."

What? That had me jerking my face in his direction. It was the last thing I'd expected to hear. I would've been less shocked if he'd whipped out a gun and shot me.

"No one. Not even Butch or Leon." He stared me down until I nodded.

He grabbed my arm, pulling me upward and toward the door. He was shuffling me into the passenger side of his truck. "Don't come back here alone. I don't want anyone to see you roaming around explosion sites. It raises suspicions."

I reached out, stopping him before he shut the door. "Why?"

Instead of pushing my hand away, he answered, "I can't kill you, and I won't let anyone else do it, either. You say nothing and you lie low. Is that understood?"

I nodded, feeling the heat of his hands as he tucked me in before he shut the door.

Chilly night air hit as he got into the driver's seat, and then we were on our way. I didn't say anything else. Wasn't sure I could hold it together enough to converse at that point. Everything I'd feared looked to be true. I focused on the scenery as I tried to force myself to stop crying. I was like a leaky faucet that couldn't be turned off.

We couldn't have gone more than a few miles before he pulled the truck over to the side of the road. Had he changed his mind? Had he decided he should kill me after all? I didn't even know if I had any fight left in me, not if I'd caused those explosions. I kept my gaze toward the outside, but I knew he was looking at me.

"We can't go back while you're like this." The words were spoken through a clenched jaw, as if he were more upset about tonight's revelations than I was.

I nodded, knowing he was right but afraid that if I spoke, my voice would crack. I knew the damn sniffles were still giving me away, though.

"I told you, I won't let anyone kill you." His voice was softer, but I could still hear the impatience.

I shook my head. "That's not it." I sounded just as bad as I'd feared. I shouldn't have spoken.

"Then what?" He leaned closer.

"Do you think I did it?" I turned, realizing his face was only a foot from mine. For some unexplainable reason, knowing what he thought, him believing I wasn't the cause, felt like a lifeline to my sanity.

His eyes seemed to absorb the pain I was feeling, and his lids shuttered lower.

I knew what his verdict was before he spoke.

"I don't know," he said, and I knew that was a kindness. Because his eyes had told me he did think I'd done it.

I tried to not make a sound, but as I took a breath, my body was racked with shudders. I leaned forward, breaking eye contact before that look in his eyes added to my undoing.

I felt Kane's hand rub my back, but the kindness made the shuddering worse, as if unlocking all that was vulnerable inside me. His hands went to my waist, and he lifted me until I was cradled against his chest, strong arms encircling me when I would've moved. The intimacy nearly undid me.

"Ollie, relax." His hand rubbed my back again.

When he said my name like that, I could hear the history in his tone. History I'd lost and was beginning to wish I hadn't.

Kane's phone vibrated in his pocket, but he ignored it. Then it buzzed again. And again.

He reached for it as I shifted off him, the phone call doing little to smother the awkwardness of the moment.

He hit answer and asked, "What?" He listened silently for a moment before he said, "I'll be there shortly." He hung up and turned to me. "There's been another explosion."

I didn't know whether to cry or sigh in relief. At least whatever had happened this time, it wasn't me.

Chapter Thirteen

I WAS LEANING BACK IN THE BOOTH, MY LEGS STRETCHED out and my feet hanging over the edge. Leon occupied the other side in nearly the same position I was in, a plate of half-eaten nachos between us. We'd been sitting like this for the past hour, along with the rest of the people in the Underground as we watched the latest news on the big screen.

The first day I'd been in the Underground, the place had been pumping music so loud you felt the bass thrumming through you, and the vibration buzzed your feet. Now the main noise that filled the place was the terrified voices of the reporters as the news went from one location to the next. After Butch had called last night, there had been two more explosions in Boston.

Had to give the reporters credit for showing up for work and not beating feet out of there, like half the population had. Actually, it might've been more like three-quarters. It was hard to keep count between the cars, trains, buses, and planes.

I saw Leon shaking his head out of the corner of my eye as the flames lit the screen.

"I can't believe they blew up more places," he said softly, still in shock over the whole thing. "I've seen a lot of shit, been so deep that I thought was going to choke on it sometimes, but I never saw something like this."

I bent a knee and used it as an armrest, glued to the horror that was playing out. They were interviewing a teenage boy that had seen one of the crawlers from the latest explosion. "Why? What is the purpose? Do they get off on the destruction or something?" I asked. It just didn't make any sense. Even monsters must have motives. But as horrible as it was, I couldn't stop the feeling of relief. Three explosions and I hadn't blacked out or disappeared for any of them.

Leon didn't answer my question, but asked his own. "And so random. Sometimes it's homes; sometimes it's stores. How is anyone supposed to figure out why?"

That was all anyone was doing. Asking questions, as they stumbled around like confused zombies muttering, why, why, and there wasn't one person that seemed to have any answers. Not the shifters or the vampires or the fairies, or Kane, whatever he was.

If the music had been playing as loud as it normally did, and we weren't all news junkies today, no one would've heard the scream of surprise that rang through the room. It took a minute for me to locate the source, but as all eyes were turned toward the main door, it was pretty easy to spot where the problem was.

Jerry was stumbling away from his post, his back to us.

"Jerry?" Leon called.

Jerry turned toward his name, his face saying it all. Something very bad was heading this way.

Jerry raised his hand and pointed in the direction of the door. "It's one of them. It's a crawler."

Everyone seemed to make the same choice at once, and instantly. Scream first and then run in the opposite direction of the monster. The most impressive people did both at the same time.

I yanked my stray foot inside the booth as the wild stampede went past, knowing they'd break my ankle if it got in their way. I wasn't sure why I wasn't running with the horde, except I guessed I was the only Shadow Walker. If this was anyone's wheel house, it was mine, right? I was the only possible captain of this ship.

But as I watched the backside of the last shifter running out the backdoor, it was hard not to wonder if I should be exempt. How did you captain a ship if you didn't remember sailing it? Because as much as everyone told me I was this kick-ass Shadow Walker, and I had all sorts of magic stored inside my head, I didn't remember a damn bit of it.

I got out of the booth, debating if I was the captain, about to go down with the ship, or a passenger about to scurry to the last lifeboat. Jerry and Leon were staring at me. Butch was crossing the floor, staring at me as well. I might not remember everything that had happened, but I felt a sort of ownership of these crawlers, considering they'd followed me around most of my life. And that wasn't all. Finding out that maybe I wasn't the monster I feared made me want to grab the wheel and prove it. Fuck. Guess I was the captain.

Although first mate seemed like a good option too,

especially when I might steer us right into some craggy rocks. "Where's Kane?" If I could find him, he'd ease right into the captain seat. Kane was a natural take-charge person. People like him were great to have around on sinking ships.

"He said he wouldn't be back until later," Butch said.

"You can't call him and maybe have him come back a little early under the circumstances?" We did have a crawler about to bang down the door.

Butch made a face that matched my sarcasm. "I just tried him. He didn't answer."

Jerry was on his tiptoes and angling his head, trying to see out the small peephole from five feet away. "It's standing outside the door," Jerry said, definitely not keeping his cool.

A loud banging echoed through the room. The four of us looked at each other, and it was clear none of us knew what to do.

Butch's face turned white. Leon's was a shade of green, which was more concerning, considering I'd seen how many nachos he'd eaten. When I turned to Jerry to get his status, he looked like he'd been smoking crack, as he took a step toward the door and then back again.

It showed how bad the situation was when the chick who had no memory, and was definitely unbalanced, was the one holding it together best. Or maybe that was why? I'd have to debate it later, as we had a monster about to bang down our door.

"Haven't you people ever dealt with monsters before?" I asked.

"Not"—Butch stabbed the air in the direction of the door—"like that!"

I couldn't help but nod. These crawlers were rough. I'd grown up on them, so I'd gotten acclimated a bit. And even then, my last memory before the gap had been of a person on the border of depression and mania.

The crawler banged again. "Let in or explode." The voice was almost painfully deep, rasping on the ears. The words were said like a person, or monster, new to speaking.

I'd seen them blow up buildings. We'd all seen it, watched it on the news. I'd seen it in person a couple of times, and actually remembered one of the times. The crawler's threat filled me with a level of doom that seemed to have come from a sad place in my soul.

I motioned for our group to close ranks a bit, not sure how good the crawler's hearing was. "If it was going to blow the place up, it would've done it already. I still think we need to talk to it. We need to know why it's here. Except you said they blew stuff up if I talked to them. You'll have to talk to it." I looked at Butch.

"Why me?" He took a step away from the group.

I wasn't sure why I'd picked him except for gut instinct. "You have the deepest voice," I said, hoping a little flattery would encourage him.

Jerry and Leon nodded in agreement. I could've said Butch had to do it because he had the sweetest demeanor and they would've agreed. They'd probably be laughing about it too, after this was over, if we all lived that long.

Butch eyed up the group and folded under the pressure. "Fine," he barked, but no one complained about the delivery. He could've added a string of insults after it and we still would have nodded in agreement.

"Start with why it wants to come in." I leaned forward and patted him on the arm.

"That's good," Leon said, stepping out of Butch's way so he had a clear path to the door.

Jerry patted him on the back, giving him a little nudge forward. Butch shrugged Jerry away, showing how he felt about that, but trudged forward.

Butch stopped in front of the door and looked back, as if to ask, *Really?*

Jerry and Leon nodded, and I waved my hands, hurrying him along.

Butch stared at the closed door and yelled, "Why do you want to come in?"

As if choreographed, we all took a step away from the door as he spoke, in case the rules had changed and anyone speaking to a crawler could unleash an explosion.

"Speak only to Shadow Walker." The words were ground out like he'd eaten sandpaper for breakfast.

I moved closer to Butch and whispered, "Ask if it's so he can blow stuff up."

Butch rolled his eyes. "Well, that's a little obvious, isn't it?"

"No." The crawler's voice boomed through the door. He'd obviously heard me.

"Oh fuck, did that qualify as speaking to it?" Jerry asked, another few feet away.

I shrugged as we all froze, waiting to see what would happen. I bit my lip, cringing. I thought back to all the things I remembered Kane telling me. Somewhere in that pile of information, I remembered a nugget of gold. He'd said crawlers didn't blow up Shadow Walkers. Hadn't blown one up in as long as he could remember. They blew up the stuff around them, but left the Shadow Walker alone. So, we were probably safe as long as I was in the building. If I stepped out, well, that might be a whole different situation.

"Shadow walker, now!" The door rattled with the force of the pounding that followed.

Or maybe he would blow the place up with me in it? I stepped to the side of the door, just in case it blew off its hinges.

Butch whispered, "What are you doing?"

I waved him off when he went to grab my arm. "Go over there," I said, shooing him toward Leon before turning my attention back to the closed door and the crawler beyond. "Will you give me your word that if I speak to you, nothing blows up?"

Jerry rolled his eyes at me, and Leon threw his hands up, like I had to be kidding.

I gave them all my best *shut the hell up* look, before asking, "I'm sorry, but what were your plans?"

"Only speak," the crawler said, no pounding this time.

"I'm coming outside. Step away from the door."

I got up on tiptoes, waiting to see if it would oblige my request, ignoring the tiny part of me that hoped he wouldn't. If he didn't, I wouldn't have to go out. Although that might not be a good outcome either.

Butch's shoulder brushed against my left one, and I stepped back to see the three of them standing close by.

"If we let you go out there alone, Kane will not only kill that thing, he'll kill us," Leon said.

Good. I didn't really want to go out there alone anyway. "Okay."

"You're not going to even fight us?" Butch asked.

"No." I shrugged. "Do you have any weapons?"

Butch and Leon lifted their shirts; both had guns on their hips. Now I knew why they always wore long shirts. Jerry pointed at his ankle. I assumed a gun was there.

I looked out the peephole again. It had stepped back about ten feet. Fuck.

And then I really got to see what I was dealing with. It might've been one of the scariest-looking crawlers I'd ever seen. It stood somewhere between seven and eight feet tall and was built like a gorilla, alternating black fur and silver scales that reminded me of snakeskin, with muscles bulging underneath. Its eyes were a red so bright that they nearly glowed, and its large, flattened nostrils flared as it breathed. Its fangs were oversized for its mouth and hung lower than its nonexistent lower lip.

Then there was the thing that was oversized below the waist. As ugly as its face was, that was where I'd be keeping my eyes. I was not making the mistake of looking below that thing's waist again.

I swiped my hand across my jeans so it wouldn't be too slick to open the door. Jerry, Butch, and Leon were lined up behind me.

"We ready?" I asked, white-knuckling the knob.

"Not even close," Butch said.

They didn't look it, either. No one could be ready for this thing. "Then let's go," I said.

I pushed the door open and stepped forward, the guys spreading out to my sides.

The creature took in my entourage, pausing on each person. I knew immediately our greater numbers didn't intimidate it. Its attention settled on me, and it bowed its upper body slightly in my direction, grunting with the motion.

Was that a greeting or something? Maybe a bow? I did the same, including a bad imitation of the grunt, just in case. Less than a second later, I heard three other grunts. I looked to my sides and saw Butch shrug. I shrugged in return. They'd obviously thought it was a good idea, too.

I opened my mouth, but it took a few seconds more before I got the words out. What if this was a trick and he was going to blow up the Underground? Stuff was blowing up anyway. At least maybe I might get some answers, and I was pretty sure the building was empty.

I held my shoulders back and acted as if I didn't want to pee my pants. "What did you want?"

"Help." Its voice was gruff but clear.

I heard a "Huh?" but I wasn't sure who had said it in my stunned daze.

Help? Did it just ask for help? It must be struggling with the language. Maybe it didn't know what "help" meant. Maybe it thought "help" meant mass death? This definitely called for some clarification. "Help with what?"

Another "Huh" came, and this time it was definitely from Jerry. I held up a hand, a silent gesture for him to shut up.

The crawler wasn't paying them any attention. Its eyes hadn't wavered from me since they'd landed there. "You help bring more crawlers over. We don't burn anymore."

More crawlers? And not the ones that only had a toe in this world, because they were everywhere. He wanted them crossed over completely. He wanted them roaming this world, where everyone would see them. The chaos that would ensue from that might be worse than the fires.

And what happened if I refused? Would it continue with the explosions? Why even ask me for help? Maybe whatever it had been doing wasn't working anymore and it couldn't bring more over? That didn't mean it couldn't still blow things up.

"I don't know how," I said.

It nodded. I took that to mean he'd give me a primer when the time came.

"Are you saying you don't want to burn?" I asked, feeling a little more confident now that I knew the creature needed me. Or thought it did. I wasn't sure I could help bring anything over at this point, let alone a crawler. Even if I could, I didn't know how.

"How many of you are here now?" I asked, not ready to give up.

It stood silently as if I hadn't asked it anything. This thing didn't even blink.

I tilted my head to the side. "You're the one that came here."

"No."

"Yes, you did come here," Jerry blurted out.

"He's not saying he didn't come here. He's saying he's not answering any questions," I told Jerry, not trusting the crawler enough to break eye contact while I spoke. "Why should we do anything for you at all?"

He stared above me and tilted his head back, and then a great burst of fire flew out of his mouth. I could feel a blast of heat as it died in smoke.

"Burn." Sparks flew from its mouth with the word.

"So either I help or you're going to burn more places down." It had looked like he meant burn down this place specifically. However unlikely, I didn't want to give him any ideas in case that had been a coincidence. "That's not a good bargain, and I think you can't cross anyone else over. I think whatever you were doing before backfired, or you wouldn't be here, so let's try again."

His brows dropped lower and his lip curled back.

Okay. I might've overplayed my hand.

I watched as his nostrils flared and his mouth opened.

I'd definitely overplayed.

"Wait. I can't agree on my own."

"You lie, Shadow Walker."

"If I start bringing your people through without an okay, I'm dead. You don't believe me?" I stepped forward, hands on my hips, wondering if I'd lost my mind with my memories. "Then do your worst, because I'll be dead anyway."

We stared at each other, neither of us speaking. I didn't think the guys were breathing. I would've sworn the birds had stopped chirping, waiting to see if the situation was going to literally go up in flames.

"You find out *soon*." A couple residual whiffs of smoke came out as he spoke.

The mood went from a tornado about to touch down on top of us, to watching it off in the distance a few miles down the road. I didn't know how soon that "*soon*" was. It wasn't now, so I didn't argue.

"How do I contact you?"

"Tell crawler to get Harg."

His name sounded like he was trying to bring up a hairball. Again, something that didn't need to be discussed at the moment. But there was another potential problem.

"And when I talk to this random crawler, what happens then? If there's another explosion—"

"No fires until I say so."

I nodded.

Harg nodded.

Then we all watched as he made his way slowly away from our building. I wasn't sure any of us breathed until he was out of sight.

Chapter Fourteen

JERRY, BUTCH, LEON, AND I WERE WAITING IN KANE'S office when he walked through an empty Underground half an hour later. I hadn't asked Butch what Kane's reaction was when he'd gotten through to him. As I stood by the window and watched him, he might as well have been striding into war from the determination of his steps and the sharpened angles of his face.

He climbed the stairs and paused right inside the door. Butch was loading up on caffeine by the Keurig, while Leon and Jerry were trying to appear relaxed on the couch. Kane's attention was solely on me, where I stood by the window, even though there were three other people in the room staring at him.

Kane's eyes bored through me like he'd just gotten back from the planet Krypton. "Who made the decision to talk to it?"

I lifted a shoulder, not feeling the need to vocalize what he already knew. That didn't stop Jerry and Leon from serving me up for dinner, as they said, "Her," at the same time.

I looked at Butch, about to thank him for not throwing me under the bus. Then I remembered he'd been the one to tell Kane in the first place, as soon as he'd been able to get him on the phone.

Kane's stare was glued to me alone, and I was pretty certain it wasn't going to shift until I acknowledged it. "I acted the best way I could in the moment. It's not like there's a manual on what to do when a crawler is trying to bang down the door."

He shifted his attention to the others. I watched with a teaspoon of glee as they shifted in their seats now. *Yeah, let's see how you like it. So quick to throw me to the wolf.*

"And you three went along with it?" Kane asked.

I couldn't have sworn that he had given them instructions to avoid a situation like that. But I wouldn't have bet against it, either.

"He was going to blow the building otherwise." Butch threw his hands up as he shrugged an *I fucked up; don't kill me* gesture. The other two sat mute on the couch, as still as a puddle in Antarctica.

"It wouldn't have blown up anything." Kane didn't wait for the thaw before he strode toward his desk, dropping his phone roughly on the surface.

Butch shot me a look as Kane had his back turned. I wasn't a mind reader, but was fairly certain that he thought I should be bailing him out of this, considering it was my idea to talk to the thing.

I raised a hand and made a face back, as if to say, *You aren't my puppet.* What happened to free will in this place?

He jutted his chin out.

I rolled my eyes, my head moving with the act. Fine. I'd take the heat, since the two Popsicles on the couch wouldn't move. "It *really* looked like it was about to do just that."

Kane turned toward me again. "It *couldn't.*"

I narrowed my eyes. No way he could be sure of that.

He gave me a look that said he was. I guessed there was the possibility that he might know something I didn't. It wasn't out of the realm, but whatever. It was done now.

He leaned against the desk, crossing his arms.

"Why does it need you now?" he asked.

I knew what he was thinking, because I was thinking it too. If they had used me in the past, whatever they'd done wasn't working anymore.

I moved away from the windows, feeling the need to stretch my legs as something struck me. I paced a bit, but then stopped once I realized I kept walking closer and closer to Kane, my mind going back to how nice it felt to have him wrapped around me.

I shook my head and took a step away from him, getting back to the problem at hand. "The ones that have been spotted so far have all been bigger and stronger. Maybe they can't get the weaker ones over the same way?"

"Plausible," Kane said, and I glanced over my shoulder to see he'd uncrossed his arms and had them resting on either side of him, hands on the desk. An image of me standing in between his legs, in that very spot, sprang to mind. I didn't know if it was a daydream or a memory, but I could nearly feel his lips searing my skin. My cheeks burned at the thought, and I coughed, even though I had no need, giving my skin an excuse for the flush.

Butch and the Popsicles might've bought it, but there was a heat in Kane's eyes that made me think he knew exactly what had been running through my mind. Might've been running through his as well.

I scurried back over toward the window, a safer distance away. "I stalled us for a little, but time isn't going to fix this problem. If I don't help, they're going to continue destroying things."

Leon finally defrosted enough for his mouth to move. "People are panicking. There isn't a single case of bottled water left in town. People think this is the end of the world."

I understood that train of thought. I was thinking it too sometimes. It certainly might be the end of Boston if things kept going this way.

"And if you do help?" Kane asked, his head tilted to the side.

The ramifications were obvious either way.

I shrugged. "There's obviously problems. I could help them through and we could end up in the same place in a few weeks. I could say no and they could blow up the whole city tomorrow. There is no right answer."

Kane thought over my words for a moment before he said, "We call a meeting."

"We're going to let those buffoons make the call?" Butch asked. "Rudy with his ancient ways, or Collin, who's just plain old stupid? Frederickson certainly doesn't give a shit what happens to anyone but him." Butch raised his hand and then yelped as hot coffee spilled on his hand.

Kane stood. "Of course not. We decide now and then let them think they had a say. If things go badly, we might need help cleaning it up. That'll be easier to get if they think it's partially their fault."

"Things go badly which way? When we help them in or when we don't?" Jerry asked.

That was the question now, wasn't it? It seemed like the difference between getting slow-roasted or flash-fried. At least with a slow roast, maybe we could drag it out long enough to find a solution. "We let them through," I said. "This isn't an idle threat. They're going to light the city up otherwise."

"What if we let them through and then they do it anyway?" Leon asked.

I glanced over at Kane, waiting for him to step in. He didn't. Maybe someone had dropped his crystal ball on cement and now the picture was all cracked and foggy. Or maybe this was a test.

"Either way, we're cooked," I said. "We've got guaranteed destruction or possible destruction. We let them in, but only because there's no other solutions right now. We can work it into the bargain that I only bring over five a month until we figure out how to destroy them, or what they really want."

Leon let out a huff. "I'm pretty sure it's not to get a job, get married, and have two kids."

"I agree with Ollie," Kane said. I guessed that meant I'd passed the test.

Butch, Leon, and Jerry nodded.

"It was better than my idea," Leon said.

"What's your idea?" Butch asked.

"I didn't have one. It was a low bar to clear."

Kane turned to Butch and Leon. "Line up a meeting for tomorrow. You know who to call. You, come with me."

I didn't realize I was the "you" until he pointed at the closet door and was staring at me.

I knew what this was about, and it had nothing to do with getting me up close and personal for a moment. He had a bone to pick with me right now. I wanted to hash this out in private too, but the closet seemed like a weird choice.

He walked, and I mentally shrugged and followed. In the closet, he moved a shelf out of the way and opened a door. If I hadn't been fairly sure that he wasn't going to kill me, I might've hesitated stepping into the pitch-dark entrance that looked like it led to a dungeon.

There was a stairwell below, and I reached out, feeling for the wall as he shut the door and all light ceased to exist in the space. His arm looped around my waist, pulling me back to the top landing. His hand shifted to the wall, and I felt his forearm brushing my side, blocking me from falling in the dark. Nope. Definitely not the move of someone who wanted me dead.

"What did you not understand about lying low?"

It was so dark that I couldn't see his face, but his heat reached out like the lure of a fire on a freezing night.

Something had shifted last night when he'd held me. I could pretend it hadn't, but my body was making a different choice as it bowed toward him, hips shifting forward as my shoulders were planted on the wall. My nipples hardened and my pulse thought it had just gotten the flag that the race was on.

"I *was* lying low. That thing came to me." I licked my lower lip, hating how breathy I sounded.

"You shouldn't have answered." There was heat in his

voice, but it wasn't anger this time. Whatever was happening, it wasn't one-sided.

"Sometimes shit happens you don't plan for." Sort of like the way my stomach fluttered when he was close and my breathing hitched, completely beyond my control.

His other hand rose, cupping my neck, his thumb grazing the side of it. My heart was beating so hard that I was sure he felt it racing against his fingers.

The arm that grazed my other side shifted. Suddenly it was grasping the back of my thigh where it joined the curve of my ass, lifting my leg up so that his hips pinned mine to the wall.

When his lips covered mine, it was as if they were claiming what was already his. And I didn't care. I was willing to surrender everything I had, at least at that moment. Right now, it didn't feel like he was kissing the past, but the person I was now.

His tongue darted into my mouth, rubbing against mine as our hips rubbed below. All I wanted was to embrace this feeling, this want that felt larger than us both, because as we came together, it felt like it must've been preordained for it to feel this perfect.

I didn't care that the guys might still be in the next room, or that there were so many questions still unanswered right now. There was only one thing that was driving me back from the emotional abyss that was Kane.

"Do you think I caused the explosions?" My question came out in breathy pants.

He didn't answer as his mouth covered mine again, but this time I wasn't swallowed back into the moment. I was jerked to awareness by his silence. I turned my head, and his lips shifted to my jaw.

"Kane, I need to know." I hated the pleading in my voice.

His shoulders tensed underneath my palms, and I knew what he was thinking, because it had been running a marathon in my mind for the last hour. Harg thought I could get the weaker ones through. Why wouldn't Kane think I might've gotten the first ones through? That I might've gotten Asher through somehow? It all seemed to keep coming back to me.

"I think it doesn't matter to me what you did."

But it did. Because if someone had been able to manipulate me into doing it in the past, odds didn't look so hot for the future. Was I a monster? Maybe not, but it didn't look good. That was clear too. I'd never tried for sainthood. My goals had never been that high. But I'd always tried to stay out of the gutter.

"Do you trust me?" I asked.

His forehead dropped to mine, the silence stifling. He didn't. And maybe he shouldn't. That didn't change how it felt to know it.

I shoved at his shoulders, but his muscular bulk stayed firmly pressed against the length of me.

"How am I supposed to trust you when you don't even trust yourself?" he asked. "You have no idea what you did, and still I'd kill to protect you. Isn't that enough?"

I bit my lower lip, wishing he was right. His tongue ran over the spot, making it clear one of us could see in the dark.

"I wish it was." This time when I shoved, he moved back.

Chapter Fifteen

THE UNDERGROUND WAS CLOSED TO ALL BUT INVITED guests the next morning for the meeting. That was easier to achieve than normal, since half the people who lived here were still afraid to come back since Harg. Bunch of wimps.

I was over at the bar beside Butch when Kane walked in. I stared out of the corner of my eye. He just stared back. All in all, the moment felt fairly awkward, since the last time I'd seen him, we'd been kissing in a stairwell.

I gave him a short nod when he stopped beside me and Butch.

He did the same before turning his attention to Butch. "Stay beside Ollie and give her a rundown as people show. They all probably know she lost her memory, but no reason to broadcast it."

"Got it," Butch said.

Kane stepped away, walking to his office as Leon made his way closer.

"Are you two not talking?" Butch asked. Leon leaned in, waiting for my answer.

"We're talking." I squinted at them, as if I were confused at the very idea of it.

Butch scratched his jaw. "Something's up."

"Nothing's up." I pointed at both of them as I saw a familiar trend about to happen. "Don't either of you make a face."

Leon shrugged. "I had no intention of making a face. None."

Butch crossed his arms, snorting at the same time. "I certainly didn't. I'm not a maker of faces."

I matched Butch's snort with a louder snort of disbelief.

Before we could completely dissolve into the ridiculous, Jerry signaled and Leon headed toward the door. Our company had arrived. All my enemies, or known ones, would walk through that door. I had a past with these people that I only knew about because I'd been briefed.

The first arrival stepped inside. A tallish man with hair nearly as black as Kane's. His deep blue suit and pocket square had a slight dandy feeling. He was followed closely by a man with auburn hair and a beard.

Butch ducked his head closer to me. "Leprechauns. They held you hostage in the basement. Rudy, the one with the dark hair, still claims he wasn't aware of what was happening. He's the top guy, so it's dubious."

First enemy up to bat. I remembered Kane saying something about how the two who had kidnapped me weren't a problem anymore, with no other details provided. I'd watched enough gangster movies to know that probably meant they were dead.

I committed those two faces to memory and turned to watch Leon and Jerry greeting the next new arrivals. Definitely vampires—even though one had an older look about him, his face was somehow still perfectly unlined. Like he had some weird vampire Botox thing going on. The woman who followed him wasn't much to look at by vampire standards, but would still be above par if you threw her into a room with a bunch of blond mortals.

"Frederickson, head vamp," Butch said. "That woman following is his new second in command, since, well…"

"Well what?" I grabbed Butch's arm to get his full attention.

Butch shrugged. "Nothing important."

I let it drop, more interested in the next arrival.

"That's Collin," Butch said. "He's the head werewolf." Two lackeys followed him, and those two I actually remembered. They'd shown up at my building, trying to hire me even before I'd met Butch and Leon.

"Is he the one who tried to help?" I asked. If getting me stuck in the Shadowlands could be called that. It was still a relief. If things turned ugly, at least he wouldn't be swinging his claws my way.

"I guess you could say that," Butch replied, thinking along the same lines as I was.

The next face I recognized from the Underground. "A witch?"

"That's Dana. She— Yeah, nothing good to be said there."

I didn't ask anything else. I knew that she'd probably been involved in some of the nasty things I'd heard about. I didn't want to cause a scene breaking things by accident.

"Is this it?" As they'd come, I'd kept hoping something would trigger a memory, but nothing had.

"We only invited the pains in the asses," Butch said. "We left the crowds that lie low out of it for now."

There were general nods and a few hellos, as you'd expect of a group thrown together by necessity but not likeability. At least I wasn't the only one not vibing with the group.

Frederickson was the first to approach me, and I gave Butch a nudge with my elbow to shoo him away.

"I'm supposed to stick by you," he said, not budging.

"You'll broadcast that I'm such a lightweight I can't be alone, even in a crowded room."

Butch put on a fake smile and then edged away, just a bit. Five feet wasn't perfect, but it was better than having him glued to me.

Frederickson took in the proximity but acted natural enough as he stopped beside me. "How are you, Ollie?"

The moment he neared, I immediately wished he'd walk away. I couldn't tell if it was a past feeling bleeding through the black hole of memories or if I hated his overdone cologne. "Good, thank you, Frederickson."

"I've been hearing that things aren't quite the same as they used to be around here?"

"Most things do change." Most people, too, but he wouldn't know about that.

"You know, there's a lot of rumors I'm hearing," he said. "I, of course, don't pay any heed to that type of talk, especially when it includes slights against my friends. You might want to think about which friends you want to keep." He wiped a hand over the front of his jacket, as if a stray fur from Collin had floated onto him.

I nodded. "I'll think long and hard on that."

Jerry dropped a thick bar over the entrance, and all eyes shot to the upstairs door when it swung open. Kane made his way down, heading toward the table. "Everyone, take a seat."

I would've grabbed the closest chair to me if Butch hadn't shown up at my side again and steered me to the seat beside the head of the table.

"All the groups sit together," Butch said, barely audible.

"Stop shoving. I got it," I told him.

I sat beside Kane, who didn't seem very concerned or aware of where I sat. Butch sat to my left, and Leon took the seat on Kane's other side.

When I heard the snarl, I thought there was going to be a fight for the other head chair. Collin stepped away from Rudy, head leprechaun, who didn't appear to be budging. Well, that told me one thing. If this were a card game of war, leprechaun trumped werewolf. I didn't know where vampires ranked, but Kane seemed to trump them all, with the way everyone seemed to be taking their cues from him.

The werewolves were on the other side, with Butch buffering me from the vampires. Kane waited as everyone took a seat, but remained standing in front of his. "As we all know, there are some new monsters in town."

There were grunts and nods around the table. Collin growled and added, "And those fuckers better learn their place."

No one disagreed with the statement, and I found myself nodding as well. I'd been feeling that way about crawlers my whole damn life.

"One of them showed up here," Kane continued. No

one so much as budged in their chairs. After the stampede out of here the other day, it wasn't surprising that news had spread. There were all types in the Underground, after all —better for everyone to keep tabs on everyone else. "We believe it to be their leader, and it wants to negotiate."

"What?" Frederickson shouted out.

"Seriously? For what?" Collin asked, his two backups taking up the growling.

Dana, the black-haired witch, stared at me, as if I were the cause of all the problems in the universe, and maybe the galaxy next door, too.

"They want Ollie to help some more of them through," Kane said. "In exchange, they'll stop torching the place. We were thinking five crawlers and no more for a month until we see if they uphold their end." He took his seat, and proceeded to kick his heels up on the table while everyone else was still absorbing that tidbit.

"What do we get out of it?" Rudy asked.

"We can say no if you want. But the crawlers seem to have an affinity for your locations." Kane shrugged.

Dana stood, shoulders squared. "The witches will help out in whatever way is needed." She smiled sweetly in Kane's direction before retaking her seat.

"I'm fine with that agreement," Collin said, rolling over pretty easy, considering.

"We'll go along with this, but"—the head vampire pointed at me—"she comes with us."

"Why in the world would I go with you?" I asked, having absolutely no intention of going anywhere. I hadn't been keen on moving into the Underground, but I'd rather live in the first level of hell than with the vampire who might send me to my death.

"She stays here," Kane said, almost at the same time.

Well, that was pretty predictable. If I'd thought about it for a second, I would've realized I could've leaned back and kept quiet. There was no way Kane was letting me leave here, no matter who wanted me to go, including myself. He'd put up too much of a fight to get me here in the first place.

"Why do you get her?" Rudy asked. "We have just as much right here—"

"She's not going anywhere. End of discussion." It was the first time Kane had raised his voice, and the room fell silent. He let the silence hang for a moment before he continued. "You can send over a representative for updates. That should be more than sufficient."

Frederickson nodded.

"Us too?" Collin asked.

"Yes. Everyone. Complete transparency. We'll handle the rest of it." Kane stood, completing the meeting before anyone had technically agreed. "Glad this is worked out. Now, if you don't mind, I've other business to attend."

He walked away from the table and over to the bar and ordered a drink from a gargoyle, as if his guests were no longer at the table.

It was a real ballsy move. If he could do that, then surely I could leave as well. I stood. "Nice to see you all again," I said with a peppy wave as I headed toward the hallway, not wanting to push my luck by hanging too close.

I didn't make it out of the room before Collin rushed over to me. "Hey, I just wanted to say I hope there's no hard feelings about that Shadowland incident?"

"Not at all." I shrugged it off, not mentioning that I might change my mind once I remembered the incident.

He smiled and shrugged a broad shoulder, a lock of freshly cut brown hair falling across a prominent brow bone. "I'm somewhat adverse to the crawlers being let out, but we have to work together in these times or we'll self-destruct."

I nodded in agreement. I would've said just about anything to have this charade over with.

Kane walked over and patted Collin on the back. Collin shifting forward was the only sign it might've been a slightly aggressive pat.

"Collin, how's it going?" Kane asked, acting as if he hadn't shoved Collin a foot forward.

"Good."

"Great. Do you have a moment?" Kane's hand was now resting on his shoulder, making it clear he was getting a moment whether Collin had it to spare or not.

Considering Collin had been easy enough at the meeting, there must've been some old business between the two.

Butch and Leon filled the gap as Kane walked Collin away.

"Well, at least you're still..." Butch's words trailed off, but I knew what he'd been about to say.

"Still alive," I finished, starting to understand how that might've started in the first place.

"Still alive," Leon said.

"See you guys later," I said, walking off as I heard them continue to talk.

"Did that feel natural to you? Do you think she forced it?" Butch asked.

"No. She definitely didn't. It's just going to take a little time, is all. Even the first time, she didn't take to it right away. She had to get nearly killed before it went smoothly. Considering how things are going, I think we'll get there."

I went to my rooms, hoping for a few minutes of peace before Kane showed and I had to go whisper to communicate with crawlers.

Chapter Sixteen

I STOPPED BESIDE FLIP, WHO WAS TOSSING BACK A SHOT AT
the bar at four in the morning. She did a little shiver as she
placed the glass down. Then she glanced over at me before
saying, "Two more," to the gargoyle tending bar. It was
clear that hadn't been her first shot, or her second. Might
not have been the third, either, but I wasn't sure what kind
of tolerance a half-fairy, half-leprechaun who was a
hundred pounds soaking wet would have.

I rested my elbows on the bar as the gargoyle poured a
clear liquid into the glasses in front of us. "I hope that's for
me." I wasn't sure there was an AA that could handle Flip.

"You look like you need it. And if what I've heard is
accurate, you definitely do."

That was the understatement of the year. Now that
helping crawlers through had moved from the abstract to
reality, a fast charbroil seemed a better option. The
message to Harg had been sent, and the doomsday clock
was officially ticking down. I had about forty-eight hours

before I began bringing over the monsters that might end the world.

She lifted her glass and held it up, waiting for me to take the other.

I did, thinking a stiff drink might be the only thing that would knock me out. "Do I want to know what this stuff is?"

"Probably not."

I clinked glasses with her and tossed it back. I put the glass down feeling like I'd just swallowed lava and it was tracing a path to my stomach. I waved my hand over my glass when the gargoyle would've refilled it.

"I know why I can't sleep. What's your occasion?" I asked, once I was sure that the liquid was going to stay where I put it.

Flip pointed at her glass, signaling a refill, and then threw that one back as well. She dropped the glass back onto the bar, declaring, "It's the end of the world."

As if the news were conspiring with her, a grey-haired man with some years showing around the eyes came on the big screen. Looking almost too gleeful, he declared, "It's the end of the world. That's what's happening. We've been preparing for this for years. We tried to warn everyone, but no one wanted to listen. Well, now, some of us will survive, the true believers." The longer he talked, the more excited he got. He pointed at the camera. "But most of you will die."

The reporter, probably half his age, and even less than that if you deducted for gullibility, hung on his every word. "Do you know what these monsters are? Are they aliens?"

"No. The people screaming fanatically about Area 51 are nut cases." He leaned his face closer to the screen, his eyes rounded, pupils dilated. "This is the devil coming for all you sinners."

I heard a vampire in the corner whimper. What the fuck? Was everyone losing their mind? Yeah, they were freaking ugly monsters, and yes, it was alarming to see them. But the devil? These people had to get a grip. And they'd had the nerve to give Shadow Walkers the nickname paper dolls? I'd sat beside these things every day for years.

I signaled for another shot of liquid lava. I threw it down and turned to Flip. "I'll see you later. I'm going to try and get some sleep."

I hoped this time it worked out better with the aid of whatever the hell that drink had been. I'd just made it to the stairwell when Zee popped up in front of me.

"Where?" she asked the air. "Okay, good."

"Hey, Zee," I said, and tried to walk around her, hoping this was a coincidence. I was too exhausted for this today, and I didn't care what business we had anymore. I had too many balls in the air as it was.

She wrapped her hand around my wrist and tugged me upstairs, not giving me a choice. The chick was as unmovable as the stone she looked to be carved from. It couldn't be luck that I'd done this very thing to the witch not days ago.

"Where are we going?" I asked.

"Sixth floor. We've got problems. I've been thinking of this for days, and I know what I feel." She was certainly feeling a lot of whatever it was, judging from her frantic pace.

"What problems?" I tugged on my wrist, but I wasn't sure she noticed. "Do we need to run the whole way?"

"I'll tell you when we get there," she said, not slowing down.

The invisible person who'd answered Zee must've also alerted Kane, because he was standing in the hall outside his apartment when we got to the sixth floor. His eyes ran over me like he expected a missing limb, or maybe a pair of horns.

Zee said nothing to him as she tugged me along, no chance of getting loose. It was like being towed behind a giant boulder.

Kane didn't ask what was going on. He stood beside his apartment door, allowing us to enter first. He shut the door after Zee had tugged me into the living room. The place had too many lights on for him to have just gotten up. Was I the only person in this building who was interested in trying to get some sleep? It was the middle of the night.

"What's so important?" Kane asked as he joined us in the center of his living room.

"This cannot leave us," Zee said to him before turning to me. "His apartment is off-limits to listening in. He did some funny stuff so we can only hear when he specifically calls us."

Kane let out a sigh, clearly not in the mood to entertain Zee's demands. "Tell me."

Zee didn't shoot for another nondisclosure, but wrapped an arm around my shoulders, pulling me in between the two of them. "There is something not normal in her head. I felt it. I *know* I did."

"We tested her for spells. It was negative." He turned and was walking away from us, toward where he left his phone on the table.

I took Zee's words a bit more to heart. I'd accepted Kane's pronouncement as gospel, but why? There could definitely be things he didn't know. I didn't trust him in any other area, and yet I'd taken that information and simply accepted it?

I would've taken up the fight, but Zee didn't go down that easy, following him across the room. "I *felt* it. Gargoyles can sense magic on a much more sensitive level than any other creature. You know this."

He turned. "Then tell me how it got past the test?"

"Whoever did this is top of the food chain. Maybe it's not just blocking memories but woven into the fabric of her mind. I don't know, but it's there, and you need to fix her." Zee popped a hip out and pointed at me, as she stared at Kane.

I'd never seen a standoff between Kane and another person, other than myself, and I was too desperate to count. If I wasn't trying to stay alive most of the time, I might not have stood up to Kane either. First, you had no real idea of what you were standing up against, since I doubted very much Kane was human. Second, even if we gave him the benefit of the doubt and threw him in the human column, Kane was the type of person you knew was made of tougher stuff than the general population. It was in the way he never seemed to fear anyone or anything, as if he'd shown up, fought the war, and won fifty times already, while the rest of us were still figuring out how to load the gun.

But there was Zee, taking another determined step toward him. "You either try and fix her or we're going on strike. And I speak for *all* the gargoyles here."

Whoa. Could Zee really declare that? The set of her

stone shoulders made me think so. A slight breeze would've toppled me at that moment. This was serious shit going down.

Kane raised an eyebrow, losing interest in his phone. "Are you sure you want to threaten me?"

Holy granite, I hoped Zee knew what she was doing, because as tough as she said gargoyles were, Kane looked like he was about to come down like a sledgehammer and dust her.

"I'm willing to die on this hill." There was no waver, no flicker of fear. She meant it.

I saw a flicker of doubt flash in Kane. A drop in him was torrential rain to a normal person. He was rethinking his position, and not because he was worried about her or a strike. The way he walked over and leaned on the back of the couch wasn't someone who was scared. I knew what he was thinking because I was thinking it too. Zee believed so much that her conviction was hard to turn away from; it was the kind of belief that ended wars—or started them.

"If it is a spell, is there something you can try?" I asked, not for Zee but myself. If there was a stone we could turn over, I wanted it turned.

Kane glanced at me. "Yes. None of it pleasant."

He was giving me the choice. If I said I wanted to try, he'd try with me.

It wasn't a question. For a chance to get my memory back? To know exactly what happened? I'd do anything short of death. "I don't care how unpleasant. I'll try anything."

I turned to Zee, not sure if there was a way to express what her standing her ground meant to me.

She smiled, as if she already knew. "Don't worry, girlie

—you're going to be paying me back in spades once we get this fixed."

I nodded. "I hope so."

WE DIDN'T START until the next morning, which was good, considering some people actually had to sleep.

Kane strolled in while I was sitting on the couch, drinking coffee, and said, "Have you eaten yet?"

I shook my head, thinking he was going to ask if I wanted breakfast first.

He didn't. "Good. Let's get started."

I jumped up, ready to go, even though that didn't sound good at all.

We made our way down to his office, into the closet, and down the darkest stairwell ever until we landed in some medieval-looking room. It was a cross between a dungeon and the sort of spot a mad scientist might hang out.

"What is this place?" I was guessing the Underground was right above us, but the aesthetics made it feel like it was an alternate universe.

"It's the only place that I know the magic won't leak out and cause a problem if things go badly."

I ran a hand over the stone walls as he watched. "Why?"

"The walls, the floor, and the ceiling have all been warded more times than I can keep count of."

The heavy door that led to the stairwell creaked open,

and Butch walked in. "What's going on? I saw Zee watching you two and then head off to pace in the alley."

"Zee thinks Ollie's memory is gone because of magic." Kane's voice didn't reveal whether he thought it were possible to fix me with potions or if we were down here for shits and giggles.

Butch nodded, keeping his features neutral as well, following Kane's lead. "Okay then."

I leaned my elbows on the stone table in the center, one of the only pieces of furniture in the place. I tried to not think about whether sacrifices had been performed on this thing, and if I'd be next.

Kane slid back a panel, revealing all sorts of bottles sitting on shelves carved into the stone.

We'd just taken a definite turn toward mad scientist. Better than dungeon, and I was ready for any potion he threw at me that could possibly fix me.

When I thought it was a bump on the head that had stolen my memory, I hadn't been happy about it, but I'd been able to live with it. I'd fallen or something. It had just happened. No malice and no one's fault. Even if I'd been attacked or mugged, and I'd gotten injured, it would've been easier to handle, an unintended consequence of living the life I had.

But this might not be an accident. Some bastard had possibly stolen months of my life, and that drastically changed my feelings on the matter. Anger boiled up, mixed with a determination that I wouldn't just accept this slight along with all the others. It was enough. It was too much.

"Do you think it's the witches?" Butch asked as Kane stood in front of his bottles.

I waited to hear what Kane said. The witches had already been added to the list I'd made last night, and would remain there no matter what his answer was.

"I'm not sure if it's anyone," Kane replied. "If it is, though, they wouldn't have the magical chops to do something like this. If they were involved, they were puppets."

"What about the vampires?" Butch asked, his list similar to mine, if in a different order.

Kane pulled down a bottle from the top shelf. "They don't have spells."

Butch took a couple of steps away from Kane and glanced at me. I mouthed, *Leprechauns.*

Butch cleared his throat. "What about leprechauns? They kidnapped her once already, and they have magic."

"Not the right kind of magic," Kane said.

Good thing I wasn't crossing anyone off my list with his answers, or I'd have no suspects left.

Butch looked at the bottle Kane was holding. "You sure about that one?" It wasn't the question but the way he asked it that had me worried.

"I'm not sure about anything other than if Zee is correct, we aren't going to dislodge the magic with anything weak," Kane said.

If this and *if* that. I got it. He was going through the motions but wasn't necessarily buying it. He was kicking the magical tires. As long as he kicked the tires while he helped me, I was fine with it. I didn't need a best friend or a boyfriend—I needed my memory back.

Kane walked over, glass bottle in hand. He pulled the stopper out and a plume of smoke escaped. "This is going to make you sick." He held it out to me. "Make sure you drink it all."

I took the bottle and breathed in and out quickly, trying to psych myself up to swallow it.

"Why can't she just rattle around in that brain for a cure?" Butch asked, eyeing the concoction I was about to chug.

"Because if what Zee said is accurate, what's going on in there might be blocking access to those spells," Kane replied. "She'll probably be able to shadow walk, but that's it."

They, whoever they were, had stolen my magic too?

I couldn't have taken the potion quicker. I chugged back the foul liquid and was relieved when I found Butch holding out a flask to chase it. I took a swallow of his and handed it back. It was almost harder to hold down than the potion.

I ran my arm across my mouth. "What was that?"

"Special whisky blend. Good stuff, right?"

I gave him a halfhearted shrug. That was as good as it was going to get while I fought my gag reflex. It had been worse than the smoking potion. A couple of deep breaths later, I was fairly certain I wasn't going to throw up. "How long does this take to work?"

"It's nearly instant if it does." Kane walked back to the shelves and grabbed a pail that was on a lower shelf. He turned and put it beside me.

I poked around in my head, checking to see if I'd missed all the memories flooding back somehow, but found nothing. I shook my head at Butch, who looked like he was still holding out hope.

I looked down at the pail. "What's that for?" I asked.

"In case you don't make it to the bathroom over there." Kane pointed off to the side.

I was about to say I wasn't going to be needing it when I had to do a mad dash. The upside of my day was that my hair was already in a ponytail. I didn't straighten back up until after every last sip of coffee I'd had that morning had left me in the most violent fashion.

I walked out of the bathroom and Butch held the flask out to me again. I took it, ready to drink gasoline after that potion came back up.

I took the edge of my shirt and tried to wipe off the opening of the flask before handing it back this time.

Butch pointed at the flask. "You can hang on to that."

I straightened, eyes still watery from getting sick. "What else you got?"

Kane didn't say anything, but he stared at me as if he were seeing someone he'd missed. He walked over for another flask.

"You sure?" Butch asked.

"Positive," I said. "I'm going to get my memory back, and then I'm going to kill whoever stole it from me."

Chapter Seventeen

I scanned the Underground as I sat in the booth, waiting for a magical miracle to strike and one of the potions I'd drunk to have a delayed reaction and actually work. Someone in this room could've been behind the spell that had obliterated my memory, and here I sat, eating a salad like a sitting duck, no idea who was friend or foe. I could've been brushing shoulders with the asshole and not know.

Flip slid into the booth and took in my sweatshirt and yoga pants that looked like they'd been slept in—plus the disheveled hair that was mostly in a ponytail and the dark circles under my eyes—before stating the obvious: "You don't look so hot."

I wasn't sure if it was my green skin or lack of sleep.

"Rough sleep." I hadn't realized that the vomiting wouldn't be the end of the side effects. Muscle cramps had interrupted the few hours of sleep I'd tried to slip in that afternoon. To top it off, I'd been trying to eat a salad to get something in my stomach when Kane walked out of his office, followed by a very happy-looking witch named Dana.

He stood outside the door for all to see, being chummy with her as they laughed over some shared joke.

Flip propped her chin on her hand and studied me intently. "You look kind of mad, too."

I shrugged. "I'm not mad."

Laughter rang down from above, and I stabbed a tomato, afraid to look at the duo the merriment came from. If I did, I was afraid the railing Dana was leaning on might break, which would be unfortunate. Kane would want to know what happened and probably deduce that my emotions had gotten the better of me. And the why of that was baffling. He'd surely make unflattering assumptions, such as me wanting him or something. That *assumption* was the only thing making me hold my emotions together.

Flip glanced up toward the pair, who were laughing again, and her long sigh drifted over to me.

I couldn't keep it in anymore. By Flip's assertion, she was supposed to be my friend, so why should I? "For someone who I was supposedly involved with, he's getting very chummy with another person who was horrible to me."

"I wouldn't exactly say…"

I looked up from my salad, fork clenched in my hand. "Wouldn't say what?"

She leaned back a bit, staring at my fork. "He's not exactly flaunting anything."

"Are you kidding? Look at them."

She looked back, as if she were missing something and had to reexamine the scene. "Well, he's just standing there talking to her."

"He could've talked to her inside the office. She was already in there with him for the last twenty-two minutes." I stabbed another tomato.

"Twenty-two? Not, I don't know, twenty? Because those two minutes…" She whistled loudly, shaking her head.

"Stop messing with me. You know I'm in a bad mood." I stared at my salad, hoping the room would remain laughter-free for at least a few minutes.

"So you're in a bad mood?" She leaned forward, her chin in her hand.

"Of course I am." How could anyone be in a good mood listening to the hyena cackling above?

"Does this mean you like him or something? Because I got the impression you were done, and I didn't think it was his doing."

"Where'd you get a crazy idea like that?"

"This is very hard to keep track of." Someone bumped into Flip's chair. She turned, about to let them have it, but then stopped and stared. "Whoa."

My head jerked up. "What? What are they doing now?"

Flip wasn't looking up, though. Her attention seemed transfixed by the door, but I wouldn't look. They'd probably made their way across the room doing who knew what.

"Flip?"

Her attention swung back to me. "Not them."

"Then what was the whoa?"

"The piece of meat that just walked in the door." Her attention was back on the entrance, and I followed her stare.

A vampire male was speaking to Jerry by the door. He was about as tall as Jerry and almost as broad. Thick blond hair cut somewhat short. For a vampire, he had a very *GQ* look, and could've modeled for Ralph Lauren.

Jerry turned and scanned the crowd before he stopped and his gaze landed on me. He pointed in my direction, and then the vampire looked at me. He smiled my way, fangs safely tucked in. It looked like he thanked Jerry and then he headed my way.

"Oooh, looks like you're getting some company today," Flip said, kicking me under the table.

"Don't get so excited. He was probably sent over by Frederickson. They'd talked about having representatives or some nonsense." Total nonsense, actually, because Kane was anything but transparent, and I had too many skeletons to swing my casket lid open.

He stopped beside my table while Flip's jaw dropped open. The guy was attractive. I could see this in a logical way, but jaw-dropping? His hair was too blond and his look too soft. I glanced upstairs again, to where Kane was walking back into his office.

"Ollie?" he asked.

I turned my attention back to the stranger and nodded.

"I'm Vincent. Frederickson sent me over." He held out his hand.

"Nice to meet you." Yep, as expected. I took his hand, trying to not react at the chill of his skin. How did Jerry sleep with vampires all the time? Although it might be nice in the heat of summer if the AC was broken.

He looked at Flip and then down at my half-finished salad. "I don't want to interrupt, but if you have a moment?"

I'd thought that the representative would introduce himself and then go up to speak to Kane. But maybe this was an opportunity to feel the vampires out. All information was good, especially when you held so little.

"Not interrupting at all. We were just finishing up." I glanced over at Flip, hoping she'd make an excuse and leave. I gave her a nudge with my toe. She sat there as if she didn't feel it.

He gestured his head toward the door. "Would you like to get a coffee or something?"

He wanted to get out of the Underground and away from all the eyes on him, and he'd caught me in the exact same mood. "Sure."

I got up and headed to the door before I'd thought it through. If we left here, we still wouldn't be alone. Kane would have me tailed, and with my luck, I'd end up with Butch sitting next to me.

"A lot of places are closed right now. Maybe we could grab a coffee at the bar?" I took a step in that direction, relieved when he followed without complaint.

I stepped up to the bar, getting ready to call for a gargoyle when Zee popped up. She placed two steaming mugs in front of us with a wink. Did she spy on all my conversations, or only ones with attractive men?

With Vincent settling onto the stool beside me, I couldn't exactly pursue the subject. "Thanks," I said, as if it were normal. She nodded and disappeared, but I had a feeling she was still listening in.

"So, if you haven't guessed, I'm going to be the liaison between you and Frederickson, if that's all right?" He smiled as he wrapped his hands around the mug, seeming to appreciate the warmth.

"That's good with me." He had a soft manner about him, the kind that led me to believe he'd pull out my chair and hold the door open. I appreciated it more than I normally would, considering my recent experiences. He might be from the enemy camp, but he was actually more pleasant than some who were supposed to be on my team.

"If it's good with you, I figured we could meet every few days or so? Then I'll be able to update all parties."

"That would work." Was I supposed to tell him about letting the crawlers in tomorrow? He was still from the other camp, and I didn't know if I wanted them there, watching everything. What if something happened that revealed my current…issues? Maybe I could steer him in Kane or Butch's direction? "Are you sure you're supposed to meet with me, though? I'm pretty much out of the loop."

"No, you. Frederickson said you." Vincent took a sip from his mug. I thought it was just for show, but the coffee level in his cup went down.

He saw where my eyes had landed. "I enjoy the taste even if I don't need it."

I averted my stare quickly. "Sorry. Didn't mean to be obvious."

"You weren't. Newcomers are always watching for it." He shrugged it off in that easy style he seemed to have. He smiled, fangs still tucked away.

I was starting to see why they'd sent him. He was charming, and if I was interested in dating right now, cold hands or not, he'd be a temptation.

"So, is there anything you—"

"Kane wants to speak to you," Butch said, seeming to pop up out of nowhere and staring at Vincent. "Now." He stood a little too close, making it clear he wasn't walking away without Vincent beside him.

Vincent nodded and stood. He put a card from his pocket on the bar in front of me. "I'll be in touch soon. Call the number on the card if you need me," he said, smiling despite the fact Butch was hovering.

I waited until Vincent was halfway across the room before I whispered, "Zee, are you still there?"

I didn't hear anything, but my coffee was suddenly topped off. I took it with me, not wanting to tempt fate in case Vincent looped back around with questions I didn't want to answer.

Chapter Eighteen

I WAS THROWING BACK A SHOT AT THE BAR WITH ZEE when Kane walked out of his office.

"You ready?" Zee asked, knowing where we were heading.

"No." Today was D-Day. It was the day I'd let the crawlers in. There was no way to be ready for this.

She slid another shot toward me. "Little liquid courage isn't always a bad thing. You got this, girl."

I threw back the fresh shot. She held out her fist, and I tapped it with my knuckles before turning toward the door where Kane waited.

He was watching as I approached. "You sure you don't want another one?" he asked, when it was clear he didn't think I should.

I got it. We were heading into dangerous territory, but not everyone had nerves of steel.

"You're not the one who has to walk them through," I said, walking past him and out the door. Butch and Leon were waiting beside a huge black Hummer outside.

"I'm sure Butch has a flask on him if you lose your buzz before we get there." Kane walked around to the driver's side, while Butch and Leon got in the back.

I hopped in the front passenger seat, trying to remain calm so I wouldn't have to ask Butch if he did indeed have a flask on him.

Kane eyeing me out of the corner of his eye didn't help the nerves. I sat on my hands so I wouldn't fidget. Butch and Leon were absurdly calm, considering what we were heading to do. All they seemed to care about was Jerry's latest vampire squeeze and how she'd found out about Jerry's previous love interest, and how there might have been an overlap both girls now knew of.

I tried to listen to the gossip instead of thinking about what was coming. The possible catfight wasn't holding my interest though.

Kane glanced over at me. I waited for some sort of backhanded comment about needing more shots.

"You're going to be fine. You might not remember, but you've shadow walked before and handled scarier crawlers."

He ran down the details of how it was supposed to go. I held his hand because he was some sort of anchor to this world, and then I went in, trying to not go farther than necessary.

None of it sounded remotely familiar, but I knew he was right. I'd done this before. Might've done all of it before, even crossing crawlers over.

I really should've had at least one more shot.

"No one else should be there." He glanced over at me again. "I thought it would be better that way."

I read his meaning clearly. He had the same fear as me.

That I might somehow incriminate myself. I nodded, having trouble talking past the golf ball in my throat.

It was just about dusk when we pulled into a cemetery on the outskirts of Boston. Harg was already standing there, surrounded by several other smaller crawlers that I wasn't sure were visible to Butch and Leon.

I got out of the truck quickly, eager to get this over with. I walked deeper into the cemetery toward Harg, as if I were walking toward my own burial. Kane was close behind, and Leon and Butch trailed a short distance from him. I was surrounded but incredibly alone.

Harg moved toward me, and I made a point of holding my ground, even when he didn't stop until he was less than two feet away. Maybe he hadn't been trying to crowd me on purpose. He was a crawler; maybe he didn't understand personal boundaries. Half the people I'd encountered at coffee shops had the same problem. Why should a crawler know better? Still, I threw him another hard-ass look. Needed to make sure it was very clear that I wasn't scared of him. Kane being close might've helped a little with that.

"How's this going to go down?" I asked.

"I'll open, then you step through but stop partway. This will force the opening wider and allow the others to come through," Harg explained while maintaining his distance. His speech still had that sandpaper roughness, but his English had improved.

"Partway?"

"Leave arm or leg out."

That didn't sound that safe. I turned to Kane, and he nodded. Then I realized I'd just relied on him again. I had to start going with my own gut.

"Five," I said to Harg. "That's the agreement and that's all I'm letting through until next month."

Harg nodded. "Five. They're waiting."

Kane stepped close enough that our arms brushed and I could feel the heat from his body. He gripped my hand as he spoke softly to me. "Don't let go of my hand and it will be fine. If our connection feels like it's fading, you turn around and walk back out. If you feel me tugging at you, you run out."

I held up a finger to Harg and tugged Kane over to the side, as if there was a last-minute detail we needed to discuss.

I licked my lips, thinking the worst. What if somehow, when I did this, some crazy flare shot up into the air and declared my guilt? What if that Asher crawler I'd said was dead walked out of the portal?

"Promise you won't leave me in there, no matter what?" I asked in a whisper for Kane alone. "You can kill me afterward, but I don't want to go down like that."

"Never. No matter what." His words had gravity to them, heavy enough that I could rely on.

Kane squeezed my hand in an *I've got your back* way. And maybe he would. I didn't know Kane that well, or didn't remember what I knew, but that was the kind of guy he seemed like. If he said he had you, he did. It was starting to become clear why I'd been attracted to him before—why I was becoming attracted to him now, whether I liked it or not.

Kane and I walked back to Harg.

"I'm ready."

Harg opened a portal in front of me, the air rippling as if it were a reflection on a pond.

I stepped inside, leaving the hand Kane was holding extended. It was as if I'd taken a step in the same landscape, but all the people had disappeared and a hazy, dim lens had been placed over the full moon, a drab duplication of the same place.

And there they were. The crawlers that were supposed to come through, all lined up and waiting. Some were scaled and others had fur, but all were horrifying in their own way. They looked like what you'd imagine was lurking in the open closet at night, or the creature that would hide beneath your bed. Come to think of it, it made me wonder if when parents told their children that there was nothing to be afraid of, were they right? Because before me now were the very monsters they feared. Maybe those youthful minds saw something the parents couldn't?

The first stepped forward, walked past me, and disappeared. Then the next, and the next. With each one, I began to wonder again if I were the true monster.

By the time the last of the five was approaching, more had gathered around, scenting out an anomaly happening.

"Can you speed it up?" I asked, smelling trouble.

It didn't. By the time it snail paced its way through, I knew I had a problem. As soon as the fifth one's foot cleared, I tried to step out, practically brushing against it as I did. But before I could, a larger crawler who'd been on the outskirt charged toward me.

It shoved into me and was pressing its way through at the same time I was. I gripped Kane's hand hard, making sure I didn't lose connection. He must've sensed the problem, because I was quickly yanked through. Unfortunately, the other crawler latched on to me, and was pulled out as well.

I fell in a tumble to the ground, Kane's hands under my arms and pulling me away from the crawler that had half fallen on top of me. By the time I got to my feet, the sixth one was gone.

Kane was beside me, looking for him too. "Fuck."

The thing was gone before we'd gotten to our feet.

I looked for Harg. I was ready to give him a piece of my mind, figuring he had something to do with this, when I saw we'd gotten company. Harg, with more crawlers at his back, was standing off with Frederickson, Collin slightly behind them. The only one missing was Rudy.

We were about to have a turf war, monsters versus monsters. My instinct was to try and stop it, but then I wondered if that was a good idea. Letting a fight break out might have its uses in eliminating either a few crawlers or a few vampires. The werewolves might be collateral damage, but some things couldn't be helped.

Kane stepped forward to break it up, Leon and Butch readying to follow his lead.

I grabbed Butch's arm, even as the sounds of growling reached my ear. "Why are we breaking them up?" I asked.

"They'll never kill the crawlers, and we might need the vampires at some point," Butch said, reading my mind.

He walked over to where Kane already was, right in between the warring parties.

"Stop. It was one crawler and he wasn't with Harg. It was an accident," Kane said.

I lost track of who was screaming what, but after a few minutes, the voices lowered and Kane left them, with Butch and Leon buffering the groups.

He walked toward me and then tilted his head off to a

farther-away spot. The way he stared at me, I was wondering if a scarlet letter had appeared on my chest when he'd pulled me back out. Instead of a whore, I'd been branded a traitor. "What?" I asked, fearing in my gut that I was about to hear something horrible.

"What happened?" he asked, and that was when I realized he didn't believe anything he'd just told the others.

"The thing charged me."

"You couldn't avoid that?"

The doubt in his eyes was as loud as thunder. And I felt the jolt that went with it. "No. I couldn't."

He nodded, slowly. Too slowly.

He'd had my back, he protected me still, and yet he clearly thought I was a monster. I heard a cracking sound off to the right and had a feeling I'd just downed a tree.

The vampires and the werewolves all charged the area where the noise had come from, thinking they'd find the crawler who'd disappeared. I knew they wouldn't.

Kane knew it too, as he continued to stand there, a billboard of doubt.

His suspicions weighed me down like a boulder on top of me. When I walked away from him, he didn't try and stop me.

Vincent stepped up beside me. "You need a ride back?"

With all the commotion, I hadn't even noticed him in the background.

I glanced over at Kane where he waited. Something told me if I said yes, Kane would let me go. Something also told me it was probably another test. I didn't care. I failed all of his tests anyway.

"Yes. Thanks."

VINCENT PULLED up to the Underground and threw the car in park.

I touched his arm when he went to shut it off. "I'm good."

He glanced at the metal door twenty feet away and his hand went back to the ignition. "Let me walk you to the door."

"I really appreciate it, but I think it's best if you don't."

He looked as if he were going to argue when Jerry swung the door open and stood right inside it.

Vincent's finger finally dropped from the ignition. "If you need anything, a ride, someone to talk to, anything at all…"

"Thanks." I nodded.

I got out of the car and headed toward Jerry, who was now back to his smiling self and not looking so much like an enforcer.

"Heard things got a little hairy." Jerry stepped outside the door, his hand on the knob as I passed him.

"Just a hair."

The blond vampire Jerry was messing around with was making her way over, evaporating any interest he had in further conversation with me.

"See you tomorrow," I said, getting a half-assed wave from him as I walked away.

The Underground was in full swing, maybe even a bit swingier than normal. The shouts and drinks seemed to be flying a little looser, and the smell of skunk hung in the air so heavily that I wondered if Pepé Le Pew had moved in.

Glad to know everyone was in such a good mood while we escorted more monsters into the world.

As I made my way to the hall, Kane's office door opened, the light shining in the dim room. He stood there, looking down at me. I didn't know what he wanted, but if he had something else to say, he'd have to come track me down. I was in no mood for more insults tonight.

Chapter Nineteen

BY THE NEXT MORNING, THINGS WERE GETTING FUNNY, and not in a belly-laugh kind of way. This was more the *my milk smells* kind of bad. And as I sipped my coffee at the bar, fixed with plenty of milk, I wished a different analogy had popped to mind.

I called into the air for a refill as I watched Butch and Leon with their clipboards hogging our booth. One by one, people slid into the booth while Butch and Leon made marks on their boards. It looked like a job interview, except I couldn't imagine what position they'd be applying for, or who'd want the current applicants.

Flip walked across the room, her eyes shooting to the interview booth as she passed before hopping onto the stool beside me. "Crazy shit, right?" she asked, looking at the big screen.

"Huh?" I turned my attention to the TV, which showed a big caravan of military trucks driving toward Boston. The reporter talked about the National Guard setting up a perimeter around the city.

"Did you hear that some soldiers on the east end spotted one in the middle of the night?" Flip asked. "They opened fire on it but nothing happened. The thing just vanished in front of them and then reappeared a few feet away."

"No. I hadn't heard." Wasn't really surprised, either. There'd be a lot more sightings if we kept letting them in. "What did they do?"

"What any sane person would do." She leaned over slightly as she said, "Ran. For their fucking lives. Then called in backup. Heard they're setting up a perimeter around the city and preparing to do a mandatory evacuation."

I nodded. Getting people out of town was a solid idea, but then what? If this progressed, if we had to keep letting the crawlers in for a while, it wasn't going to be a localized problem. They'd spread. I was surprised it hadn't happened already. Why was it only in Boston? And did I even want to know, when I was the only Shadow Walker I knew of that happened to live in Boston?

I turned my attention back to the trucks, but that wasn't where my interest really was. I nudged Flip and nodded to Butch and Leon, who were sitting with Jerry's blond vampire now. "What are they doing?"

She leaned in a little closer. "Getting ready for shit to go sideways."

"How is that getting ready? They look like they're interviewing for jobs."

She pulled her fluffy blond hair and twisted it into a knot on top of her head, as if she were preparing to get down to work. "According to my conversation with Casio, who talked to Maria, who—"

"Who's Maria?" I asked, and sipped some more coffee.

"Leggy blond vamp that was diddling Jerry before he moved on to the new one. Doesn't really matter other than the credibility of my sources."

A face flashed through my mind, and a swaying pair of hips. I nodded. I did remember the previous blond vamp. Without her, I wouldn't have been able to sneak out to check the site of the explosion.

Flip continued, "So Maria overheard Jerry talking to Butch when she was, let us say *conveniently*, outside his apartment door in the middle of the night just happening to listen in. She repeated it to Casio.

"They're narrowing the herd. You're either pledging support or you're out. Kane's cutting the fat."

Flip kept her eye on the booth. "My guess is there won't be too much fat to cut. If shit gets worse, this will be the safest place in the city. There isn't one person here that's going to leave willingly. Kane tells them they've got to dig shit holes in the alley, and they'll be digging shit holes all night long." She let out a laugh that sounded like it was fueled by nerves. "Thank God I don't have any brawn."

I glanced up at Kane's empty office, wondering where the man who had ordered this had disappeared to. I took another sip of coffee when I should've been guzzling potions to try and get fixed. He'd been in the wrong to accuse me yesterday, but it looked like I'd be the one who had to track him down. Man, that grated on the nerves.

I swallowed the last of my coffee and my pride in the same gulp, then put my mug down and stood with conviction. I was getting myself fixed, no matter what I had to swallow. "Have you seen Kane?"

"In the basement pissing off the gargoyles."

"You sure? I didn't see him pass by all morning."

"Why would he pass by? The basement door is in the hall." She pointed to the same hall where the elevators were. "When you find him, make sure you tell him I'm too small to dig ditches. You know, just in case."

I gave her a thumbs-up, not bothering to explain that my opinion counted less than a single snowflake in a blizzard right now. The hallway was empty as I examined it for a door I'd somehow missed. I ran my hands along the walls, trying to find a secret entrance. I looked around for a good ten minutes before I called Zee.

She popped up immediately. "Why aren't you with Kane trying to get fixed? We're never going to get back to work if you're slacking."

"I'm trying to find Kane to do exactly that. Flip said he's in the basement, but I can't find it."

Her chin snapped back at the same time her hip shot forward. "He's putting more shit down there? We're already crowded." There was some elaborate huffing and puffing before she said, "Come on. I'll bring you."

She reached toward the wall and a door appeared. A plume of smoke flooded the hall with its opening. All of a sudden, I saw gargoyles coming and going everywhere.

"How did I miss this?" I asked.

"Because you were supposed to."

"Are they always here?" I watched as they passed.

"Usually."

"So all those times I thought I was in the hall alone…?" I ran through the moments, wondering how many things I'd done that were cringe-worthy.

That was how Kane knew I'd dragged a witch into the stairwell so quick.

"You may have been or may not. Us gargoyles like privacy. We spent years on display. It was too much." Zee waited for a gap in the flow of traffic heading up the stairs. "Come on."

The place was massive and filled with gargoyles, some of whom were staring at the supplies being loaded along the side wall with dirty looks. It looked as if Kane's supplies were taking up about a tenth of the space, with gargoyles stacking more boxes and crates as I watched. There was no Kane, though.

But wow, the rest of the place was jaw-dropping. I'd had no idea of the hustle and bustle going on down here. I hadn't realized gargoyles existed in these numbers. Quite a few liked to smoke cigars, so the place had a strange fog.

"Don't you guys have air filters down here?" I asked, a strong stream of smoke hitting me.

"Too drafty. This is much nicer, don't you think?"

"Sure. I can see that." If you had a vendetta against lungs, it all made perfect sense.

As I moved farther into the room, my eyes streamed tears from the stinging. I got a better sense of what was going on. There were tables all over the place. The basement was divided into different districts. One corner had four or five tables with gargoyles bent over hand-rolling cigars. Another area had sewing machines running, and the brown monogrammed leather they were working on looked quite familiar. I was fairly certain this wasn't an authorized manufacturing center. And it didn't matter what area they were in, they all had a drink in their hand.

I grabbed Zee's arm. "What goes on down here, exactly?"

"You know, a little of this, a little of that. It's work hours, so it's a bit more uptight than normal. If I were you, though, I wouldn't come down at night. Might be too much considering…" She waved a hand at my head, as if I was too delicate, since I was broken.

It was a bit much now.

The strangest part of it was this seemed to be right under the Underground, the spot where Kane's dungeon/mad-scientist lab was.

"Thanks for showing me the place," I said. "Going to go find Kane."

As I turned, the man himself was on his way down the stairs.

I walked toward him, and we ended up meeting beside all the supplies. "What's going on? Why the stockpiles?" I asked, testing the waters with the only thing that popped to mind, even though I already knew.

"Getting prepared." Short and clipped—that was the best he was giving.

My pride told me to walk away, but then I remembered I'd swallowed that because I needed him.

"That's a good idea." There. I'd even flattered him a little.

He crossed his arms. "Did you need something else?"

The bastard knew I did. He'd insulted me and I was supposed to grovel? Right now, the idea seemed as tempting as chugging sand. "So I'm at fault?"

"Did you have a nice ride with Vincent?"

So this wasn't even about his false accusation? "You

mean as opposed to walking or riding back with you as you stared at me like I was a traitor? Oh, *dandy*. Thanks."

I said "thanks" the way most people said "fuck you," then walked away. I'd figure out something else, somehow. Maybe I could negotiate with Harg? He had magic and we were bartering with him anyway. Anything was better than dealing with that asshole.

I walked up the stairs and toward the elevators, but an arm turned me in the opposite direction. I'd been so mad that I hadn't realized Kane had followed.

"What?" I snapped as he propelled me toward the Underground. Then I dug in my heels, making it clear he'd have to carry me if he wanted me to move one more inch.

"You want to drink potions and throw up or do you have better plans?" he asked, raising an eyebrow.

That was it? I was supposed to just skip into the basement with him? "Not unless you admit you're an ass."

He tilted his head forward, both eyebrows raised. "I'm offering to help you."

"Why? You don't believe my mind has a spell on it. You think I'm blowing things up for shits and giggles." I gave him a hard stare, "You. Don't. Trust. Me."

I turned toward the elevators again, and he grabbed my arm, stopping me. I looked at his hand with disdain. "You want to help so badly? Admit you're an ass."

His jaw shifted. "If you admit you're stubborn and occasionally delusional."

That one bit a little. Not like a shark bite, but a small dog? "Fine."

"Then fine. Now can I *please* make you sick?"

I shrugged, feeling a little better. Or enough to take his help, anyway. "Fine."

Chapter Twenty

THIS WAS THE SECOND DAY IN A ROW WE WERE BACK AT potions. Kane had looked for me this morning and I knew it had been his way of apologizing. He had to do it somehow, since he wasn't so good at verbalizing them.

"Do you need a break?" he asked, watching me from the comfortable armchair he'd had moved to the basement.

I'd decided to call it a basement, instead of a dungeon. Dungeon made me think he was torturing me with concoctions that didn't work, instead of helping. I liked to think of the couch I was sitting on as another apology for the other day. Otherwise, he'd only moved it here because his sitting in the armchair while I had nothing would've definitely marked him as the ass I'd called him.

The coffee table was a nice touch as well. I'd like it more if it didn't have all the concoctions lined up on it.

And there were a whole lot of glasses at this point. We'd branched into fairy spells, some strange stuff the dwarves had suggested, and some gargoyle concoctions Zee had brought over. I couldn't remember where the thick black one on the end had come from, but it smelled like a decomposing body. I was saving that goody for last.

I'd made it through four already and had only thrown up three times, so I was considering the fourth a win.

"How can I possibly take a break with everything happening? There might be something in my head right now that could fix my memory and I can't get at it." I leaned forward, wrapping my hands around a glass filled with a yellow slime that was topped with a mold-green foam. "Maybe I should go back into the Shadowlands. That's where I was shadow kissed. Maybe I can find that crawler again?"

"You won't even recognize it if you do."

I flopped back in the couch. That wasn't why he didn't want me to go back. He didn't trust me. Walking into the Shadowlands for someone such as me was akin to dipping your soul into pure power. From what I knew, I'd have access to endless amounts of spells.

Tough pill to swallow when Kane didn't trust me. Or maybe he thought, injured as I was, I might get hurt or stuck? Might as well continue with a streak of optimism, since I wasn't willing to disturb the newly found peace.

He leaned an elbow on his armchair, staring at the glass in my hand before his eyes slowly made their way to my face. "You quitting for the day?"

I thought I heard a challenge in that question, as if he wanted me to admit he was right. It was the fastest way to get me to keep going.

"Nope." I tilted the glass and the slime ran into my mouth. I placed it back on the table and then leaned my head back. This one wanted out immediately, but I locked down my throat, breathing through my nose.

It wasn't until good five minutes later, and after a cold sweat, that I felt confident I'd won. I opened my mouth, taking in a deep breath.

"Why is it that everything you have has the same side effect?" I asked.

"It's not what I'm giving you. It's you. As a Shadow Walker, you're repelling foreign magic."

"How is that possible? What about the spells the witches did? I heard my clothes kept falling off."

"They spelled the clothes. Your body rejected them. It was your magic that made that work so well."

"What about my memories?"

"Different magic, and they probably got a strand of your hair. Your hair is dead. It's not going to repel anything."

If I could only repel everything. Unfortunately, I was a magnet for anything from the Shadowlands.

Oh fuck me…

Was I a magnet for them, too? Was that why they all stayed in Boston?

I leaned my head back again, breathing through my nose as another wave of nausea hit. Something was making me sick, but it wasn't the potions this time.

"What is it?" Kane asked, as if he could sense I was out of sorts. It was odd to have a stranger be able to read me so well, especially when he'd been checking his phone and shouldn't have noticed every stupid move I made.

"So, you'd never ever kill me?" I asked, noticing he'd put his phone on the table, as if he'd found something else more interesting at the moment.

"We've covered this."

"Can you say it again?" I'd feel a lot better about this if

I got it reconfirmed. I wasn't sure how many other people would be coming for me if my theory was correct.

"No. I already promised. There is no renewal process. That's not how promises work. You keep the ones you make."

Had to give it to him. That was a pretty good answer. But still… "And there's no loopholes, right?"

He leaned forward, resting his arms on his legs. "Ollie."

I got it. He wanted me to spit it out. He already thought my hands were covered in blood, and I didn't think I could fall any further in his esteem. Might as well say it.

I bent a knee to my chest and hugged it there. "Have you noticed that the crawlers seem to be localized to Boston?" It was one of those non-questions you asked when you didn't have the balls to come right out and say what it was you wanted.

"I hope there's more to this breakthrough of yours, or I greatly overestimated your intelligence," Kane said.

I let out a short laugh. Arrogant bastard. On the plus side, he didn't think I was stupid—most of the time.

He waved his hand in a rolling motion.

"Do you think that it has anything to do with me?" I asked. "Like, maybe they have to stay in a certain perimeter?"

"Yes. That has occurred to me." He picked up his phone again, leaning back in his chair and swiping.

Seriously? Did he not see the pitfalls of that? I got up and took his phone. He didn't fight me for it, either, relinquishing it easily. I glanced down at the screen as I placed it on the table.

"Blackjack?" He was gambling online while I feared

for my life. I was crazy to say it, but now that I'd brought up the subject, he should be giving it his full attention. He clearly hadn't thought this through or he wouldn't be playing cards. "What if we find out that getting rid of me gets rid of them?"

"Then we'll find another way to get rid of them or start charging rent." He pointed at his phone. "Can I get back to my game now?"

I picked up his phone and moved it to the other side of the table, as if that would stop him if he really wanted it.

"I'm a liability." I definitely shouldn't have just told him that. It was a confidence you'd only tell someone you trusted with your life. Why had I done that? A promise was only words.

He didn't respond, and I found myself staring at the ground. I lifted my gaze to see if I could read his normally unreadable expression.

"For one," he said. "I made a promise to you that I broke. You told me that you thought something bad was going to happen and I told you that everything was fine. It wasn't."

He'd told me this before, but I hadn't heard it like I was hearing it now. Just as my memory loss tormented me, this was his cross to bear, and it was no less painful. From the look in his eyes, it might've been even more so.

The tension in the room swelled as I stared at him. I knew that when I wanted to reach out and comfort him, I was entering dangerous territory.

I glanced at the table instead. It took another couple of seconds for the spell to break.

"You quitting yet?" he asked, the playful jab back in his voice.

"Nope."

I WAS SLAMMING down another concoction when Leon appeared. As I saw him, a little part inside me hoped that something truly horrible had happened, something that would require me to not drink the decomposing body that sat waiting in a glass.

Kane turned toward him, pulling his eyes away from his gambling. "What's wrong?"

Leon shrugged in a way that told me this was a common nuisance and not the calamity I'd hoped for. "Ernie, the police chief, is here."

Kane let out a sigh that said it all. "Okay, give me five minutes. She could use a break anyway."

I was too sick to show surprise, but I hadn't thought he'd truly understood how horrific this was. My throat was raw and I'd wiped more tears from my eyes than when I'd lost my dog at ten.

Leon nodded and left as Kane turned his attention back on me. "Anything?"

I consciously tried to remember something. Anything. Even a hint. "Not yet."

"This one could take a little longer, so let's wait it out for a bit. I've got to go handle the chief anyway." He picked up the black concoction to put away for another day, and I didn't try and stop him.

He paused by the door, watching me as I got off the couch slowly.

"You need help?" he asked, looking ready to come over, sweep me off my feet, and carry me if needed.

I didn't mind the idea of being carried, but the sweeping off my feet was a real concern. The more time I spent with him— when he wasn't being an ass—the more I wanted to.

And he thought I was maybe the worst person to ever live and didn't trust me as far as he could throw me. He was probably waiting to help me because he didn't want to leave me here alone.

"I'm good," I said.

He waited for me to precede him, and I knew it was more about making sure I didn't fall down the stairs than checking out my assets.

He was already halfway up the stairs when I asked, "How'd the police chief get here, anyway? I thought this place was warded so no one could find it unless they had magic or something?" Or I'd thought Kane had said that. I'd gotten so much information in such a short time that I wasn't certain of anything. It was one big confusion. I glanced back and realized maybe he *had* been multitasking when he had me go first. Worse, I liked that he was checking me out. I turned back around as if I hadn't noticed.

"It's a weird glitch," he said. "He's got some leprechaun blood in him. Warding places so people don't find things doesn't work on leprechauns, even if there's only a drop of the blood running through their veins. They're like hound dogs. They sniff out magic miles away."

"The police chief is a leprechaun?"

"No. Leprechaun numbers always remain constant. If

one dies, one can be born. They can only fill one spot. But a few hundred years ago, twins were conceived. There was only one true leprechaun born, but the other ended up with a touch of magic too because it was in the blood. The magic from that drop has lingered for generations. It's a very rare occurrence."

"I thought Flip was half-leprechaun?"

"She is, but she has no leprechaun magic."

I got to the top step, not realizing how heavy the door was when Kane stepped close behind me, his front brushing my back as he reached past me to open it. The last time we'd been close in that spot it had gotten a little hot and heavy, and I found some more pep in my step to move into the office.

Kane walked over to the window overlooking the Underground and waved a hand to Leon. "Don't mention the leprechaun thing to the chief. He has no idea."

The worn leather couch was a perfect seat to watch this spectacle happen. A tiny drop of blood and he could still sense this place? I found it absolutely amazing.

A minute later, a man, with a few extra pounds in his midsection and a bit of frost in his reddish hair, appeared in the door.

"Ernie, what can I do for you?" Kane asked, as he shifted some piles of papers around his desk. Just another day of business, as if he hadn't been in the basement feeding me magical concoctions that sent up plumes of smoke and smelled like bats flying at midnight.

Ernie walked farther into the room, nodding in my direction before turning to Kane.

"Kane, I know some weird things happen here—*so* weird my guys pretend they don't even know about this place, or this street"—he threw his hands up as the absurdity seemed to strike him—"or even the few blocks around it. And I've got this funny feeling you know what the hell is going on. Don't tell me you don't know about the monsters." His cheeks were rosy from blood pressure that was probably popping up like a bad game of Whac-A-Mole, and the sheen on his forehead said his nerves were worn down to nubs.

I liked Ernie immediately. He wasn't aggressive, and I could sense he was slightly intimidated by the way Kane took over a room, but he stood his ground anyway.

Kane stopped moving about the office and walked around to perch on the front of his desk, folding his arms as he measured his words.

The dilemma was as clear and painful as a busted nose. Too much information could start a stampede of shit our way, worse than a herd of buffalo. But Kane clearly liked Ernie. I could tell because he was willing to speak to him. I'd noticed in the last week that you could measure how much Kane liked somebody by the number of syllables he was willing to spare.

"If I could explain to you what was happening, I would," Kane said. "I can't. Honestly, I'm not sure you'd want to know anyway."

Ernie's shoulders dropped while he reassessed his approach, looking like a person trying to size up if he could swim to shore or not. "Can you tell me this? Should I get my guys out of here? They want to stay and help, but I'm figuring this to be something that's a one-way ticket to hell."

"In the long term, I don't know how much leaving will help. Short term, it might be a good idea."

"I'll tell my guys," Ernie said, in a voice that sounded as if Kane had sent him to his demise.

"This doesn't come back my way."

Ernie nodded. "It won't." He glanced over at me and then back to Kane. "You staying?"

Kane had the nerve to laugh, as if Ernie had asked the devil himself if he was going to leave hell because he couldn't take the heat. "Of course I'm staying. I don't get pushed out. I do the pushing."

Ernie left and Kane looked over to me.

I shook my head, letting him know that I still hadn't remembered a thing.

Chapter Twenty-One

IT WAS THREE IN THE MORNING. THAT WAS WHAT MY CLOCK said when I woke to Kane standing at the foot of my bed. Again. It was so reminiscent of him showing up after my last blackout that I immediately thought back to what I'd done last night. Lain in bed feeling like garbage for five hours. Figured that I'd remember every lousy minute of that.

"Do you ever knock?" I sat up, shoving hair gone wild out of my face.

"No."

"Well, don't you think maybe—"

"Before you start, we've had this fight before and I won." He walked over to the closet and started flipping through it.

"So what's that supposed to mean?" I asked, sitting up, glad I'd slept in a t-shirt. "And why are you going through my things? Have you no boundaries?"

"To answer your first question, just because you don't

remember doesn't mean I have to re-win a previously won fight."

"How do I know you won? Maybe you're trying to trick me."

"Clearly I wouldn't have to trick you. And to your second question, I hardly see what getting you moving has to do with boundaries." He turned to me, clearly annoyed as he said, "Where are your jeans?"

"In the dresser drawers where people put them." I got there before he could flip through my drawers and hustled him out of the way. "Where are we going at three in the morning?"

He leaned against the doorframe as he watched me shuffling through my clothes. "I've got a location on Harg."

I didn't need to ask why. I'd been wondering myself where Harg was. The only "why" I had was why it had taken this long. Or had it?

I grabbed a black t-shirt and my darkest pair of jeans. Clothes in hand, I shooed Kane away with my hand. "Get out. I'll be dressed in two minutes."

"Get out?" he asked, looking at my hand as if he found it alien. "Are you shooing me from your room?"

"Yes. If you can barge in, I can kick you out."

He smirked, sending a little buzz of awareness through me. No one should look that sexy and arrogant at the same time.

Luckily, he left before I invited him to stay.

"HOW MANY CARS DO YOU OWN?" I asked ten minutes later, my hands on the wheel of his Tesla.

"Too many to drive. Turn right," he said, looking at a dot on his phone.

"Is that him?" I asked.

"It's the person following him. Turn left." He reached over and shifted the wheel more when I almost clipped the curb. "How many times have you driven?" he asked.

"Enough."

"Let me guess, you didn't care to carpool?" he asked, referring to the crawlers that used to hover all over me.

"Not really." They'd nearly driven me to a breakdown, but that wasn't a topic I felt like delving into. I had more pressing matters. "How long have you been following him and why are you bringing me now?"

"Maybe I just found him?" He didn't look up from his phone as he watched the dot. "Turn right."

Sure he did. I swung right. "I'm glad we've come to a place where we can be so open and sharing with the flow of information."

"I'd answer your questions, but I can't remember all the details right now." He gasped loudly. "I must've blacked out," he said with fake shock in his voice.

The teasing didn't make the urge to punch him go away. "Awfully convenient," I said, throwing his words back at him. "You do know deep down that you can be a real ass, right?"

"I consider it one of my better qualities." He pointed to the side of the road. "Park. We need to go on foot from here."

He pocketed his phone as if he hadn't just given me a harsh dig and I hadn't called him an ass.

I got out of the car, convinced there was something seriously off with him. "Can't you act like a considerate person for any length of time?"

He ducked in between houses, and I followed him.

"You mean considerate and sensitive like Vincent?" he asked, keeping his voice low. "Sensitive and considerate doesn't keep people alive."

Vincent? Were we really back to that? What was Kane's beef with him? I would've asked him, except he put his finger to his lips and pointed forward. Harg was close.

We crossed the street, coming upon a cemetery. It had an iron fence, the kind that didn't have a good spot to place your foot unless your legs were six feet long.

Kane turned and, with his hands on my waist, lifted me over. Then he was beside me, grabbing my hand and pulling me up from where I'd landed awkwardly, even though I'd gotten over first. *Definitely* not human.

We walked slowly then stopped behind some shrubbery that divided the different areas, Harg clearly in view a hundred feet away.

He was standing in a clearing that was surrounded by smaller mausoleums that looked as if they could've been designed by one of our gargoyles. He appeared to be talking to someone, but no one was there. The closest crawler was a good twenty feet away, and looking in the wrong direction.

"Can you see who he's talking to?" Kane whispered.

Now I knew why I'd gotten an invite. How many times had he tried to figure out this mystery before bringing me in?

Although I wasn't going to be much help. I stared, not

believing my eyes. How could I not see anything? I saw *all* the monsters, *always*. I kept staring, but there was nothing there. What was he talking to?

"No. There's nothing…" I narrowed my eyes. "Wait."

"What?" Kane's eyes fixed on me, looking as if he wished he could crawl into my head and see for me.

"There's a shimmer in the air. Kind of like when a portal opens." I fixed my stare on one spot and tried to focus better. Nothing else was showing.

"Is it in a shape? Can you make out a form?" he asked, wanting more information, and he didn't want to wait for it.

"No. It's blotchy." The moonlight shimmered against it here and there, but it was impossible to make out a perimeter or what I was actually looking at.

I heard a crawler hiss ten feet away and turned toward it. It growled before running off, like the shepherd it resembled. Seconds later, it was in front of Harg, who turned in our direction, seeming to stare right at me. I didn't know if he'd come for us or how ugly this moment might get.

We waited, and at that moment I thought about what Kane had just said about Vincent, and knew in my gut it was true. I was glad it was Kane beside me and not Vincent.

Then Harg did what I least expected: he nodded in acknowledgement and walked away.

Chapter Twenty-Two

KANE WAS LEANING AGAINST THE BAR, AND DANA KEPT her eyes transfixed on his lips as he spoke. Dana, the witch who'd tortured me. She lifted her fingers and trailed them down his bicep before leaving them resting on the forearm he had leaned on the bar. Their bodies angled toward each other as if they were a couple.

I focused my eyes back on my sandwich. Trying to not stare, I ate my lunch while everyone else ate their dinner. That was what happened when you had to get your sleep piecemeal.

I was going to eat my meal here. It didn't matter if Kane was in the room, and flirting with enemy number one. She used to be down around three or four, but after further consideration, I'd decided to bump her up the ranks due to being irritating.

"Her fingers are still in action," Flip said as she ate across from me. "Would you like a play-by-play so you don't have to look? Because it might get awkward if you punch her in the face, considering you aren't together anymore, by your choice."

"No." I bit into a piece of bread that tasted like it had come from the recycling bin, and knew it wasn't the cook. It was the atmosphere. "Yes."

"So is that a no, or a yes, you want a play-by-play?" I could hear the hesitation in her voice.

I looked up at her with both eyebrows nearly touching my scalp. "*Yes*."

"Just wanted to check, is all." Flip took a couple more bites of her dinner, her eyes wandering around but always lapping back to Kane. "I didn't think you even liked him anymore. You always seem to be fighting."

"I don't. Just watch." I couldn't explain it myself, and if I tried, my skin was going to burn. I couldn't tell her how when I walked into a room, he was the first person I searched out. Why? I didn't know myself. It didn't make any sense. It had to be blocked memories leaking through somehow. What else could it be?

I heard Flip shifting around in her seat, and I looked up to see her biting her lip. It couldn't be more obvious that she wanted to say something but was holding back. Flip holding back was like trying to stop a tidal wave. You couldn't do it. Best you could do was brace for the impact.

"What?"

"Left hand just came in play." She was starting to sound like a boxing commentator.

"His left or her left?" I asked, leaning forward.

"His left. He just gave her waist a squeeze."

He might as well make out with Dana right there at the bar. I put my sandwich down as my fingers shook, trying to remain as calm as I could. Accidentally breaking something would definitely be awkward.

"Keep eating. People are looking," Flip said, then laughed like we were joking about something.

I picked the sandwich back up, smiling like Flip was the funniest person I'd ever met. I chewed and then swallowed what felt like a bowling ball.

"I don't know what's going on with you two. I mean, other than the obvious, that you broke up. You did break it off with him, right?"

"Yes." I shrugged. "It's hard to be in a relationship with some guy you just met." And thought that maybe you were a monster and had not a lick of trust in you. The list of problems went on and on, but it didn't seem to stop the feelings that piled up, poking me in opposite directions.

"I don't want him. I just don't want him with her." Dana wasn't a good person—at all. She'd done horrible things to me, and there Kane was, about to get it on with *her*. It was quite logical why I didn't want them together when I thought of it like that.

"Oh, okay then." Flip's eyes opened wide, but then returned to normal as she shrugged. She looked like she's just had a silent conversation with herself. "His right—"

"Don't tell me." I stood. "I've got to get out of here before I accidentally break something." After the last time, I'd gotten a vague idea of where the threshold was, and I was fast approaching it.

She nodded, making me think I should run out of there before I found out what Kane had just done now.

I started toward the hallway and then made a sharp turn toward the exit. Less damage to be done outside if I didn't calm down quick enough. Jerry stiffened as he saw me approach. "Jerry, I need some air. If you don't open the door…"

He looked over my shoulder to where Kane was sitting, then sucked in some air between his teeth. "Don't go far," he said, swinging the door open.

There was no one on the street, but that wasn't unusual around here, and even more so lately. I was more surprised when they did linger outside. All the monsters inside were afraid of the bigger boogieman down the block.

I paced away from the door, wishing I had something to do out here, instead of looking like what it was—that I was having a bad day and needed air.

I walked a little more, aware that Jerry might be staring at my back through the peephole. I went just far enough that I could duck around the corner out of sight.

I banged my head on the brick wall I leaned against, closing my eyes as I thought back over every step, every decision, that might've led me to this place I was now. Maybe I should've just kept kissing Kane that day? Then maybe he wouldn't be at the bar with Dana right now. But I had a really great reason for pulling back. He hadn't trusted me then and he still didn't.

But her? Did he have to keep hanging out with her?

My eyes were still closed when I felt a slash across my neck. I opened them as I gripped my throat, my hands trying to stop the bleeding. A vampire I didn't recognize stood in front of me, smiling, fingers dripping in my blood.

I fell to the ground at his feet as he said, "Die, you whore."

Chapter Twenty-Three

My cheek was against cement, my attacker's boots in front of me. Ugly boots, with green plaid trim. It angered me to have ugly boots as my last vision. I tried to hold my hands to my throat, gushing warmth oozing through my fingers. My vision was blurring and my grasp weak. As I lay there, it was odd I was even still awake. I felt like I was dying. Considering the damage he'd inflicted, shouldn't I already be dead?

"Fucking die, already," my attacker said, hatred thick in his voice. His knees bent as he stooped to my level, probably to see why I was alive.

Even he thought I should be dead, and he was probably experienced at this sort of thing. I knew the slim thread of life I clung to was about to be snipped.

Before he could, there was a blur off to the side, accompanied by a breeze. The vampire's ugly boots lifted off the ground. There was a thud of something heavy hitting the ground, followed immediately by a second thud.

Kane appeared in front of me, his eyes taking in the

damage done. "Ollie, hang on. I've got you." His hand pressed over mine, gentle but firm, trying to keep pressure there without cutting off my air. His other arm hoisted me up partially. "Jerry, go to—"

"Kane, let me help her," Frederickson said, kneeling in front of me. "She'll never make it otherwise. I can save her. It's her only option."

Where had he come from? Had he been sitting back watching the attack?

Kane tensed, contemplating it too. Death or Frederickson. It wasn't that clear-cut. I wasn't sure if he hadn't been watching from the end of the alley. Maybe this was a setup?

That I was still alive made me begin to doubt that Frederickson was my only hope. Maybe I had more time than anyone thought? How had I not died already? I wanted to say all this, but staying alive and awake seemed to be the extent of what I was capable.

I felt Kane's arm squeeze around me. Somehow I knew this meant his was going to let Frederickson do it, like a final hug before he handed over my fate. Except that thought was much more poetic than the reality.

"As her maker, you will release her immediately," Kane said.

Oh shit. Here it came. I was going to be a vampire.

"Of course—after the initial phase, anyway," Frederickson said. "It needs to be like that or—"

"Just do it."

Kane knelt in place, my upper body resting against his lap and arm. My head lolled to the side as they argued the details. They fell silent, and I had the worst feeling that it was because Frederickson was opening his wrist up for me. I'd heard that was how they did it.

Maybe this was the only way? And even if it were a trap, I'd find my way out. I didn't want to be a vampire, but I wanted to be dead even less, or at least the kind of dead that no longer spoke. I'd take Frederickson's type of dead over *dead* dead. Being a vampire would be just another compromise of life.

I heard other people approaching, and then Kane barked, "Everyone back inside." The sound of shuffling feet receded. I heard Jerry, and then Butch, yelling and telling them to get back.

As I lay there, my head supported by Kane, I saw a shimmer ahead. It was exactly like the shimmer I'd seen Harg talking to. Whatever it had been, it was here now.

As it got closer, I waited for some response from Kane or Frederickson. There wasn't one. They didn't see it.

"Craw…" I said, only getting the first syllable of "crawler" out before warm liquid was dripping into my mouth and down my throat.

Frederickson's wrist was pressed firmly against my lips, and there would be no more speaking. Whether or not I wanted his blood was no longer a choice. It was done.

It felt alive, as if it were fizzing and bubbling against my damaged flesh, easing itself inside of me. A hand ran over my head, trying to soothe me through the process.

My eyes shifted to the shimmer that was now nearly on top of all of us, and I was stunned by the overwhelming power I felt surging over me. This thing, whatever it was, was potent on a level I'd never experienced.

And *still*, neither Frederickson nor Kane seemed to sense it. It hovered close to all of us, and I wondered if even Frederickson's blood would save me now—or them, for that matter. Were we about to die? I tried to speak, but Frederickson seemed to force his wrist firmer over my mouth, clearly wanting me to drink his blood, be one of his. Maybe he feared I'd try and abort this transfusion?

All the while, the shimmering moved closer to my hand that lay limp on the ground, until it was right above it. It bit down on the spot where I had the mark of being shadow kissed. The stabbing pain made my body jerk.

"Slow down. You're hurting her," Kane said to Frederickson, as his fingers grazed my forehead.

I tried to shake my head and realized I couldn't move. I wanted to say it wasn't Frederickson, but I couldn't speak. I was frozen, and not from weakness. That thing had done something to me. All I could do was lie there.

The pain on my hand relented for a moment, and a grey mist filled the air a few feet above our heads.

"What the hell was that?" Kane asked, sounding like he was about to rip Frederickson's throat out.

"I have no idea. Maybe it's something to do with her Shadow Walker blood?"

Teeth bit into my hand again, and somehow didn't hurt quite so much this time, as if it had been numbed. I could still feel the vampire blood coursing through me, mending as it went. But instead of seeping through my body, it now felt as if the fizzing and bubbling was traveling through my mouth, and throat, then down the arm, where the creature was biting me.

"That should be enough," Kane said firmly.

"A little more to be safe," Frederickson said, making sure he got his hooks into me as best he could.

"No. That's enough." Kane pushed Frederickson's wrist away from my mouth. "Why isn't she moving yet?"

"It might take a little bit to fully work. Her injuries were extensive."

Kane's fingers grazed my neck, which felt like it was healing, even as I barely moved because of whatever the other creature was doing to me. It released my hand again, and then released another grey mist.

If Frederickson or Kane noticed it this time, they didn't remark upon it. Kane gathered me up, cradling my body to him as he stood. "I'll find you if I need you."

"I'll need to bring her with me. It's part of the process." Frederickson's desperation reeked like rotten eggs on a hot summer day.

"I told you, I'll let you know."

The creature that glimmered rose with us, and then there was a swooshing feeling, as if my arm was attached to a vacuum that was sucking my cells dry. I found I could finally move my head, and I tried to catch a glimpse of what was happening to me. I couldn't see much, but I heard a drawn-out "Shhhh," as if it were telling me to keep quiet and lulling me to sleep.

Chapter Twenty-Four

A WARM HAND BRUSHED MY CHEEK AND THEN MOVED OVER my forehead.

"She's still warm," Kane said, sounding as unsure as he was capable of.

I opened my eyes and realized I was in my apartment, on my bed.

Kane had his fingers placed on my neck, his brow furrowed. Butch, Leon, and Flip were all standing around the bed, staring at me as if I were a zoo exhibit. It made sense—I was a newly made vampire.

Kane sat on the bed beside me. "How do you feel?"

"Pretty good. I guess that's normal?" I looked out the window, seeing the dark sky. I ran my tongue over my incisors. They felt the same. Maybe they wouldn't pop down until I got hungry. Was I hungry? I looked back at the people staring at me, seeing if I had an urge to sink my teeth into their necks. No, definitely had no urge to do that.

"Does it take a while to kick in? Maybe by tomorrow? How long have I slept?"

Kane reached out again, grazing my throat. "I've seen the transition before. Another day isn't going to get rid of your pulse."

"How *do* you have a pulse?" Butch asked, stepping forward and squinting. Leon was taking a step back, and Flip sat down on the other side of the bed, gaping.

"I definitely have a pulse?" I asked, looking at Kane.

"Yes."

I put my fingers to my throat. Yeah, still ticking away.

That thing, the Glass Monster, it had cleaned the vampire blood, sucked it out of me. I'd felt it. But why? That didn't make any sense.

I'd thought I might've imagined it, but I guess I hadn't. If I had, I would've been dead right now, or undead. Definitely in some sort of dead category.

None of this made sense. "Does this vampire thing ever not take?" I looked around the room, hoping for answers.

Kane was the only one who responded. "No."

"You said Asher did something to me that kept the crawlers away, right?"

He crossed his arms. "Yes."

"Maybe whatever he did could protect me from all sorts of stuff?"

"Nothing else happened?" Kane tilted his head down, glaring at me from beneath dark brows, his eyes as intense as ever. He knew I was holding back. It was in every line of his posture. But the tilt of his head was a bit softer, as if he were going to give me a little time to spill. I didn't know how long, but a little. Or maybe because he'd been there the whole time, it was hard to accuse me of pulling a dirty trick?

Not to mention that it could've been some sort of near-death vision. Maybe it hadn't even happened and the theory I'd just fed him about Asher was the actual truth.

The Glass Monster, for lack of a better name, had saved me. If it wanted me to keep quiet, I would. Especially since Kane had been sitting at the bar with Dana, my nemesis, while I was being attacked.

"You saw everything I saw," I said, playing on my hunch. "You were there with me—*after* the attack, anyways." I did some of my own glaring. Who was he to even question me?

"So that's the way you want to play this?" he asked, getting his back up.

He could stare me down all damn day. All I had to do was think of him standing at that bar and I was ready for war. "Exactly that way."

I sat up a little straighter, putting some steel in my spine. That's when I noticed my bloodstained shirt looked like a Rorschach test and my hands were stiff with dried blood. And there was a lot of blood. It appeared as if I'd emptied every drop I had and then cycled through some more. How *was* I alive?

I stumbled out of bed and I walked a few paces to the last open spot in the bedroom.

That vampire in the alley almost killed me. Considering how much killing I'd supposedly done, I guess indignation was a bit much, but that didn't stop me from feeling it.

"Did anyone identify the vampire who attacked me?" Because the first thing I was going to do after I got my head back on straight was track down Ugly Boots.

"I've already taken care of him." I didn't miss the look Kane then gave Butch, or the quick nod he got in return.

I remembered my attacker's feet leaving the ground in a whoosh. Those had been pretty loud thumps afterward. I guess someone had made sure to hose out the fleshy bits already.

Kane had protected me. He'd killed him. A vampire. In seconds. I wasn't sure if I should thank him and give him a big hug or take off running, because what the hell kind of monster was he? Maybe I should be happy he was moving on to Dana.

"Do we know why?" I asked. "He didn't say much to me." If we didn't, it was going to be hard to question him now that he'd been washed into the gutters. I stared down at my hands, walking into the attached bathroom before anyone answered.

I turned the faucet on, letting it get as hot as it could as I ran my hands beneath it. Red and then pink filled the basin.

Kane came and leaned in the doorway. "Frederickson said your attacker was the maker of the vampire you killed in the mall."

"And Frederickson just happened to appear? Seems a bit odd." I added globs of liquid soap to my hands.

"No doubt he took advantage of the situation. And if he had succeeded in converting you, I think there might've been many reasons he would've given to delay releasing you from his maker's bond." He shrugged. "But I don't think he's behind anything else. We have bigger issues than him. If he becomes too much of a problem…"

If Frederickson got in the way, he'd be dead. Kane ended the sentence with another shrug, as if that was all it merited. It wasn't even a strong shrug but a halfhearted attempt.

How was it that I, the one who was capable of releasing what amounted to demon creatures onto this earth, was the only one Kane wasn't ready to kill? There had to be something else to it that I didn't know. And it couldn't be lovesickness, or why would he be at the bar cozying up to Dana?

"Are you okay?"

I glanced up to see him staring at where my hands were turning raw under the heat and scrubbing.

"I'm fine. I'm sure you've got things to get back to. I know I interrupted your meeting with Dana earlier." I turned off the water and dried my hands, hoping he'd say something about what he was doing with her. Not that it was my business.

He straightened. "Get some sleep."

Chapter Twenty-Five

I'D LAIN LOW FOR THE ENTIRE DAY, NOT WANTING TO DEAL with the crowd in the Underground, where they could all confirm I was still human.

Being a Shadow Walker was bad in this crowd. Being a Shadow Walker who let in monsters was really bad. But being a Shadow Walker who let in monsters and was such a freak that she was immune to vampire blood? Off the charts.

Chairs screeched as people hurried to move out of my way when I walked into the Underground. It seemed that people were maintaining a twenty-foot distance at all times, fearing I'd go nuclear at any moment.

I didn't look up at Kane's office. Or I didn't look up for long. The booth we always sat at was empty, but I made my way to the bar, where Flip was already seated.

"How are you holding up?" she asked, looking over the new flesh lining my neck.

"No scar." I'd worn a V-neck on purpose. Let everyone get their look and be done with it.

I glanced up toward the light shining through Kane's office and then looked away quickly.

"He's alone up there," Flip said. "I'm keeping tabs."

"Thanks, but it doesn't matter."

She snorted. I ignored her.

I was still there, leaning against the bar next to Flip, when the procession started. It began with the door opening and a vampire walking in, holding four dozen red roses. He paused as Jerry pointed at the bar. The vampire started right toward us.

"Flip, are you dating someone you haven't told me about?" I asked.

She turned toward the vampire. "No. My relationships only span from dusk to dawn, and those are the good ones. You don't want to know about the bad ones."

Before the first vampire got a few steps in the door, another one followed with another bouquet. Then another. All heading our way.

I looked at Flip, trying to see what she was making of this. Her face smoothed out and then expanded as her jaw dropped and her mouth turned into a large O, like Flip had just gone through her own Big Bang.

The vampire, a young—or at least appearing that way —man, stopped in front of us. "Ollie?"

"Yes?" I asked, expecting him to ask me for more directions to get to his true target.

He didn't ask for anything. He held out the bouquet. I took it even as the next vampire was putting his bouquet on the bar beside me. I put the bouquet I was holding down and took out the card as everybody in the Underground watched.

OLLIE,

THERE'S many roses in the world but there's only one Ollie. I'm sorry for the pain caused by one of my kind. Please don't let that taint your opinion of me. Looking forward to our next encounter.

VINCENT

"VINCENT? THE HOT VAMP?" Flip nearly yelled.

I turned to give her a glare where she stood, hovering over my shoulder like a parrot. "I didn't want everyone to know," I said.

"Like you were going to hide this," she said as the procession continued. It didn't stop until there were ten bouquets lined up on the bar.

The door of Kane's office opened and he stepped out, looking down from above like a lion smelling an intruder in his territory. His expression was blank as he surveyed the garden lined up on the bar.

"Did you sleep with him?" Flip had the decency to whisper this time.

"No," I responded immediately, making sure to add a little indignation into the word. Hopefully a firm answer would slam the door on the subject.

"Some touchy-feely? Get friendly with his hang-low? Maybe some kissy-kissy down there?"

I should've known better. "*No.*"

Flip walked around me, staring at the roses and shaking her head. "You're telling me he sent all these bouquets and you did nothing? Because how the hell does that work? I can't even get flowers when I put out. Seriously, the things I've done, and I've never, ever—"

"Please shut up. People are listening."

She glanced around and then snapped, "Mind your own business!" She walked back and stopped close to me. "You sure you did nothing?"

"Nothing." I didn't know if this was a romantic gesture or a manipulation to make it look like something was going on. But why would he do that?

I felt Kane's eyes burning into me, and wondered if it was to drive a wedge in my situation here. If Frederickson couldn't recruit me one way, maybe he was trying to have his man recruit me through other means.

If they were planning on using me, then I had no qualms about using them right back for information. Maybe they knew something about what had happened to me? If the potions weren't working, and they didn't seem to be, I'd have to try different avenues.

I turned, feeling eyes burning into me. Kane stared straight at me. He turned his head, looked in the direction of his office, and then stared at me again for another few seconds, making sure the message was clear. If there was any doubt, he left the door wide open after he walked back into his office.

"Uh oh," Flip said.

"Can you get rid of these?" I asked.

She nodded, and I walked across the floor toward the

stairs. The worst part of it was that I wanted to go into Kane's office. I didn't care why he was calling me, either. I didn't even like the guy, but I had this urge to be near him. I wondered if this was how it had been before I'd lost my memory.

Kane was seated when I walked in. He looked up, leaning to the side a bit. His body relaxed but his eyes were hard. "Nice flowers."

I ignored the comment.

I'd watched him flirt with Dana. He didn't deserve an explanation. We weren't together. Every time he looked at me as if I'd betrayed him, I remembered he'd made that choice.

"Sit. We need to talk."

So, he was going to take the first shot. I shut the door, making my way toward his desk, but passed the chair and moved to the couch. I might as well be comfortable. I had a feeling this was going to be a long one.

The couch was worn leather that hugged you like a glove when you sat down. Definitely the right choice.

I kicked my feet up on the table in front of me. "What's up?"

He was leaning back in his chair, watching me while trying to pretend he wasn't. But he *definitely* was. Was it my feet on the table? Whatever was bothering him, it didn't look like he was going to share. Maybe he didn't like people on his couch? Well, if he was going to make me sit here with him, complaining or accusing, that was too damn bad for him.

"What was it you wanted?" I asked.

"You look as if you're getting pretty comfortable with Vincent. And considering the attack yesterday, there's something you should know about your past with the vampires."

I closed my eyes as I put a hand over my forehead. This wasn't going to be good.

"Which is?" I might've groaned.

"You've killed more than one."

I definitely groaned as I slid a few inches lower into the couch. How had I managed to do so many screwed-up, crazy things in such a short time? Had it even been me? Maybe I had a crazy doppelganger running around Boston.

I spun and kicked up my feet onto the arm of the couch, feeling the need to be fully reclined before I heard anymore.

"Who and how did I do it?" That put my death toll at three, if I didn't include the deaths from the explosions, of which I feared I had culpability somehow. How did I forget killing them all? Had I been a complete wrecking ball? What kind of animal had I turned into?

"It was a vampire named Alexandria."

I thought back to Butch's cryptic action and words when Frederickson had walked into the meeting with his new second in command.

"She was Frederickson's second in command," he said, his voice closer as he confirmed my fears.

Kane was leaning on the partial wall that helped form the alcove the couch sat in. I hadn't realized he'd moved while I'd been in the midst of tallying how much blood I'd spilled.

"It was provoked. She was trying to kill you. You killed her first." Another shrug. How could he brush it off so easily?

Right now, I wished I could. Although there was probably a reason he did. Who knew what his count was up to?

Still, it was a kindness he was doing me, and I nodded a silent thanks. At least I'd had good reasons all those times. I was a well-intentioned killer. That sounded *much* better on a résumé.

"How did I do it?" I asked. "Second in command. She had to have been strong, right? Are you sure I killed her? I can't see how that's possible." I sat up. That didn't help, so I stood, hoping to walk off some of the unease over my death count going up again.

"You turned your blood into poison as she drank from you. Butch and Leon helped you clean up afterward." Kane walked back to his desk calmly, flipping through a couple of pieces of paper that were lying on it.

"Why didn't you tell me this before?" I asked as I took a step toward him.

He stopped looking at his mail and turned to lean on his desk, crossing his arms. "Because at the time you didn't seem to be handling all the details that well, and this was something you were better off not knowing. You'd act more natural with them."

"I see." So that was it. He'd decide what I needed to know and when? No. Not a chance. "My memory might never come back. You can't manage me anymore. I need to know the things I've done. No more half-truths. Is there anything else?"

I glared at him as I waited. That was what he'd been doing all along—managing me. Deciding what I should know and doling it out here and there.

"That was it."

I nodded, not sure I believed anything anymore. I was

losing faith that there was anything honest between us at all. I walked to the door.

"Ollie, don't trust Vincent. He wants something."

I didn't bother answering. Kane was the last person to lecture me on who to trust.

Chapter Twenty-Six

THE PEOPLE HANGING AROUND THE BOTTOM OF THE STAIRS cleared before I was halfway down. It wasn't because they needed to go somewhere or do something. It was for the best, anyway. I wasn't looking for company.

I turned to head toward the elevators when Zee popped in front of me. "How come you look so healthy?"

"You mean because of the attack?" I asked, hitting the elevator button.

"I mean, why aren't you guzzling potions?" She stepped in front of the door when it slid open.

Because they aren't working. I wasn't ready to admit it out loud yet. Kane knew it too. There was a reason he wasn't mentioning it. "Taking a couple days until I'm sure there isn't any side effects from what happened." Hopefully I'd come up with a better plan in the meantime.

Zee looked like she was going to pop back out, but stalled, gazing around the hall, seeing the way people saw me and then turned. "Why don't you come downstairs and hang out?"

"I was going to go lie down for a while."

"No, you're coming with me." Zee took hold of my arm, and I knew how this went. I didn't bother fighting. There would be no escape.

She swung open the basement door.

"I thought it wasn't good to go down there at night?" I asked.

"It's better than the sad-sack stuff going on up there." She pointed one dragon-length nail upward. She did have a point.

The basement was in full swing. Drinks were flowing, and "Havana" was blaring as people danced in the center of the room. Card games were going on off to the side— gargoyles puffed away on Winston-sized cigars and sipped amber liquid from snifters. It reminded me of the Underground, before it had turned into a twenty-four-hour news cycle. But the gargoyles didn't seem to be worried. But then again, gargoyles were a lot harder to kill and had been around for a very long time. Seemed it took a lot more than a new breed of monster in the world to rock them.

"What's your game? Stud, blackjack, Texas? There's craps over there." Zee pointed to different areas around the room as I took in the setup.

"Zee, I don't have money to gamble."

"What about the money we made before you…"

I was barely listening to her, most of my attention on the door behind the craps table. It was too sturdy looking to lead to another room or closet. "Zee, where does that door go?" I asked, pointing to it.

"That? Nowhere important." She tugged me toward the other part of the room.

"Zee, that door gets me outside with only gargoyles

knowing, doesn't it?" And I'd learned one thing: for the most part, gargoyles didn't care what you did, as long as it didn't bother them.

"I don't want to talk about the door. Let's get a drink?" She started pulling me again, but I dug in and was ready to sit my ass on the floor if needed.

Finally, she turned, and the look on her face made it clear she knew I was leaving out that door, either with her help or without.

I looked at her stone face, a face of someone I truly believed was a friend, and laid out the ugly truth. "Zee, the potions aren't working."

She didn't look surprised, but she waved a fist in the air as if she wished it weren't so.

She was still shaking her head as I continued. "I was nearly killed in the alley. I need to get answers, and I think I've got a better shot of trying to get them alone." I watched as the information slowly sank in and could see the resolve fading. Her head was turned partially away, but her eyes were on me.

"Why alone?" she asked, probably not understanding why I wouldn't want Kane at my back for protection.

"Because people don't talk in front of Kane, especially not the ones I need to talk to." *Definitely* not the ones I wanted to seek out now.

She glanced around the room, checking to see if anyone was paying attention to us before she asked, "Who do you need to talk to?"

"Harg." I didn't bother adding that he was just a means to get to the Glass Monster. It *had* helped me. Maybe it would help me again. But it didn't want contact with anyone else. That was brutally clear. But first I needed Harg, since he was my only connection.

If I got out of here, I'd call over a crawler and see if Harg would talk to me. Kane probably knew exactly where Harg was. After all, he'd known he was in the cemetery, among the mausoleums.

I gripped Zee's arm firmly, not that she'd notice. "You know where Harg is, don't you?"

She froze. When a gargoyle froze, it was hard to tell if they'd spontaneously died. Then her forehead dusted.

"Tell me."

"I'm not supposed to—"

"Do you want to get back in business or not?"

I stepped back as a large plume of dust hit the air.

"Fine." She headed toward to the exit, and I followed after her. She opened the large door, which looked as if it weighed two hundred pounds, and waved me outside.

I thought it was going to let me out into one of the alleys, but it let me out nearly a block from where I knew the Underground to be. So wait, maybe Kane's basement was under the Underground—but where the hell had I just been?

"Do we have a location?" she asked the air. "Okay, that'll have to do." She dug a phone out of the back of her Daisy Dukes and pulled up Google Maps. "You sure about this?"

"No, but that doesn't matter."

She nodded. "Do you want me to go with you?"

What I would've given to have backup, but not for this trip. "I've got to do this alone."

She shook her head, giving me a slew of directions as she pointed to the map on the phone. Go two miles this way and then a mile that way. Luckily, I was a pretty fast walker.

I dug in my back pocket and handed her my cell. "Can you put this in my room?" I knew it was the first thing Kane would check if he knew I was out and about.

"Sure," she said as she dusted up some more, knowing she was getting deeper and deeper into the conspiracy as she agreed.

"If I get my magic back, I swear, I'll work my ass off at whatever it was we were doing."

She pocketed both phones, not looking convinced I'd be able to uphold my promise. I turned to leave, wanting to get going as soon as possible.

I turned back to her before she'd made it inside. "Hey, Zee, you mentioned money I made before I disappeared?"

She turned, hand on the door. "Yeah?"

"So we'd made decent money?"

"Don't you look at your bank account? Between what we made and the witches paying restitution, you've got to have at least a couple hundred grand." She shook her head as if I were a dippy human and walked inside.

That fucking bastard. There was no way Kane hadn't known. He knew I didn't need his place and he'd let me think I had nothing, not a dime, so he could yet again control me.

Chapter Twenty-Seven

I PROBABLY COULD'VE BORROWED A CAR FROM ZEE, BUT I hadn't wanted to. I didn't want to drive through the streets. I wanted to feel what was going on around me. Get a sense of the city that you couldn't get breezing past at forty miles per hour.

I didn't see the gangs that hung out around the Underground as I walked. As I got farther away, I didn't see many people at all, even though there hadn't been a fire in a while. Harg was holding up to his bargain right now. No one was blowing anything up. But there were still crawler sightings near daily.

Still, it was good to walk the streets again. This was my city, it always had been, and I wasn't rolling over and giving it up easy.

I neared the area that Zee had said Harg would be, expecting him to have possibly moved. But he was there. I could feel the magic brewing in the air before I saw him. I turned the corner and Harg was in the distance, standing on the opposite corner, as if he were waiting for me.

He walked down the center of the road toward me. I took a step toward him, then another. I wasn't sure what would happen once we met. I had no back up this time. It was just a Shadow Walker against a crawler.

The closer we got, the more I thought of running. If I ran, I'd look scared. And maybe I was, but that didn't mean I had the luxury of showing it. I needed answers before the next attack came. Another few moments and we were standing a few feet apart.

"Nice night." I shoved my hands in my pockets, as if this were normal, me and a crawler chatting it up on an evening stroll.

He nodded. He didn't move to leave, but he didn't move closer. He was giving me my space on purpose, respecting my boundaries.

I looked up and around, then at him again, a little too low this time. If he was going to walk around this world, putting on some pants would go a long way. It wouldn't fix the horns, red eyes, and teeth that looked like they'd shred you in one bite, but it was a start.

"You might think about investing in some pants."

"Pants?" He said the word as if it hadn't made it into his vocabulary yet.

Why was I the one who was going to have to explain the birds and the bees to a monster? I didn't even have children yet. I looked over to the side—since he was so tall, it was an easier view. "Your stuff. You're going to scare people with it."

"Stuff?"

I pointed at his genitalia. "That. That is one scary-looking penis."

His head dropped, as if he were surprised.

"Yes. Scary. You need to get pants." I wondered if I'd be so brazen if he didn't need me alive to get the rest of his fellow crawlers through. Yeah, I probably would. You couldn't walk around slinging a two-foot dick and expect to blend. Even if he didn't have all those other monster things going on for him, people would still be running as long as that was hanging loose and swaying all over the place.

He continued to stare down until the awkward level hit a new low.

I waved a hand in the air. "Forget it. That's not why I'm here. What do you know about what happened to me? My memory and being attacked?"

He shook his head. I wasn't sure if that meant he wouldn't tell me or didn't know. Either way, I wasn't getting an answer.

"Was I there when you crossed?" I asked.

He stood stoically, and I wanted to leap up and choke the words from him. This was starting to look like it had been a waste of time, but I hadn't hit him with the big one yet.

"What about the creature that saved me? Who is it and why did it help me? Don't tell me you don't know."

"Can't."

He might've regretted not being able to help, but that didn't appease me. Not even a little. I was tired of not knowing anything, including what I'd done last month. I was sick of having no control.

"But you want my help? You better reevaluate, because unless I get answers, I'm not crossing one more crawler, and I don't care what you blow up or what deals you strike." I was completely full of it, but I was also full of rage. I'd lost my past, my throat had been nearly ripped out, and I'd almost been turned into a vampire. Nothing was off-limits to me right now.

His lips rose slightly, and I didn't know if he was going to growl or sink his teeth into me, and I didn't care. I'd turned my blood into poison before, and I'd figure it out again somehow.

After some huffing breaths, his lips relaxed. "I'll ask."

"You'll speak to the other one? He's in charge?" I asked, wanting clarification of the pecking order. I'd suspected as much, but that meant nothing.

Harg nodded then looked as if he had something else to say. He reached out a clawed hand, but stopped short of touching me when I jerked back.

"Have to work together," he said, staring at me as if he'd graced me with the greatest wisdom.

They covered that bullshit back in little league, and they didn't have anything like him on the team.

"Yeah, we'll see," I said.

He dropped his head, before turning around and walking away. Well, at least I'd made it through my first one-on-one with Harg.

I was still watching the corner Harg had disappeared from, enjoying the solitude, when the crawlers scattered. I wasn't sure if Zee had gotten nervous and given me up or if it was another gargoyle. It didn't matter. I'd done what I'd needed for now.

I waited, knowing he was walking toward me. He stopped beside me.

"What are you doing? These creatures are all over the place and you're their ticket in. Do you realize how this looks, hanging around out here having private meetings?"

I knew exactly how it looked. Right now, I really hoped Kane was as true to his promises as he'd said.

I looked him dead in the eye. "You can't have it both ways. You want me to trust you, tell you everything, so you can micromanage my life, while you tell me nothing, including how I didn't even need your help. I've got a bank account full of cash that you didn't mention but I'm sure you knew about." Anger welled up like venom pumping through my veins. Of all the manipulative things he'd done, him and Dana at the bar was the thing I couldn't drive from my mind.

"I'm not your banker."

"No, and you're not my keeper, either." I walked around him.

He grabbed my wrist. "What were you speaking to him about?"

"*I* was trying to get the truth," I shot back, not bending a hair.

"If I hadn't taken control, you'd be dead." He spoke as if I were too steeped in naiveté to possibly understand.

"And what about the secrets? How do they keep me alive?" I yanked my arm free and walked away, too fired up to hear anything else.

I'd walked ten feet or so when I heard him say, "Abandinus."

I waited for some spell to freeze me in my spot. Nothing happened, and I kept walking.

Chapter Twenty-Eight

I WALKED INTO THE UNDERGROUND, HAIR WILD FROM THE wind on the walk back. The place cleared around me as if I were as wild and dangerous as I looked.

The light in Kane's office was off. I'd sensed him following me, not that I'd seen him. The booth was empty, Butch and Leon out and about somewhere, probably handling Kane's secrets. Flip wasn't around either, and I barely recognized the guy at the door.

I turned toward the bar, feeling better about throwing back a stiff one when I wasn't sitting alone in my rooms. That was when I found one friendly face.

Vincent sat there, looking as if he'd been waiting for me. He wore a warm smile, which should've been an oxymoron for a vampire but wasn't for him. I walked over and didn't care that I'd killed their second in command, or about the rest of Kane's warnings. Vincent might have answers, and even if he didn't, he wasn't calling me a liar every other day.

Vincent met me before I'd made my way over to him,

his hand resting on my lower back as if it belonged there. "I'm glad to see you looking so well."

"Thank you for the flowers." I settled onto a seat beside him, where a bottle of red wine waited with two glasses. "Did you have company?" I asked.

"Just hoping I would," he said, handing me the second glass. "I tried to reach out to you but was having trouble getting my call to go through."

I took a sip before calmly saying, "I don't get very good reception in my apartment." Was that bastard blocking numbers on my phone? Was he completely out of control?

Vincent nodded, pretending he believed me. He topped off my glass. "The compromise with the crawlers seems to be working. No new explosions so congratulations."

"Thank you." Bringing monsters over wasn't quite what I'd ever expected to be congratulated on, but I took another sip of wine. It ended up being a gulp.

His eyes shifted over my right shoulder and then returned to me, his shoulders tensing.

If that hadn't told me Kane had just walked in, the crawlers that lurked in the corners, still half in this world and half out, scattered.

I wasn't going to look. It didn't matter if he was back and watching me right now with Vincent.

I looked. Oh yeah, my self-control was *rocking*.

I wasn't the only one who couldn't seem to ignore Kane. Dana, whom I hadn't noticed when I walked in, beelined it over to him so fast that I was surprised her heels weren't smoking.

Kane smiled in greeting.

That was when I stopped looking.

Kane was right about one thing: Vincent wanted something but it wasn't my head on a stick. It was a lot more basic than that. I drained my glass and leaned in closer to him. It was a conscious choice with Vincent, instead of the visceral reaction I had to Kane. But Vincent was a salve to my ego, which was hanging in shreds, along with other more important parts.

Vincent refilled my glass and then moved closer. "Do you want to go somewhere else?"

Dana's laugh rang across the Underground. I slid off my stool, resting my forearm on Vincent's shoulder, then wobbled closer. The wine was surprisingly strong.

His hand moved to my waist, steadying me. His head dipped closer, his lips by my ear. "Are you all right? Maybe I should help you to your apartment?"

I wanted to want him. I really did. But I didn't.

I meant to move back, put the brakes on what I'd begun, but landed a hand on his chest instead. Damn wine.

He wrapped his arm around my waist and escorted me toward the hall.

"Vincent, I'm not ready to go up yet." *And definitely not with you.* I'd need another bottle of wine, and maybe not even then. As much as I hated it, there was only one man I wanted in my bed, and he wasn't an option at the moment.

"Ollie, I'm only going to get you settled. You drank too much."

I nodded. Maybe that wasn't such a bad idea.

As drunk as I was, I still knew the moment Kane joined us in the hallway. It was as if I could feel each step getting closer until he was there, his arm wrapping around my waist and shifting me from Vincent to him.

"What are you doing?" Vincent asked, as if shocked Kane would get involved. "I was going to—"

"Won't be necessary. I've got her," Kane said as he swept me up in his arms. We both dipped slightly as he hit the elevator button.

Vincent stared at both of us, leery of turning this into a fight. "Ollie, are you—"

"Go before you piss me off and I have to put her down." Kane's muscles tensed.

I'd seen Kane shrug off murder one too many times to not get a little worried.

"I'll see you tomorrow, Vincent. I'm very tired," I said, waving as Kane carried me into the elevator. The doors couldn't close quick enough. "He was only trying to help me upstairs."

"Sure he was," Kane said. "How much did you drink? You cannot get this sloppy around one of them. You might slip up, and I don't have time to kill people this week."

"We weren't even talking about business."

"Well, that's fucking wonderful," he said.

"Where's Dana?"

"I have no idea."

Because he'd abandoned her to protect me. I should still be mad, but it was hard to stay that way when he kept watching out for me.

I didn't say anything else. I didn't want to argue. All I wanted to do was snuggle against Kane while I had a plausible excuse to do so.

He opened the apartment door. "For future reference, you aren't fucking somebody in my building."

"Why?"

"Because it's my building and I say so. Apparently that's the upper limit of my patience."

"So you can fuck anyone you want here but I can't?"

"Nobody is fucking anybody."

Even in my fuzzy brain, it slammed home. Maybe he hadn't slept with Dana?

"What if I left?" I asked.

"You won't. Whether or not you're ready to admit it, you like being around me."

I was about to tell him he was crazy, but wasn't sure if I could pull off the denial. Better to pretend I hadn't heard anything. I couldn't have spoken anyway. I was too shocked over where the conversation had turned.

He dropped the arm from under my knees, and my body was sliding down his, oh so slowly, as if he was as hungry as I was for the contact. I swayed into him, my hands grazing his chest and then his shoulders, and nothing about this was an act. If anything, I was holding back, but barely, my tongue darting out to wet my lips as I tilted my head back to look at him.

"How much did you drink?" he asked, his voice huskier than it had been.

"I'm not drunk."

He poked my shoulder. I toppled back onto the bed.

I thought I heard him curse as I bounced.

"Yeah, you're sober," he said.

"That wasn't fair. You've got freakishly strong fingers," I said as I lay flat on the bed, not attempting to move. Movement seemed way too complicated at the moment.

He pulled off one of my shoes and then the other,

before lifting the side of the comforter and folding it over and tucking it around me.

"Kane?"

"Yes?" He was still close beside me.

"Why do you protect me the way you do? It's not like you love me or something."

He brushed a strand of hair off my face. "Go to sleep, Ollie."

Chapter Twenty-Nine

MOVEMENT ON THE BED TOLD ME THAT SOMEONE WAS IN the room with me. That person didn't smell like Kane, so it might be clear to open my eyes. Still, it was a gamble. I'd practically dry-humped him before he left me last night. Actually, maybe I had and forgotten. Things were a bit hazy.

"Ollie? You alive?"

I should've known it was Zee from the cotton-candy perfume, but my brain was currently like an engine trying to fire up on watery gas. Eyes open, I proceeded to turn over with supreme caution.

Zee held out a cup of coffee to me.

"Thanks." I sipped slowly before putting the cup on the nightstand. "I feel like hell. I didn't think I drank that much."

I thought back to last night. How many glasses of wine did I have? I'd thought maybe three. Yes, wine always hit me pretty hard, but it shouldn't have done that much damage. I'd barely been able to stand.

I took a couple more sips of coffee, trying to clear my head. "I think there was something in my wine."

That was all Zee needed to be off and running with the topic. "You think Vincent drugged you? Maybe he wants to sleep with you. You should watch out for him. He's cute, but I think he might be bad news."

I sipped more coffee, staring at Zee over the rim. "No, I don't think Vincent would've done that. And I know how most people feel about vampires, but he's a nice guy. And even if he weren't, would he do it in the middle of the Underground with so many people around? That doesn't make any sense." I got out of bed, realizing I was still in my clothes from last night.

"Maybe he wasn't sure how much to give you?" Zee asked, watching me.

I didn't like the crinkle that had formed on her forehead as she said it. Then I thought about the way she'd topped off my coffee without appearing. "Zee, did you slip me something?"

"What? Me?" The dust kicking off her forehead plumed.

"Zee!"

"I did it for your own good." She jumped off the bed and was about to poof away.

I latched on to her arm before she had the chance, gripping her stone wrist for dear life. "Drugging is not the way to have good friendships. Why would you do that to me?"

"I had my reasons." She tried to pick off my fingers, but there was no getting loose. As soon as she pulled one hand off, I gripped with the other.

"So Kane would step in and I'd end up sleeping with him?" I asked.

She finally stopped pulling at my hands. "Did you?" she asked, all the heat of her fake anger turning into hopefulness.

"No." I let go of her arm, sensing her urge to run was over.

"Shit."

She stomped off into the other room, and I followed her. "What if Kane hadn't seen me?"

"As if! That man's eyes barely leave you. Look, you don't remember what you and Kane were like, but I do. I'm not letting you lose that." She sat down on the couch, arms crossed, staring at nothing.

I stood directly in front of her. "What we were. Not what we are."

She rolled her eyes at me. "That's fucking bullshit and we both know it. You might not remember, but your heart beats the bongo every time he's near."

I perched myself on the arm of the couch as she stared at me, daring me to deny it.

I finally held up my hands. "Okay, maybe there's some underlying feelings, but friends don't drug friends."

There was a long, painful pause as I stared her down.

"Sorry." She gave me a halfhearted shrug as she looked everywhere else.

"Really? That's all I get?"

"It's not like you're dead. I don't know why people get so sensitive about shit." She was shrugging and bobbing her head so much that she was leaving crumbs on the couch.

I planted my hands on my hips. "Don't do that again."

"Fine." She jumped to her feet and started tugging me along again. "Come on."

"Where?"

"To the basement. There's a new batch of purses coming through, my treat."

"That doesn't make up for drugging me," I said, although my feet were no longer dragging.

"It does a little," she said.

"Maybe a little."

KANE WAS WALKING through the hall when I was coming up from the gargoyles' basement.

"You seem to like it down there."

"What? I like them." I shrugged.

"That's all?"

"Yes, that's all. Why, do you think I'm trying to stage a coup and steal all the gargoyles?"

He raised his eyebrows. "No. Not even close to what I was thinking. You couldn't pull off a coup against me. The gargoyles love me."

Worst part of that was it was true. Hell, Zee had just drugged me to try and get me in bed with him.

The crowd scattered as I walked into the Underground. I'd gotten used to it, but for some reason, at that moment, with Kane watching, I hated it. I headed toward the bar off to the side of the room, where I tended to go when I was alone.

"Do they always do that?" Kane asked from behind me.

I'd thought he'd gone up to his office. I hadn't realized he'd been behind me watching the crowd part like the Red

Sea. Great. Just what I wanted to do today. Explain my daily interaction with the monster bunch.

"No," I said. Why was he not going up to his office? "I don't know what that was about."

"You sure?" he asked, stopping beside me.

"I know you feel like your intellect is untouchable, but I think I can answer this question sufficiently. It's not the norm."

I called for a gargoyle and asked for a tea, hoping Kane believed my lie and I could salvage some pride. He leaned against the bar, looking casual, but I'd caught on to when he was faking a while ago.

I stirred some honey into the tea as he stood silently beside me. "If you think I wouldn't—"

"Shh," he said. "I'm listening."

The only thing playing was the news on the big screen. "Are you deaf?" They had the sound blasting. How could he not hear that?

I would've continued, but he laid two fingers gently over my lips. It wasn't a harsh action, but gentle, especially as his fingers grazed my cheek next and he didn't even seem to be paying attention to what he was doing. When his hand kept moving to settle on my neck, as if it were meant to be there, I was having a hard time keeping my breathing in check so he didn't realize how his touch affected me. Luckily, he was too busy staring at the crowd to notice. But his thumb was nearly resting in the base of my throat, making my heart kick in like a jackrabbit's.

I wasn't a virgin. That I remembered clearly. I'd had a man's hands on my body, my breasts, my ass, all the necessary. But the warmth from where his hand lay, right above my fluttering pulse, felt more intimate than the one-night stands I'd had.

Then his hand dropped and he walked off without another word. As if he hadn't been touching me.

I ordered a shot as he walked toward his office with purpose. He didn't go all the way up the stairs, though. He stopped halfway and then just stared at the crowd. The volume on the television lowered without Kane asking, and everyone fell silent. He had that determined look I'd seen so often. This time it was being directed at specific spots in the crowd.

What the hell was up with him? I didn't have to wait long to find out.

Kane took one last sweeping glance as he straightened. "The next person who walks away from Ollie when she enters the room will find themselves being hosed out of the cracks in the alley."

There were a couple of gasps, but no one said anything.

"That's all." He turned and walked to his office.

I didn't know whether to be mortified that he thought I couldn't handle myself or blush because he'd threatened to kill anyone who snubbed me. It was the scariest and sweetest thing anyone had ever done for me.

It was like Kane's version of a dozen red roses.

Chapter Thirty

WITHOUT A KNOCK, KANE THREW OPEN THE DOOR AND stepped into the living room. His theory about not being able to have the same fight twice, when I didn't remember the first fight about knocking, was absolute bull. I was about to tell him so, until I saw the set of his shoulders and the line of his mouth.

I got off the couch and met him just inside the door. "What happened?"

"There's been another explosion, down by the harbor." Anger rolled off him.

Harg. He'd double-crossed us. While I was sitting here, trying to figure out my next step…

Shit, did Kane think I did it? "I was—"

"I know," he said, stopping me short when I would've laid out my morning minute by minute.

He believed me? Maybe he was starting to trust me a little. Although I didn't know if I trusted myself, except I remembered every second since I'd gotten up.

"I know where you've been all day. Come on, we've got to go."

Well, so much for trust. Whatever. I didn't trust him either these days. At least we were on equal footing. And I couldn't focus on Kane when I needed to kill Harg.

"You know where he is?" I grabbed my phone off the table, leaving everything else behind.

"No, and we don't have an ID yet," he said.

"So we don't know who did it? It might be one of the ones I let through for him?"

"Or it might've been a crawler who came through before. We don't know."

WE HAD to work our way around the explosion and the cordoned-off area. That was what the police, the fire departments, and the National Guard did now—rope off the area and let it burn. They said it was safer. It was true. Everyone knew they couldn't handle the monsters, including themselves. Still, they made it a tad inconvenient to get close. We found a gap where some of the soldiers were busy drinking coffee and keeping their distance.

The good thing about the cordoning off was that once we did get past it, it was clear for a good five blocks in any direction.

The blaze was easy to spot. It was a high rise on fire this time. It looked like the crawler had blown it up, starting with the upper levels.

"You feel anything?" Kane asked, as we stood across the street, but in the shadow of another building.

"Yes." As I watched the fire from this close, there was a buzz in the air that made my hair stand on end. It made me want to duck farther into the shadows. That was how I knew we had to get closer.

"I say we go in there." I pointed to the building next door. "The windows are pretty close. If he's still in there, we might be able to get an ID."

He nodded, and we crossed the street as quickly as possible, trying to stay out of sight the best we could. The doors to the building were already open, either from the force of the blast from the building beside it or previous looting. When we walked into the storefront, the racks were on their sides and looked picked over. Kane tugged me behind him toward the employees' section, and then the back entrance.

We took the emergency stairs in the hallway up to the fourth-floor door, which was locked. He gave it a kick, and it swung open to a small office that had a plaque with the name Hayes Accounting hanging on the wall.

We were steps from the window when Kane froze and so did I. The buzz I'd felt before was suddenly amping up until it was almost hard to pull in a deep breath from the intensity. Kane ran at me as what was about to happen was still registering. The place was about to blow, with us in it.

He grabbed me around the waist, and then I was being thrown against a cinder block wall and pressed into the corner of the room. His body covered mine, as he reached over and pulled a filing cabinet down on top of him.

I tried to shove him out of the way, but he didn't budge. "We've got to run," I said. "We'll burn to death."

"Take a deep breath—"

The loud explosion wiped out the rest of his sentence. I

sucked in air and held it, knowing I wouldn't have another chance.

The sweep of heat rushed over us, sucking up all the air along with it. I kept my eyes squeezed tightly shut as I waited for the burning to start. Worse, I waited for Kane's hands to fall slack where they wrapped around me, the feel of his weight on top of me as his body went limp. I should've forced him to run somehow. Maybe we would've made it.

The initial blast blew over us, leaving heat in its wake. I was alive but Kane was still. He'd saved me and now he was dead. I felt myself start to shudder as sobs ripped through me, even as the smoke choked me. The worst of the blast was over and I was terrified to open my eyes, though I knew I had to get out of there before smoke inhalation did what the blast hadn't.

I felt Kane's weight pull from me, but I was still afraid to open my eyes. I didn't want to see the last bit of life fading from him. Not him. He was the most alive person I'd even met.

The filing cabinet was shoved away.

"Ollie?" he called, and his hands had moved to my shoulders and were tugging at me now.

How was he still alive? I opened my eyes, scanning his face. He pulled me to my feet as his clothes were dropping off him, the back of his pants and shirt fluttering to the ground in charred ashes. I didn't want to see his back, but he grabbed my hand and was pulling me after him through a maze of fire, giving me no choice.

His flesh was marred with ash, but beautiful unharmed skin showed beneath, where the soot had rubbed off.

He was moving too quickly for someone injured. We

exited the building, the buzz of magic now gone, and we were none the wiser—except that one of the crawlers on the loose wanted one of us dead. If it was Kane they wanted, they were going to have a hell of a time killing him, from what I'd just seen.

We didn't stop until we were back at his car and he was popping open the trunk. He handed me a water bottle before he pulled out pants.

"How are you alive?" I asked, still staring at him as if he were a ghost.

"Their fire doesn't harm me," he said as he stared at me, his hands dropping to his sides. He looked as if he expected me to run screaming.

That was probably what I should've done, too. Run like hell. He wasn't human. No one could've withstood that and been able to shelter me if they were. But I didn't want to run anywhere. I wanted to hold on to him for dear life.

"Are you afraid?" he asked, and I wasn't sure if he meant from what we'd escaped, or him.

"No." Maybe I should've been scared of both, but I wasn't. Overwhelming relief left no room for any other emotion.

Unlike myself, he was radiating anger. It pulsed from every tense muscle on display, but something in his eyes softened. He didn't want me to fear him, and that casually asked question had held untold weight.

"Why were you crying back there?" he asked, his thumb brushing over my still-moist cheeks.

"It was…a lot." I couldn't stop staring at him. "What the hell are… Forget it. I don't care." And I didn't. All I cared about was that he was alive, standing in front of me. It was as if that blast had burned away all but what mattered. As I stood covered in soot and ashes from the fire of a monster, I somehow felt cleansed of all but what mattered.

BUTCH, Leon, and Jerry were waiting for us outside the Underground when we pulled up. Jerry whistled as we got out of the car.

"What the hell?" Butch asked, while Jerry and Leon stepped closer, sizing up my charred clothing.

"Were you watching the news?" Kane asked.

"Of course we were," Leon said.

Butch sucked in a loud breath. "Don't tell me—you were in the second building?"

"We both were." Kane turned to me. "Talk to one of the crawlers. Tell them we want a meeting with Harg by tonight. I want the crawler who did this, or they haven't seen what a fire looks like. I will blast them out of the only home they have."

I didn't think much surprised me anymore, but my mouth gaped. He could torch the Shadowlands? Was that possible? "You can do that?"

"I don't bluff."

That seemed a hair extreme, even to me. "I know they blew up another building—"

"They didn't just blow up another building. They blew up a building with you in it."

He wasn't kidding, and I was more unstable than the

night Zee had drugged me. I didn't even need a push. I was ready to topple over with a light breeze.

Kane loved me. I didn't know why or for how long, but he did. It was the only thing that made sense.

I glanced at the guys, expecting to see my shock mirrored there, but no one else appeared surprised. Did they not notice, or had they known?

Kane pointed down the street. "Tell that little ugly one over there. He probably knows right where Harg is," Kane said. "I'd tell him myself, but I can't get close enough to even talk to the things."

"Uh huh," I muttered, still stunned, even as everyone else acted like it was business as usual.

"They're out here too?" Butch asked. Kane must've nodded, because there was a lot of cursing behind me as I walked over to the little one Kane had suggested and passed on the message.

I'D JUST STEPPED out of the bathroom, hair dripping and a towel wrapped around me, when I found Kane leaning against the bedroom door. I didn't pick a fight over knocking. I was afraid to do anything that might make him leave.

I simply asked, "What are you doing here?" and then prayed my body wasn't thrumming to life only for him to leave.

"I think you know." The heat in his eyes left no question why.

I wanted this, and yet the problems hadn't disappeared just because I craved him more every day.

"You think I'm a monster," I said, even as my heart pounded and I found myself stepping toward him.

Was I really ready to sleep with this man? A person who thought the very worst of me? I should be kicking him out of my rooms, or at least asking him to leave nicely, since he owned the building. I didn't. I stood there, in nothing but a towel, hoping he would stay.

He didn't look at me like I was a monster. He looked at me as if I were a goddess.

"Then you're the most beautiful monster I've ever seen," he said, stepping closer, his finger trailing along my exposed flesh as he leaned forward and kissed the base of my throat.

"What if I do something else? Black out again and another explosion happens?" If I slept with him, and he looked at me the way he had in the past, I knew without a doubt I'd shatter.

"I don't care if you're an angel or a monster. I want you, and that's all that matters." His hand grazed my waist.

"And what happens when you don't anymore?" I dipped my head, staring at his shirt, where I laid my hand, feeling his heat beat beneath.

"That's the one thing I know will never happen. Wanting you has become as ingrained as breathing."

When I lifted my eyes to his, I could see it there, how much he really did want me. But that was now, cocooned in this room, in his building, without the world pressing in.

"And if wanting isn't enough?" I asked, hoping he'd tell me what I suspected.

"I think it is."

His hand went to the towel, and I let him tug it free

even without hearing the words. It swooshed to the ground, and I didn't try to stop it. My arms dropped as the towel did. At that moment, I knew I might've taken the first step on the road to hell. I might wake up tomorrow and realize I was wrong, that he didn't love me and he'd never want me again. I knew I'd risk all the torment that might lie ahead for this one moment.

His eyes soaked me in as water dripped from my hair, trailing rivulets down my breasts before dropping lower. I pulled his shirt open so I could feel his flesh, the smooth hardness underneath my hands.

He grasped my hips as he dropped his mouth to lick the moisture from my skin. His arm circled my back as his tongue teased one nipple before he took it into his mouth and sucked hard, my back bowing into him, my fingers curling into the thick, dark hair.

My breath hitched as his hand grazed my ribs and then moved up and forward until he was cupping my other breast.

The flat of his palm grazed over my nipple on its way up toward my neck until his fingers were threading through my hair, tugging my head backward as he moved in closer, his shirt grazing the flesh of my chest.

His eyes burned into mine before his head dipped closer, but instead of his lips closing over mine, they grazed my ear as he said, "I've been waiting to taste you for an eternity."

He walked me backward until I felt the dresser at my back, and he hoisted me upon it, his head dropping lower. Two fingers entered me, hooking forward and rubbing in such a glorious way, right before his tongue joined them. It trailed to my clit and then teased, licking gently at first before sucking hard. I called out, my shoulders and head banging against the wall as I came undone.

His grip tightened and his lips were finally on mine, his tongue delving between my lips like he owned my mouth. Right now, he did. He could have my mouth, my lips, every part of my body, as I feared he already had my heart.

I shoved his shirt the rest of the way off him. His eyes captured mine as he backed away and stripped out of his pants. When he stood before me in nothing but beautifully sculpted muscle, my body ached to be pressed against the length of such strength and become one with it.

His stepped back between my still-spread thighs and slipped an arm around my waist. I wrapped my legs around him as he lifted me then turned to carry me to the bed. I was falling backward as he followed me down. He grabbed my hips and lifted them.

Without warning, he was seated all the way in me, his entrance smooth, since I'd been ready from his first touch.

He didn't move for a minute, but I didn't know if it was to allow me to adjust to his girth or if he was as close to the brink as I was. I moved forward on the bed and he tugged my hips back, seating himself deeply within me again.

He pulled out so slowly that I was nearly undone. I wrapped my legs back around him, urging his pace, but he continued slowly, leaning over me, his forearms taking his weight as his chest grazed mine.

He dipped his head, his tongue delving into my mouth as he continued to drag out the pace.

"Kane," I said, groaning out of a combination of pleasure and frustration.

"I won't share," he said, pausing above me, his pace going from slow to nearly stopped, the head of his cock teasing my entrance.

"Ollie," he said, and I realized he was as serious as I'd ever seen him. He wanted an answer.

"Neither will I. Now give me what I need."

He had the nerve to smirk as he plunged back into me, sending my nerve endings into a frenzy. He followed it with an urgent pace that made me lose myself as I'd never done.

I was lifeless on the bed, feeling like my muscles had been given their pink slip. Kane turned on his side, tugging me into him.

"I wouldn't have pictured you as a cuddler." I regretted the words as soon as I'd said them. Would he pull away now?

His leg parted mine. "We aren't cuddling. We're breaking between rounds. Even boxers get a couple minutes."

From the feel of him, I didn't think it would even be that long. His mouth sent shivers down my spine as he nipped at the back of my neck.

"Kane, what do you want from me?" I asked, before I slipped back into caring about nothing but where his hands were touching me or how his body felt against mine.

"Everything." There was a gravity to the word that wiped out any frivolity I might've given his answer.

"I think you've already gotten that," I said, adding a soft laugh afterward, trying to convince myself it was just a joke.

"I've barely sipped from the chalice."

He cupped my breast, holding me against him. My body arched, like I was an addict searching for its drug, forgetting about tomorrow or consequences.

Chapter Thirty-One

WE PULLED INTO THE CEMETERY, BUTCH AND LEON IN THE back, with Flip sitting between them. I was buffered by Kane and Zee in the front. Kane hadn't wanted to bring Flip or Zee, but I'd insisted they be included. If he had his boys, why shouldn't I have my girls?

We got out of the truck, and Kane stopped me when I would've started walking.

"You ready?" he asked, his hand smoothing back my hair the only indication that things had changed between us. After we'd had sex, I'd fallen asleep for a few hours and woken to business as usual.

"I've got this."

When he smiled in response, the intimacy was there, too. Things had definitely changed if you knew where to spot the signs.

"Oh yeah, they slept together," I heard Leon whisper to Butch.

"They have no idea how loud they are," I said to Kane, before turning to walk farther into the cemetery.

Leon was falling in step on my other side, but Flip shoved him out of the way so that she could walk beside me. Kane was generously allowed to remain on my left.

Harg wasn't here yet, but I knew he'd gotten the message. If he didn't show, he'd be condemned as guilty by all. If he did, I didn't know where we'd go from here.

I stopped walking and crossed my arms, looking for any sign. "You think he's going to show?"

Kane stopped beside me. "Yes." There was no question in his tone.

"Well, when he eventually does get here, you give me the signal and I'll smoke his ass," Flip said, bouncing along beside me.

"You're going to kill him?" I asked, trying to sound confident for her, even though there was no known way to kill crawlers.

"Yes," she barked, like a five-foot ball of dynamite.

"I'll help her," Zee added from right behind us, her heavy steps a stark comparison.

Kane shot me a look as if to say, *Yes, this was a splendid idea you had.*

I didn't have a chance to shoot him back a response before the sound of tires on gravel had us all spinning around.

"Oh look, it's Frederickson and there's his puppy Vincent, coming to sniff after you like a dog in heat," Kane said, dryer than a hundred-year-old skeleton.

We all stopped, watching as the car continued to speed until it screeched to a halt.

"Harg isn't here yet. Should we tell them to get lost?" Butch asked.

Kane shrugged. "No. They won't make a difference

either way, but I want to know what roads they've got spies set up on for the future. These unscheduled meetings are becoming tedious."

As we watched Frederickson and Vincent get out of the car and approach, a four-seater pick-up truck pulled into the lot behind them. Collin was driving and had three men with him.

The cursing in my head was drowned out by groaning around me.

Frederickson was out of his door and then in front of us in a blur. "We're supposed to be called for matters like this." Collin was still getting out of his truck with his crew.

Well, at least the leprechauns weren't—

Another engine revved in the distance. The lights were visible next before it turned in the drive.

"Ah shit," Leon said, as Rudy, everyone's favorite leprechaun, pulled up with a few of his men along.

"Why wasn't I informed of a meeting?" Rudy asked, as he came closer. His perusal of me made it clear he thought I'd somehow maneuvered things.

"It was last minute," Kane answered, bringing the attention that had landed on me straight to him.

"I didn't hear my phone ring," Collin said, probably having heard everything with those damn dog ears of his.

"You would've been caught up to speed," Kane said.

"Except—"

Kane didn't give Rudy a chance to finish. "You're here now. Keep your distance or you'll get booted." Kane turned, giving them his back as he waved me along.

I walked with him, wondering how I'd made more enemies than Kane. Or had I?

"One of these days, things are going to be different,"

Collin said, reinforcing my fear that Kane had angered everyone.

"Let me know when that day comes," Kane replied. "Until then, shut up." After that, no one spoke.

We made our way deeper into the cemetery, keeping an eye out for trouble. Kane and I seemed to decide to stop at the same time, as if in tune with each other. Still no Harg, but an abundance of other crawlers, only half in this world.

I said, "Maybe I should call one of them over and see if…"

I wasn't going to have to call one at all. One was coming right to me, which was now an oddity, especially with Kane near.

It was about the size of a small deer, with none of the cutesy charm. It stopped directly in front of me, as if it knew why I was there. It turned and took several steps away, before turning back to me, waiting.

Kane stepped forward with me. The creature looked at him and shook his head.

"Harg wants to speak to me alone," I said. As if Harg had been waiting, he stepped into view fifty feet or so away. Beside him was a rippling glimmer in the air.

Kane walked forward anyway.

"I have to talk to him alone," I said, putting a hand on Kane's arm to stop him.

"He doesn't make the terms." Kane's eyes were set on Harg.

"*I* think I should hear him out." The Glass Monster, whatever it was, was here. Maybe it was here to give me answers, or maybe not, but it had saved me before. Why would it kill me now? Why would it even be here? It had never accompanied Harg before. What if it had my answers?

Kane's gaze shifted to me. "They tried to blow you up."

"And you said yourself, we don't know if it was him. Kane, I think I've got to do this." My hand still on his arm, I gripped him as if I might never touch him again before asking, "Are you going to trust me?"

"It's not about trusting you."

"But it is." If he couldn't let me make my own choices and trust that I had the best intentions for all of us, then whatever we were would never have a future.

I could see the battle he was having within himself, and I really needed trust to come out the winner. If he fought me on this, would I turn him away next time he showed up in my bedroom? No. Not the next time or the time after that, but I would eventually. Because if he couldn't give me trust, our relationship would be fitting of the paper doll tag I'd been given. Eventually we'd get torn and worn out until what we'd thought we were wouldn't be recognizable anymore.

He nodded, his movement strained, as if his body was rebelling over what he'd decided. It was as if he'd handed me the sun in the sky; that was how deep the feeling burned in me.

He turned around and stepped a few feet back, as if not trusting himself to be near and allow me to continue on alone.

"What are you doing?" Frederickson asked.

"She's going to talk to him," Kane said, as if he'd backed this play from the beginning.

"Alone?" Collin asked, and I could hear the fear in his tone. He thought I'd screw this up.

Actually, I might. But the crawlers wanted to talk to me, and me they'd get.

"She's just a—"

"She's a lot more than *just* anything," Kane said, cutting off Frederickson.

I heard more grumblings, but I ignored them as I stepped forward, following the twisted-looking deer until it swerved off right before Harg.

I didn't hesitate once I was in front of him. "You broke the deal."

I resisted the urge to rant and rave like a lunatic. Kane wasn't the only angry one. As the relief that he had trusted me faded, the fear that had shaken me during the blast returned and turned to rage. If Harg had been behind it…

His chin tilted up. "No."

"Then what was the explosion?"

"Not one of ours."

"Really? Well, that's awfully convenient." I wanted to roll my eyes when I realized I'd stolen Kane's line again.

"I'll get rid of him." He grunted and pounded on his chest.

"You'll get rid of the crawler that did the explosion? How am I supposed to believe that?"

His eyes skimmed over my entourage, seeming to stop on someone before landing back on me. I turned, wondering what he'd seen that had caught his attention. They stood as a group, Kane clearly in front to stop anybody from coming forward.

I turned back to Harg. "Why should I trust you? You

could be lying. I could walk out of here and have another explosion tomorrow."

"Not do to Shadow Walker. Not to Abandinus."

Abandinus? What was that word? That was the second time I'd heard it. The first time was from Kane's mouth. What did it mean?

"What is Abandinus?"

"You know," Harg said, his eyes flicking back to my group.

I didn't know, but it was clear he definitely thought I should. My embarrassment over my ignorance kept me from asking anything else on that matter. The crawler knew more about what Kane had said than I did.

"How can I be sure? Can you at least answer my questions?" I stared straight at where the air was glimmering. "Who is this?" I would've pointed, but I didn't want everyone staring in our direction to know it wasn't just me and Harg.

"Not now."

"Yes, now. I need answers, unless you want your world torched." What the hell was this monster not comprehending? I'd passed on the message. He knew what loomed.

He beat his chest once. "Give you something."

Before I could ask what, there was a mouth outlined in the glimmer, and then a wave of heat flowed over me. Panic raced through me. I felt the magic but forced myself to stay calm. If I screamed bloody murder, that was exactly what I'd get. I didn't know who would be the victor, Harg or Kane. I was still standing and breathing, still alive. My gut had said to trust this creature, and that was what I would do.

"What was that?" I asked, teeth clenched as I waited for the worst.

"Gift. You'll see." He bowed slightly. The glimmer beside him disappeared, and Harg walked away, fading out of sight quickly.

I walked back toward the group, wondering what bull-shit I was going to be able to come up with in the one minute I had. I only moved forward from sheer will because I was panicking inside. What had it done to me? Was I a ticking time bomb or something? I had no answers, and something very strange had just happened that I definitely couldn't share with present company.

As soon as I laid my eyes on Kane, warmth spread through me, but that wasn't alarming. I'd been feeling that for days. It was when Frederickson stepped forward and I could taste my dislike of him, much stronger than it had been, that I knew something was up. My eyes shot to Rudy and coldness spread through me. I looked to my group, Butch and Leon, Zee and Flip, and I wanted to cry for the joy I felt. I wanted to hug each of them. I couldn't remember my past, but I suddenly remembered the love I'd had for them.

"What happened?" Kane asked, stepping close.

The rest of them were all gathering around me and staring, waiting, while I was reeling from feelings that I didn't understand. What had that creature done to me? How? Whatever it was, I needed to pull it together until I got out of here.

"Harg didn't do it," I said.

"And?" Rudy asked.

"He's going to fix it." My fists clenched as my heart pounded just from hearing his voice and being near him.

Cracking tree branches sounded in the distance as I tried to breathe through my nose. Or should I be breathing in through my mouth and out through my nose?

There was another loud crack, and this time it was thunder close by. Didn't matter how I breathed. Neither seemed to be working. Whatever the Glass Monster had shaken loose seemed to have affected my magic too. I couldn't get a handle on a spell, but I felt the magic coursing through me, chaotic and wild.

Rain dropped down upon us. I could see Collin and Frederickson taking steps back, widening the divide between our groups.

"Fix it? How?" Rudy demanded, the only one fixed to his spot.

"I think we should discuss this another time," Kane said, sounding diplomatic for once.

"I said he'd fix it." The rage I was feeling was off the charts. What had his people done to me? A bolt of lightning, not ten feet from us, finally jarred Rudy out of fighting mode and into flight.

Hands steered me toward the truck we'd taken while others gave hurried goodbyes. In the truck, surrounded by people I cared about, my pulse calmed, and the rain that had begun to pour let up.

I couldn't remember the last time I'd been so happy. Or freaked out, because I had no idea what the monster had done to me or how long it would last, or what might come next.

Chapter Thirty-Two

I DIDN'T KNOW IF KANE HAD GIVEN THEM SOME SORT OF signal to not ask questions, or they sensed that I was off, but no one said anything on the way back. Maybe they were afraid that I'd bring lightning down on them, too. I didn't know and I didn't ask. I sat there quietly on the way back to the Underground, digesting all the feelings that washed over me.

We got out of the truck, Kane beside me, and he dismissed everyone as the two of us headed directly for the elevator. Kane walked over to his apartment door on the sixth floor, waiting. I went to him, and for the first time since losing my memory, I walked into a room and felt as if I belonged.

He followed me into the apartment and shut the door behind him, then stood, watching me as I settled onto the couch.

"What happened?" he asked.

"I need a drink. Do you have anything to drink in

here?" It was stupid question, since I knew he did, but I wasn't ready for more complicated speech yet.

He moved to the cabinet and poured me a glass. I took it with a shaking hand and threw it back, without bothering to ask what it was.

"I asked you to trust me, and you did. Now, I'm going to take a leap of faith and trust you." I didn't know if I was telling him, or convincing myself that I should. I was so far in now that I knew this was the best move. Kane hadn't killed me yet, and I trusted his promise. "The thing that was talking to Harg was there."

Kane's jaw tensed and his eyes narrowed. "Did you know before you decided to talk to Harg alone?"

This wasn't a leap so much as it was throwing myself out of a plane, five thousand miles up. "Yes."

"And you wait to tell me now?"

"I had good reasons, as you've had when you've held back information from me." I wasn't so sure how strongly I felt about some of his reasons, but he could hardly deny the similarities.

He tilted his head forward, eyebrows rising, as if he couldn't wait to hear the rest.

I looked down at my empty glass. I held it out, silently asking for a refill. "I might need it."

He grumbled but took it and poured me another. Then he took out a second glass and looked at me.

"Might not be a bad idea," I said.

He shook his head and brought both our drinks back over with him. He handed me one and then sat, waiting.

I took a sip instead of downing it. Might need to keep my wits about me. "Whatever it is, it saved me from becoming a vampire. After I got attacked outside the

Underground, it was right beside us when Frederickson was giving me his blood."

Kane leaned in. "How close, exactly?"

"Real close. He might've been brushing against Frederickson for all I know."

Kane's jaw clenched. I watched as he sipped his own drink.

"I couldn't exactly speak at the moment, but as I lay there, I could feel Frederickson's blood flowing through me, but then the creature sucked it out through the same place I'd been shadow kissed." I glanced down at the mark right beside my thumb as I remembered how strange it had felt. I finished telling him how it seemed to ask me to not say anything and how I'd thought maybe it had been a near-death hallucination.

Kane listened, not trying to strangle me once. Finally, after I was done, he asked, "You didn't feel anything different afterward?"

"Not that time." I took a larger sip. "But this time was different. It gave me something. Or technically took something…I think. I have no idea.

"When I walked back after talking to them, I had these strong feelings associated with everyone. I remembered how I felt, not why, but the emotions flooded me."

I put both hands around my glass, sipping and watching Kane over the rim. I waited to see if he'd ask what I'd felt when I saw him. I wasn't sure whether I should come clean and say I'd already felt so strongly that it hadn't mattered.

I was relieved when he asked, "Can you remember anything besides feelings?"

"No." It didn't even matter. I knew how I felt about

people. I knew who I loved, and he was sitting right in front of me. I shifted my gaze away from him before I blurted it out.

"At least now I understand why you almost brought a monsoon down on Rudy." Kane stood, as if it helped him think. "Why would this creature keep helping you?"

He stared off as he tried to piece together the puzzle that had been plaguing me for days.

"I don't know. But he's done it twice." I flopped back on the couch. I watched him try and sort through the mystery, and felt exhausted, overwhelmed, and damn if I didn't feel like I was in love with him.

The more I stared at Kane, the more the feelings kept flooding through, much more intense than they had been.

He came and leaned a hip along the back of the couch, looking down at me. "Maybe it was afraid you'd fall under the influence of Frederickson?"

I tilted my head back. "Well, at least Harg and that other creature aren't stupid. But why would one of them try and kill us while another one was trying to help me?"

He bent forward, leaning his arms on the back of the couch, near my head. "One of the last times you went into the Shadowlands, you said they appeared to be warring amongst themselves. Maybe this is some sort of civil war? We appear to be in Harg's corner."

It would make some of the pieces fit. I closed my eyes, trying to see a path forward. "I should talk to Harg again. I should've gotten more answers. I was so rattled I—"

"No. You did the right thing. You got out of there when you should've."

"But if this creature could do this, maybe he could restore my full memory?"

"At what price? Let's make sure nothing else happens before you have any more interaction with them."

I opened my eyes to find him in the same spot, staring down at me. He wasn't looking at me like I was a monster anymore, though. The way his eyes fixated on me made me feel parched.

"I think we should try some more of your concoctions from hell."

"You sure?"

"Yes. If whatever happened rattled something loose, which I think it did, maybe it'll make a difference now." I sat up, wanting to leave before I was asked to or I threw myself at him. Just because I'd slept with him didn't mean he'd want me hanging around him every moment.

"Where are you going?" he asked, wrapping his arm around my stomach when I stood to leave.

I froze. "I was going to lie down."

He pulled the hair away from my neck and tilted my head back toward him.

"There's a bed here."

I opened my mouth to ask if he was sure, but his kiss stopped me.

Chapter Thirty-Three

I STARED AT THE LAST POTION ON THE TABLE IN KANE'S basement. It was the black stuff that smelled like it was a decomposing body.

"You sure? This one is a rough one." Kane stood and reached forward, about to pick up the rotting body and take the choice from me.

"No." I grabbed the vial before he did.

He didn't fight me for it, but he did say, "I'm not sure how much more of these you can handle."

"I can take a little bit more." I could take a lot more to have some control over my magic back. The memories and spells—it was if I could sense them right beneath the surface, taunting me.

He looked at me as if I'd just said the sky was neon purple.

"I can do it. I *need* to do it."

He shrugged, as if to say, *It's your body.*

Hands shaking, I threw it back, feeling pretty satisfied

with myself when it didn't immediately want to come right back up.

I WOKE as Kane was laying me on the couch in his office, mid-berating. "I don't know why the hell I listen to you. Clearly you have no idea what your limits are."

"Yes, I do." I wiped a hand across my mouth, afraid I might've been drooling or something.

He stepped back and crossed his arms. "Really? Then why did you pass out?"

"I said I knew I could take it, as in it wouldn't kill me. I didn't say I'd stay awake through it."

He stood at the edge of the couch, the comfy one I wasn't budging from. "I don't think that's what you meant at all, but I'll give you this one."

"It definitely was." I yawned, and my eyelids were getting heavy. "I might need a few more minutes before I can stand, though."

He was smiling as he made his way over to his desk, something about this situation feeling comfortingly familiar. It made me think back to when I'd caught him looking at his couch at different points when I'd come here before.

"Did I use to nap here a lot?" I asked, as I watched him get comfortable behind his desk.

I saw the immediate tensing in his body. "Do you remember that?" he asked.

I let out a deep breath. "No." Nothing had changed. My memories were still gone. I was starting to believe it didn't matter how many potions I drank or what Kane could find for me next. They were gone.

Kane was fiddling with his phone, but I knew he was as disappointed as I was.

"The dent in the couch that conforms perfectly to me was a tip-off," I said, trying to lighten up what felt like a ton of bricks falling on me.

He lifted his head. "There's other potions out there, but a break might not be a bad idea."

He didn't think there was anything else out there that would work. Neither did I.

Before I could answer, a knock proceeded a sickly-sweet voice. "Kane?"

I don't know if Dana had sucked on some helium before coming here, but that wasn't what she'd sounded like when I heard her away from Kane.

I rolled my eyes as Kane said, "Come in."

She sashayed over to his desk, pretending she didn't see me right there, as obvious as could be. My stomach did a flip-flop with every step she took. Not that it mattered. Kane wasn't even glancing at her. He liked me, and I had nothing to worry about. Yes, he didn't say he liked me, but he did.

But I still couldn't forget the picture of them laughing and standing at the bar.

"What did you need?" Kane asked.

She perched on his desk, leaning toward him as she crossed long legs. "I've got that thing you've been asking for."

That got his attention. "You're sure this time?"

"Yes."

What was going on with them? What thing? I guessed telling all only went one way.

It didn't matter. It wasn't my business—as long as I didn't see them sleeping together. Then I'd kill him.

He stood, waving her toward to door. "Dana, I'll catch up with you in one moment."

She walked out, continuing to ignore my existence.

Kane grabbed a set of keys sitting on his desk. "I'll be back in a little while."

He was watching me as he gathered his things and got ready to leave. He was waiting to see if I was going to have a meltdown of some sort.

"Okay." *Nope. No meltdown here. Do what you must. And if I find out what you have to do is something bad with her, then I'll do what I have to, even if it kills me.* And possibly him, too.

He walked closer to the couch. "You took a leap of faith last night. You're not calling it quits already, are you?"

"I didn't say a word." I'd only thought it.

"Not trusting is easy. Trusting?" He let out a slow whistle. "I usually don't trust anyone until I've known them for at least a decade." He smiled. "But I trust you. Sometimes you just have to go with your gut."

If we were in a dark alleyway, I knew he'd have my back. That was a pretty large amount of trust. But my heart? That was a tougher one.

He leaned down, brushing his lips over mine. "You're very cute when you're jealous."

"I am *not* jealous."

He had the nerve to laugh at that before he left.

I BANGED on Flip's door, not knowing what else to do, since Kane wasn't back and my faith was wearing thinner by the hour. I'd been packed solid with faith for a good couple of hours. By eleven that night, my faith was waning.

She opened the door and I bulldozed my way in.

"What's wrong with you?" she asked, watching me park myself on her couch.

"Nothing." The word came from between clenched teeth.

"Nothing? Because it looks like we're getting ready for another rainy season." She sat down beside me, crossing her legs and muting *Grey's Anatomy*. "You can't look like you're about to commit murder and say you aren't. You have to have a reason or you're crazy and need to be insti- tutionalized."

"I slept with him. Then he went out to do something with Dana and it's almost midnight." Wow, I was a light- weight with this withholding stuff all of a sudden. It was like a contagion that spread through you.

"Ohhhhh." She nodded and leaned back, getting more comfortable.

"No, no 'ohhhhh.' Why aren't you trying to make me feel better? I'm being irrational. Just because he went to do something doesn't mean he's going to sleep with her. You need to be telling me these things." Maybe I should've tried Zee. Why had I thought Flip was the best one for this? Butch. I should've gone to him.

"I completely agree with everything you just said. Plus, he doesn't like her like that. You might not know this, although I have told you, but I'm partially descended from Cupid. I *know* these things." She patted my shoulder.

"You're sure?" Maybe Flip hadn't been the worst choice.

"I told you, it's in my blood." She sprang into a litany of her family tree. By the time she got to her great-great-grandmother on her mother's side, I was rethinking Zee.

My phone buzzed in my pocket. "I have to go."

Flip's phone buzzed before I got to my feet. "So do I."

"Kane?" I asked.

She nodded.

"YOU CALLED?" I asked, layering on some frost. If Kane hadn't, I'd probably have lain low until I accidentally bumped into him. Not that I was mad. I had no proof he'd done anything wrong. But him disappearing with *her* for hours certainly didn't put me in my happy place.

But still, here I was, at his place, because when I knew Kane was looking for me, I had a hard time not appearing. That was the biggest problem with Kane, besides all the others. And there were lots of problems. He was secretive, arrogant, bossy, and the list could go on and on...

But the biggest issue with him was how I felt about him. I was a sinking ship and I wasn't even trying to bail out the water anymore.

Butch and Leon were already in Kane's apartment, along with a girl who couldn't have been older than eighteen. Her thick, wavy brown hair was half tucked into a sweatshirt way too big for her.

"What's going on?" I asked.

Kane walked farther into his apartment and pointed at the girl. "I want you to meet Tawny. She's a very bright witch in from New York who has a gift with memories."

My lips parted, but before I could ask, he shook his head. "We're going to use her to start eliminating suspects that might be involved with what's going on." He turned to Flip, who was next to me. "Flip, why don't you make yourself comfortable?"

She nodded, giving us some privacy.

"I've been using Dana to snoop around but she's not good enough at memory spells to break through whatever is going on," Kane said.

"You have?" I asked, thinking back to all those times I'd seen him with her. "Why didn't you tell me?"

"Initially?" He lifted an eyebrow, as if it were obvious.

He had a point. "I mean, once we were getting along."

"The witches hate you and you hate the witches. I was working Dana over to get a name of the best person she had after she failed. She was happy to help, since it seemed to be annoying the hell out of you. You were annoying the hell out of me near daily, so"—he shrugged —"maybe I didn't mind poking back a little."

"Why didn't you tell me today?"

"I don't know." He shrugged again, and I wanted to shake him to death. He knew exactly why he didn't tell me. He liked getting under my skin.

"That wasn't nice." I poked him right in the center of his chest.

"Neither was telling me to go screw right after losing your memory without so much as having a conversation about the situation." He said it nonchalantly. Knowing how

I felt now, if he'd done that to me, it would've been crippling.

I glance over at the girl, who looked barely more than a child. "Could she possibly... Is there any way she might be able to..." I ran my fingers over a lock of my hair.

"Possibly. But it's up to you."

I stared at him, and then bit my lower lip as I tried to hold back the tears. He believed me, finally, maybe more than I believed myself—believed that if I'd had something to do with the crawlers coming in, I'd been used somehow. That was all I needed. Just one person solidly in my corner.

He was watching me, waiting to see if I understood.

I nodded, just slightly, but that was all he needed, because he knew me.

"Okay. What do we need?"

Kane turned to the girl. "Tawny? Can you break down how this works?"

She fiddled with the rips in her jeans, clearly not used to being in a position of authority. "Um, I need hair from each person we want to look into. Like, a lot would be good, but I could probably make do with even a strand if I had to. Shit might be blurry, though. Nail clippings—now that's the good shit, especially if you want me to look into vamps, since their hair is even deader than normal. Were-wolf hair isn't great either, but those suckers are so hairy that you can usually get a lot."

"Who should we start with? There's no lack of possibilities," Leon said, his foot resting on the end table as he relaxed on the couch.

"We make a list," Kane said.

"Frederickson is going to be tough, but I can handle him," Flip offered.

"I'll get Vincent," I said. Out of everyone, he'd been the kindest to me. The least I could do was try and clear his name.

Butch went into a kitchen drawer and grabbed a pen and paper.

"Butch, grab me a pair of scissors," I said.

He handed them over, and I cut a small chunk of my hair and then held it up. "Tawny, is this enough, or do you want more?"

"That's fine," she said, looking nervous.

I handed it to her. "I know it's a long shot, but you never know."

Butch settled in, beginning his list, and Leon and Flip gathered around him, as he wrote down anyone who could've been involved. Tawny got up, looking over their shoulders, although she didn't have anything to add.

I'd been so overwhelmed with everything else going on that I suddenly realized I'd forgotten something. I made my way back to where Kane was standing.

"Abandinus," I whispered into his ear. "Should I know that word? That's your name, isn't it?"

He smiled, leaned over, and brushed his lips against mine. That was all the answer I got. Turned out Kane had started his leap of faith before I'd even realized.

Chapter Thirty-Four

ABANDINUS. THE ONLY INFORMATION THAT CAME UP WAS A single bronze feather inscribed to him, calling him a god. At least the arrogance made sense. God of what, though? Figured if he was some type of god, he'd be the only god nobody knew anything about. Secretive to the end.

I pocketed my phone and headed into the "god's" office. He better not think I was going to pray to him or anything. He might be a god, but he was still Kane.

The Keurig was humming, and I smelled the piping-hot French vanilla that Butch was waiting to get his hands on. I gave him a nod before turning my attention to the god sitting behind the desk, legs crossed, his heels propped on the surface. He looked more devilish than godlike.

A chair brushed my leg, but I didn't sit in it. I wasn't sure if this was going to be a friendly encounter after he heard what I had planned.

He was waiting, giving me his full attention. When Kane looked at me now, I saw the softness in his eyes, so different than when I'd first met him. I had no idea what

Kane's past was, but I knew I wanted him no matter what his dark history was. And it was dark. That I was sure of, god or not. I might not know the injuries and sins, but I could see the scars. There was a reason he'd been single for so long. Just as I had.

Sometimes when the wounds were too deep, the scar tissue that formed was tougher to penetrate. But I didn't see scars or walls as he looked at me now. I saw the same longing that burned in my chest.

"You look tired." His eyes didn't leave mine as he waited for me to reply. He knew I was and why.

I didn't answer, not even when his eyes said I wouldn't be getting much sleep tonight, either. Although I hoped the coming lack of sleep wouldn't be due to fighting.

"I wanted to let you know my plans for this afternoon. You're not going to like them." There, at least that was out of the way.

Kane leaned back and shifted, most of the softness disappearing as he geared up for a fight. "What are they?"

I smiled widely. "Before I tell you, remember, we trust each other now."

"That bad, huh?"

"Let's just say I might have to spend a lot of time on my knees praying to make up for it."

"Then I hope it's very bad," he said, a gleam in his eye as the rest of the occupants of the room groaned.

I WAS SITTING across from Vincent in one of the only

places still open in Boston. It was a small coffee shop run by a couple in their eighties who said they'd rather die in Boston than leave. Kane had mentioned the place, while also mentioning how he liked their grit.

It was surprising they hadn't been overrun with looters, since they were the only place left that had supplies. When I'd asked Kane about it, he shrugged as if he had no idea. He knew exactly why they hadn't been. When I strolled in, I'd noticed some familiar faces hanging around the corner, all with yellow bandanas, which confirmed it.

"Thanks for meeting me here, Vincent." I held my hands around the warm mug of tea.

"Of course. I'd been hoping you'd call," he said, leaning toward me and placing a hand on the table not far from mine.

"Sometimes I just need to get out of there, see a friendly face. I've been having a tough time of it. I wanted to tell you, I really appreciate the kindness you've shown me." I reached a hand across the table and rested it on his.

"I really do want to be there for you."

When he smiled, he looked so sincere that it made me want to spill my guts, lay it all out. But I wouldn't. I'd agreed to terms with Kane before I came here. I'd adhere to them. And this was for Vincent's own good.

I asked him how things were going for him lately, and he filled the time with talk about social politics and lots of fluff that didn't really tell me anything of importance. Still, I nodded as if they were the most interesting things I'd heard all week.

When I asked about his boss, Frederickson, he gave the usually boss gripe. Again, nothing of use to me. Not that I was there for that, but a couple of gems of knowledge might've been nice.

I took the last sip of my tea. "I better get back. People are always monitoring my comings and goings over there." That was especially true at the moment.

"I'll walk you out," he said, getting up as I did.

We made our way over to the Caddy I'd borrowed and stopped in front of the driver's door.

I smiled, the way a girl smiled at a boy when she was interested. There was guilt involved in leading him on, but I'd clear his name and he'd be thanking me. You didn't want Kane on your bad side, and Vincent was getting very close to making that list.

I ran a few fingers down the front of his shirt.

He stepped closer. "When I didn't hear from you, I wasn't sure."

I closed the gap.

His lips covered mine, and I reached a hand up, running it through his hair and then tugging on it, as if I were so overtaken by his kiss. In truth, it wasn't a bad kiss. But I wasn't overtaken by anything. I had to force my body to soften, instead of the automatic reaction I had to Kane.

I pulled back when I felt like it had been just enough to make the interest believable. "I really need to go."

"I'll talk to you soon?"

"Sure."

I drove back to the Underground, wishing I'd had a better way of accomplishing that in a timely manner. Either way, it was done.

I strode up to Kane's office, the door already open, as

if he'd known exactly when I would arrive. He didn't look any happier than I felt as he waited, sitting on his desk.

"He's going to be innocent." I dumped the strands in Kane's waiting hand.

He fisted them. "This was a one-time agreement, so you better not have any more plans. I don't care how much praying you plan on doing."

"I don't." I stepped in between his legs, resting my hands on his waist. "Any word from Tawny on mine?"

"She's trying, but nothing yet."

I nodded as his hand came up, rubbing my back in the most delicious way.

He resisted letting me go when I pulled away.

"Where are you going?"

I moved out of his reach as he watched me go to the knob of his door and turn the lock. "I like to pray in private," I said, smiling.

Chapter Thirty-Five

I'D WAITED A FEW HOURS FOR A MESSAGE THAT VINCENT was exonerated, but no news had come. As I wasn't familiar with this whole process, maybe it took a while to sort through memories? They probably didn't come with a Dewey Decimal system.

By the time dinner had come and gone, and there was still no sign of Kane, my linguine felt like a cinder block sitting in my stomach. What had Kane seen? Was it not even Vincent's memories? Were they mine? Were they so bad that he wasn't going to speak to me again? Was he having my things packed up right now, about to throw me to the curb?

He protected me and cared for me, but I knew there were certain things you didn't come back from. Some deeds were too bad to live with, like being the cause of a major city being destroyed by monsters. And I might've done that—unknowingly done it, but I didn't think that mattered much when it was on your résumé. He'd promised to not kill me. He hadn't promised to never stop wanting me. But he'd never said he loved me or offered any future, either.

By the time Butch and Leon were strolling into the Underground, I was rushing them like a lineman that had gotten recruited in the first round of the draft.

"Where's Kane?"

Butch and Leon shot looks back and forth.

"For once, can you people just tell me without the damn faces?"

Of course, this elicited new and confused faces. I waited those out without another word, afraid they'd need to look in the mirror next.

Butch scratched his jaw. "He's with Tawny still, using your old rooms on sixth."

I didn't wait for anything else. Whatever had happened, whatever was to come, I wanted to know now. And if it was bad, I'd live with it.

The elevator had never moved so slowly as the floors lit up, one by one, before finally delivering me to the sixth floor. I pushed open the door, not feeling the need to knock when technically it was still my apartment, even if I wasn't doing much sleeping there.

The witch, Tawny, was wrapped around herself in the armchair, looking as quiet and meek as ever. Kane was seated on the couch in front of the floating image, leaning forward as some random footage of someone driving down the street played.

He didn't notice me when I walked in the room, which was completely unlike Kane. He noticed everyone, always. His awareness was off the charts, and I'd never seen him lost in thoughts the way he seemed to be right now. My legs felt as wobbly as a new colt's as I walked closer.

"What's going on?" I asked, coming to stand beside him, afraid to sit. It would be easier to pretend I wasn't humiliated at getting thrown out if I wasn't sitting. Unless I fell. That would definitely be the worst.

"Nothing good," he said, with a deep sadness that made me want to pull him from the room and ask who'd died.

He didn't sound angry—or not at me, anyway. So, maybe I hadn't been caught doing the worst deeds imaginable?

"What did you find?" I asked.

"Tawny, can you replay that last clip we were watching?" he asked, sounding so unlike himself. For a man that had always seemed composed, the strain was startling.

Tawny's eyes darted from Kane to me and then back again before she nodded. That bad? I did some Lamaze breathing, or what I thought was Lamaze breathing from the stupid stuff I'd seen on TV. If it got women through labor pains, maybe it would get me through this without breaking anyone's bones or furniture. I gripped the arm of the couch, still afraid to sit.

Tawny chanted under her breath and the air began to shift in front of us, like a kaleidoscope changing colors and patterns. The image grew brighter until it became a new scene, washing out the previous one.

Someone was walking through a hallway. It looked as if the building had been abandoned and had sustained significant damage. The walls were charred.

The person climbed a flight of stairs before making a right turn into a room. The air was sucked from my lungs, and no amount of Lamaze could prepare me for what I saw. My body was slumped on the ground, lifeless at the feet of a man, his upper body completely cast in shadows.

Was I dead? No. That was stupid. I couldn't have been. I was standing here alive, right now, and I didn't feel like a zombie. Seconds dragged on as if I'd pressed a slow-motion button on time. The dead me, the one on the floor in the image—her chest finally moved. A sickly wheezing sound escaped her lips.

"What the hell is this? What did you do to her?" It was the voice of the person's memories we were viewing, the voice I'd just heard earlier today. It was Vincent's voice.

My fingers dug into the arm of the couch. That was the only thing keeping me standing as I felt the ax-sized knife lodged in my back.

Kane got up and stepped closer, letting me know he was there for me without smothering. It was his style. He'd give as much comfort as I was willing to take. Although, from the looks of him, he needed it more than I did. What was wrong with him?

Vincent shifted, drawing my attention back to the picture. He hadn't been a part of whatever had just happened to me, but he'd been involved somehow. He knew a lot, from the looks of it. And yet he'd pretended as if he'd never met me until that day in the Underground, when he strode in and introduced himself.

Vincent squatted beside me, checking the strength of my pulse before standing up again. I still couldn't see who he was with, though.

"Can you get a clearer picture?" I asked Tawny, hoping to identify the other man.

"Dude, I ain't a 4K TV," Tawny said.

I reassessed her. Maybe not so meek at all. Or maybe the greyish tone to her skin meant Kane was pushing her too hard.

"She's been at it for a while." Kane ran his hand down my back, his signal to not kill the new kid. I was more concerned about him doing her in than me.

"Why are parts so dark?" I asked, not caring who answered.

"Because he wants to forget," Kane answered. "That's why the voice of the other person sounds strange. It's distorted, or I might've recognized it."

I kept my attention on the picture as Vincent stood. "What happened to her?"

"Did you think it was going to be easy?" the shadowy man asked.

Vincent groaned, as if he were remorseful, but it wasn't enough to take the sting from the burn. He'd known. All along, he'd known.

Shadow Man nudged me forward with the toe of his boot. "You need to dump her close to the Underground. Don't let her die. If she does, shit could go sideways quick. We already almost lost her, and you don't want to know what happened then. One of those crawlers nearly lost its shit on us. Her dying isn't an option. Get her close to the Underground and we'll make sure she gets found. We can always grab her again when we need her."

"What happens when she wakes up and tells him?" Vincent asked.

"She won't remember anything. The ugly fuck said her mind is going to be fried because of what we did," Shadow Man said.

"How bad will it be?" Vincent asked. "Is she going to be a vegetable?"

A fucking vegetable? I heard a crack, and then Tawny shrieked. Oops, there went the end table.

"Nah, just a memory gap. She's lucky. If we'd used her any more, it might've wiped out years, and that's if she made it."

"You never said—"

"Your boss knew everything. Now hurry up and get rid of her." Shadow Man walked away.

It hadn't been a spell after all. And "boss"? It had to be Frederickson. Who else?

"Those damn vampires," I said.

Vincent picked me up, and I felt violated and weak. Vulnerable. I rubbed my hands over my arms, disgusted.

"That's why the potions didn't work and you were coming up clean," Kane said. "It *was* magic that screwed up your memory, but not a spell."

"At least I know." That was the best I could come up with at the moment. The only bright spot. I knew I'd been betrayed. Yippee.

I was sure I'd be hearing an "I told you" so any second. Kane had been right. He deserved it.

But he wasn't saying much of anything and he didn't look happy. He looked resigned and maybe a little tired— or sad, even. It was as if he'd taken this well-worn path enough to remember how bad it felt. It made me wonder who'd been smart enough to con him.

"How did you know not to trust him?" I asked, giving him his due.

"You learn the signs after a while," he said, not even a hair of gloating.

"And what were the signs with Vincent?" What had I missed that he'd read so clearly?

"He's ambitious. Never trust anyone who is more concerned about *where* they are in life than *who* they are. They never seem to mind stepping over a couple of bodies on their climb up."

They were fitting words, as I was one of the bodies Vincent had just stepped over.

"This isn't the worst of it," Kane said, and I knew that other shoe I'd been sensing was about to drop. "Tawny was able to pick up a little from your memory as well."

I shuddered, but got control of myself quick enough. What had I done that Kane was acting so weird? As I waited for Tawny to do her thing, I could swear my heart stopped a handful of times. My fingers grew ice cold where they hugged my arms.

The image shifted again, but this time it was all blurry, just blobs of shapes, like a camera out of focus. I could hear speaking, but it was garbled.

Until my voice broke out clearly: "Please, you don't want me to do this. You don't know what you're asking for."

Tawny started explaining. "Because your memory is a mess, it's just a hazy clump of nothing. It's amazing I can even get this. But that's about all I can pick up."

I watched the blurs, trying to find something clear as the picture continued. The garbled voices filled in until I spoke again.

"No. I won't—" My words were cut off as a sob came out. I could hear the swish of something but not make out what I was being hit with. If I had to guess from the sound, it was something significant.

The attack sounded vicious, and I heard groaning. More garbled words and me refusing. Both the refusals and the groans grew weaker and weaker.

That was where those bruises had come from. I'd been tortured. I should be devastated, and maybe I would be at some point. But at that moment, all I wanted to do was sag in relief. I hadn't let them through willingly. I'd been tortured, and I might not have even been conscious.

I wanted to celebrate, but I was the only one. Tawny looked as if she'd been through it herself and was ready to cry.

I turned to Kane, hoping to see the same expression on his face that I was feeling. I'd been forced, and it looked as if I'd gone down swinging. So why did he look haunted?

"Did you have bruises?" Kane asked, not a drop of joy on his face.

"I had some faded ones." I'd never been so eager to provide information as I was right now, knowing it vindicated me.

"Someone probably healed you as best they could before they dropped you off. Most likely Vincent." Kane turned toward Tawny. "Keep trying to get it clearer."

Tawny waited until he turned his back before she rolled her eyes, making it obvious this wasn't the first time he'd said that.

He turned toward me, with a hand at my back ushered me out of the room and into his apartment, and shut the door.

Why wasn't he as happy as I was? I hadn't done it on purpose. I might not have done it at all. Maybe they'd figured out a way to use my mind somehow without me doing anything? Did he not realize how great this was? How I'd agonized over this day after day?

He stopped right inside the hall and boxed me in with his frame, still not remotely as happy as I felt.

His head dropped, his cheek grazing mine. The tension was rolling off him, and I didn't know what to do but stay still and wait it out. Why was he acting so crazy?

"Kane? This is good. Even if I was involved, I didn't do it on purpose. Now you know for sure."

"I should've known for sure anyway." He pushed off the wall, his palms flat on the surface as he finally met my eyes. "I let this happen. You were mine, and you got hurt. Nothing about this feels good."

I cupped his face. "But we can at least move on from it now."

"I don't know if we can."

"Why?"

"Before, I was forgiving you for something you didn't even do. Once you remember, I don't know if you'll forgive me."

"Forgive you for what?"

"For thinking you could be that person."

"But I'm not—"

He cut me short before I could tell him I wasn't mad. Not even a little.

"You don't understand yet. We weren't just a fling, some casual hookup. I loved you. I never said it, but I should've, and so many times you were sick of hearing me."

Was he trying to take my legs out from underneath me? Was that the plan? Because if the wall hadn't been at my back, I would've hit the floor. This man, this arrogant bastard who protected me, carried me to bed and pulled off my shoes for me, held my hair back when I got sick—this godlike man was telling me he loved me.

And instead of kissing me, he walked away.

Chapter Thirty-Six

BUTCH WAS EATING A BAGEL WHILE LEON HAD HIS PHONE out, snapping pics of his bacon and pancakes. I couldn't eat a bite as I sat in the booth with them.

I hadn't seen Kane since he'd left his apartment last night. I'd waited in his place, jumping at every creak I heard, but he hadn't come back. Even if he needed some space to think about us, what about the vampires? We had work to do and he took off? Or was that where he was right now? And he went off without me?

I pushed a barely touched bowl of fruit away. "Did Kane say anything to either of you last night?"

"We already told you, no." Butch turned back to Leon. "Who eats bacon and pancakes? It should be bacon and eggs."

"See? That's your problem. You're too rigid. You need to embrace new things," Leon said.

"Are you two worried at all?" I asked, interrupting their little tiff.

They both turned to me and said, "No," at the same time, as if I were the crazy one.

Butch pointed at Leon's plate. "I embrace things that work. Bacon and pancakes don't. Look at them. Those strips are getting soggy with syrup."

"You're getting very uptight, do you know that?" Leon asked, more serious about this than Kane missing.

"Look at that soggy mess. That should be a crime to do to crisp bacon. I'm going to have a word with the gargoyles—"

"You need to move on from this," Leon said.

I stood. "If either of you hear from him, call me, okay?"

"Yeah, sure." Butch waved his hand and they went back to their argument.

I stopped by Jerry, who was manning the door, and pried his attention away from the newest blonde walking past. "Have you seen Kane?"

"Huh?" His eyes were focused on the blonde's cleavage.

"Jerry!" I put myself in between him and the blonde. "Have you seen Kane?"

"No. Been gone since last night." He only looked at me for a second before he stared over my head.

He was useless. I had one last person to turn to for information. I walked into the hall, where it was quieter.

"Zee?"

"Yeah?" She popped up almost immediately.

"Have you seen Kane?"

"No. Hang on." She lifted her ear to the air and then looked back at me. "He's off the grid."

"What's that mean?"

"Means no one has a location."

"Let me know if you pick up something?" I asked.

"You got it."

I turned toward the elevators but then went back to the Underground. I'd go wait in his office. It had the best view of the place, and I'd know the second he walked in.

I made my way toward the stairs but froze. The crawler that had been at the cemetery the last time I saw Harg, the little deer without the charm, was standing beside the exit door, watching me. I watched back. It took a step closer to the exit. It wasn't watching. It was waiting.

Did I go to it? I glanced at Kane's empty office and then back at the creature. What if it knew something about Kane? Sometimes the best you could do was go with your gut. My gut was telling me to follow the creature.

I walked toward it and watched as it disappeared through the closed door. As I neared, Jerry turned toward the blonde, as if he didn't notice me. It was a bit suspicious. These crawlers might've had more influence in this world than any of us had imagined.

The sun was warm on my skin as I stepped outside, looking for the crawler. It was waiting for me about fifty yards away. It turned the corner once it saw me following it.

I'd followed it for a mile or so when it finally disappeared. I stood waiting for a few seconds before Harg stepped out from behind a building, the air shimmering beside him. The Glass Monster was there.

I continued forward until I was standing in front of Harg. "Why are you here?"

He bowed his head. "We have a deal to offer."

Deal? Did they know where Kane was? "What?"

"Heal you, but you let more of us in, many more, and now."

I was shaking my head and stepping back before I even said, "No." There was no way I'd do that, not for my memories, not for anything in this world.

"Must," Harg said, following me. Magic was pumping into the area, and I knew it was from the Glass Monster. "We show you."

"I don't care what you show me."

I turned, hoping I'd be able to leave, because I'd made a gigantic mistake. I shouldn't have come here at all. What had I been thinking? My gut clearly sucked at decision making.

I ran a few steps and the Glass Monster was in front of me. A wave of his hand and I didn't see the street anymore.

In front of me was a portal, with crawlers coming out. Collin was standing there as they passed into this world. It took me a few seconds to notice a girl's body lay straddling the opening, lifeless as she was being trampled by crawlers as they walked over her.

Holy shit. Collin was Shadow Man.

I turned to find Harg right beside me. For the first time in my life, I willingly grabbed a crawler. "Stop them! Those are your people!"

"Not ours."

"You're warring among your own?" It was a civil war.

He nodded. "Must go now or both worlds lost."

"Are you the one who saved me?" I froze, my hands dropping as pieces finally started to fall into place. He didn't answer right away. "When they took me, did you save me?"

"They killing. I fought." He bowed again.

Just as the sixth crawler had fought through when I'd brought the others in. He'd pushed through and saved me.

Harg beat his chest. "Both times."

He'd gotten me away from them both times?

"Must go!" he said. "Now!"

Collin was letting them in at this very moment. That hadn't been in the past. It was going on right now.

What the hell did I do? "I can't go without—"

"Must."

"I need an anchor!" I dug my phone out and fumbled as I dialed. It went to voice mail. "Kane, dammit, where are you? When you get this, you need to track my phone and come to me immediately."

Harg latched on to my arm. "No more time. They have new. We must go!"

It was all so clear now. Collin hadn't been able to use me, but they must've found another Shadow Walker. He wasn't messing around this time. He would bring as many crawlers through as he could.

This was bad. So bad that I didn't have time to waste. I either went now or this might be beyond hope. Boston might be gone before Kane answered. We couldn't kill one crawler here. What would we do with the amount Collin had flooded in?

"You'll get rid of the ones coming in?" I asked, knowing we didn't have much time. But if that wasn't the plan, we were lost anyway.

Harg nodded.

"Let's go."

The Glass Monster moved closer until it seemed to move into the very space I stood, enfolding me in itself.

Everything blurred and then darkened until I was standing in the same cemetery that Collin was in, but far on the other side.

The crowd of crawlers all turned toward us, along with Collin. He waved them toward us, and we were down to seconds before they were on us.

Harg opened a portal right beside me, and bellowed, "In."

He didn't have to. The horde of crawlers shook the ground as I inserted my leg and arm into the opening, leaving my head out. Without Kane by my side to ground me to this world, I felt the pressure to be pulled completely into theirs. I stood, straddling both worlds, hoping I wasn't dooming ours, wondering if I'd end up like the other Shadow Walker I'd seen. If I'd already sealed my fate.

Crawlers appeared on every side, surrounding us, too many to count. Collin was behind them somewhere, but I couldn't see him. All I saw was crawlers.

Fire headed directly for me but Harg let out his own, canceling it out. It backed off the smaller crawlers, but probably not for long.

Then ours started running through. They had been waiting on the other side, and poured out, flying past me, at times pushing me in their haste.

It was only moments later that the entire place was in a blaze, as if I were in the heart of a volcano. It was as if the world was on fire. Harg's army had been ready.

Harg never left my side, torching every creature that neared. But even if the flames didn't kill me, the fight to straddle both worlds was draining me quickly. I felt as if I were barely hanging on as I stood in the center of it all.

The pressure to be pulled through to the other side was

growing, or my grip on this world was weakening. I fell to my knees, feeling like I was going to be torn in two if I didn't relinquish to the pull.

Kane burst through what looked like a wall of fire, charred and blackened, without a stitch of clothing left. Then he was there with me, wrapping his arms around my arm and neck, every part of me he could to ground me to our world as more and more crawlers continued to pour out.

"Close," Harg yelled.

Kane pulled me out and to the other side, and I sat there on the ground, wrapped in his arms, surrounded by dying fires as Harg's crawlers finished up the rest of his enemies. I could still see part of the Shadowlands, though, as if the portal struggled to close with so many escaping.

As I watched, the transparent shape of the Glass Monster walked across the landscape. He never turned to me, but stopped where I could see a vague outline of his two-legged form. The creature's chest expanded and then released a fire to end all fires, filling the Shadowland landscape as far as I could see in nothing but flames.

There was one way to kill a crawler. The flames of another crawler. It was killing all its enemies.

"It was a civil war after all," I said as I watched. "They had to get their people out so they could nuke the enemy."

I watched on, and then the Glass Monster shrank until it was the size of a small bunny. It looked back through the opening of the portal at me and stared for a moment, before hopping off.

I started to struggle to my feet. "The other Shadow Walker? They have another one here."

Kane held me to him. "She's dead. I saw her body as I passed."

"It was Collin this whole time," I said, sagging into him, my back against Kane's chest.

"I know."

"How?"

"Because I was interrogating Vincent. He told me about Collin, and that he'd struck a deal with Frederickson."

"Collin was here."

"He's no longer a problem."

"Do I want to see?"

"Not much *to* see." Kane pointed in the direction of one of the many piles of ashes still burning out around us. "He was being cooked while you were still half in the portal."

"Is Vincent alive?"

There was a pause. "Mostly, but only because he healed you. That might change by tomorrow."

I nodded. "Why didn't you call me? I would've gone with you."

"Because I didn't want you to have to. I've put you through enough."

I stayed like that, limp in Kane's arms, as Harg's creatures continued to char the rest of the crawlers left behind. Like a military patrol of old, they moved around the area checking bodies for signs of life, charring anything that twitched.

Slowly, as all the fires died, Harg stepped in front of us.

He bowed slowly and then said, "I'll hunt and then I return home."

I nodded. He'd round up any creatures that had escaped and go back. That was his only reason for being here in the first place. To empty out the Shadowlands until there was nothing left but his enemies. And then the Glass Monster had taken care of those.

"Last thing." Harg pointed toward where the portal had finally closed. The Glass Monster was there. It took a deep breath and, like the first time, a warm breeze washed over me.

Kane's arms circled me as I let out a soft breath.

"Ollie?" Kane asked, having probably felt something too.

I couldn't speak, though. They flooded back, memories so thick that I couldn't believe I'd ever lost them.

How had he not trusted me? Now that I remembered, I understood. We'd been a team. He'd become my best friend, not just some guy I'd fallen for.

I pulled from his arms and turned to him, searching for the words to ask him why.

"You remember." It was bittersweet, and he knew it. I could hear it in his voice.

I'd remembered all the good times, and they now put the bad times in a harsher light.

"Yes." I crossed my arms and wrapped them around myself. "I still don't remember the missing week, or the night of the explosions. I remember everything else."

He looked at me the way he had right after I'd lost my memory, as if he were mourning my loss, and now it all made sense. And I didn't know what I wanted to do. Whether I wanted to comfort him or rail at him.

"Can I help you back? You can rest until you figure out what you want to do."

I nodded. He knew what I was feeling, had guessed at it. Knew I might leave again, and this time it might be for good.

The hurt was so thick that I didn't know if he was entirely wrong.

Chapter Thirty-Seven

I STROLLED INTO KANE'S OFFICE THE NEXT MORNING, NOT bothering to knock. I hadn't seen him since I'd gotten back yesterday, and he hadn't pushed. He'd given me my space. But it was time.

Butch and Leon were standing beside the Keurig, fighting over a single French vanilla, when I stepped inside. They both turned at the same time.

"Is it true?" Butch asked.

I'd thought of all sorts of ways to break it to them. But there was really only one way that did it justice.

"Still alive," I said, with a huge smile on my face even as a tear ran down my cheek.

I could see the trepidation on their faces as they both paused. Leon spoke first. "*Really* still alive? Are you faking?"

"*Really* still alive."

"She's still alive," Butch said with a voice that matched my teary eyes.

"She is. She's still alive," Leon added, then turned and hugged Butch. "She's back. Our girl is back."

"I am. I really am." I watched them hug each other. "And why aren't you hugging me?"

They turned and nearly plowed me over, including me in their hug, all of us laughing.

And then Kane walked in and the mood shifted suddenly, tension falling over all of us as he stood looking on.

"We gotta go get French vanilla, you fuck," Butch said to Leon, hitting him in the arm.

"I know. I'm a total ass. Completely used them all up," Leon agreed.

They both stuttered out goodbyes, shutting the door as they left.

Kane and I stood across the room from each other.

"I want you to know, you have no one left to worry about. I took care of Frederickson this morning," he said.

I let out a soft breath. That was good to know. "Thank you. Did you find out how they got a crawler out in the first place?"

"Once I stopped recruiting Shadow Walkers, Collin continued. He managed to use one to get a single crawler through. That started everything. Apparently, just as you can get shadow magic, you're also very susceptible to it."

"Frederickson told you this?" I asked.

"It took a while, but yes."

"Do you have a few more minutes to talk?" I asked.

"Of course," he said, the expression on his face nearly killing me.

I waved toward his chair behind the desk. "Maybe you could sit?"

He did, accommodating my request like a man that thought I was about to sentence him to life in prison.

I headed toward the chair but then walked around to Kane's side of the desk and perched on the corner, similar to what he'd done so many times.

"You know, I was really mad— No. That's not true. I wasn't mad. I was hurt."

Kane looked at the floor for a minute before he met my gaze and said, "I know."

I could see him grip the arms of the chair, as if he wanted to reach out to me but wouldn't.

I nodded, swallowing the lump still in my throat. "But it got me to thinking."

He leaned back, watching me, not even a whisper of the arrogance he normally had showing.

"Do you…" I let out a soft laugh before I could finish, thinking back on what I was going to say.

"What?"

"Do you remember when I asked you if you were the devil?" I couldn't stop smiling at the notion. I'd really thought it was a possibility. I wasn't completely wrong.

"Yes. I believe the Rolling Stones prompted the question." He smiled, but it didn't hold much joy.

"I can't put all the blame on them." I angled my legs a little bit closer to him as I crossed them. His eyes took in the movement.

"The thing is, even then, whether I admitted it or not, I was falling for you. If you had turned to me and said you were the devil, I doubt it would have mattered."

His lips softened a little but I wasn't sure if he knew exactly where I was going with this yet.

"So, when I lost my memory, I know things didn't look good—"

"I should've known," he said, as if he'd been saying it over and over to himself.

"Agreed. I think you should've known too. You knew me." He really had. Then the reality of how bad it looked set in, and how I'd turned from him and rejected him. If he'd turned from me like that, not even wanting to hear about what we had or willing to think it over, I wasn't sure how rational I would've been either. I might've treated him like he was a stranger too, as if I hadn't known him at all, because that might have been the only thing that would've saved me from an emotional hell.

But even then, when he'd thought the worst of me, and I'd wondered the worst of myself, he'd wanted me. Just as I'd wanted him, even when I wasn't sure what might've been lurking beneath.

I took a deep breath and continued. "You know how when we were in the building after the explosion and you saw my phone?"

"Of course. And I'm—"

I leaned forward, putting my fingers softly to his lips, the way he had to mine in the Underground that day. I knew he was going to say he was sorry or that he should've known. But I didn't need to hear it again.

"Just hear me out." I moved my hand to his shoulder as I got off the desk and closed the distance between us. I bent one leg, moving to straddle his lap and resting both hands on his shoulders. He reached out to balance my hips as I did, his expression showing a glimmer of hope. "When we were in that building, and you saw my phone, proof I'd been there, I was terrified."

He reached up, cupping my face as he listened. He didn't try to speak, but I saw the sorrow, the regret in his eyes.

"But I wasn't afraid of you hurting me. Even then, when I was thinking the worst of myself, I didn't think you'd ever really hurt me. I did think maybe you'd turn your back on me, and for some reason, that was the hardest hurt to bear.

"But you didn't turn me away. You protected me. You still wanted me. You accepted me in spite of it. You thought *I* might be the devil and you still wanted me, just as I had wanted you. The way I still want you."

His hands tensed around my body as his eyes burned my soul. "Are you done?" he asked.

It wasn't sarcastic. It was genuine.

I nodded, and he threaded his hand through my hair, and when he kissed me, I didn't need to hear anything else. It was all there in his touch. All the sorrow of what we'd gone through, the anguish of his guilt, and the passion of his possession, because I was his and he was mine.

SIGN up here to be notified of new releases by Donna.

Find Donna on the web at Donnaaugustine.com

Check me out on Facebook https://www.facebook.com/Donnaaugustinebooks/

ALSO BY DONNA AUGUSTINE

OLLIE WIT
> A Step into the Dark
> Walking in the Dark

THE KEEPERS
> The Keepers
> Keepers and Killers
> Shattered
> Redemption

KARMA
> Karma
> Jinxed
> Fated
> Dead Ink

THE WILDS
> The Wilds
> The Hunt
> The Dead
> The Magic

Acknowledgments

I'm pretty lucky that my list of people to thank is so long. Camillia J., Christine J., Tammy K., Lori H., Ashleigh M., Donna T. and Lisa A., without your help, this wouldn't be the book it is.

(The exact level of book this is I'm leaving open to you, the readers, to determine. If you determine it's bad, there were a lot of hands in this cookie jar. Just saying.)

If you've read my books, and I'm assuming if you've gotten this far you have, you'll know that I *might* be kidding about what I wrote in the parantheses. If you don't know that I'm kidding, you probably haven't made it this far. I probably offended you before the second chapter and we're safe!